Could there be a greater danger than love?

HOW COULD HE THINK OF LEAVING WITHOUT telling me? Aurelia tried to say the words aloud to Daria, and they came out, "How could he leave without me?"

"Do you want to go?"

"Yes." Well, there it was. The truth.

"Then go." Daria crossed the room and opened the wardrobe. "Just"—she paused—"don't hurt him, Aurelia."

Hurt *him*? Aurelia felt numb. "What do you mean?"

Her friend returned from the wardrobe with wool stockings and Aurelia's battered riding boots. She did not release them. "You must know."

Know what? "Daria." Aurelia's tone was threatening.

"He's in love with you."

The world stopped. For one long, outrageous moment, Aurelia let herself consider the statement. He had *kissed* her. Once. And saved her life. More than once.

But the idea that he could be in love with her did not—could not be true. "That's nonsense." She had tried to let Robert know she wanted to spend time alone with him on the way to Sterling. And he had rejected her. He was *still* rejecting her.

Daria handed her the stockings. "Honestly, Aurelia. There's nothing wrong with being in love."

Aurelia was not at all certain of that.

ANNE OSTERLUND

speak
An Imprint of Penguin Group (USA) Inc.

SPEAK
Published by the Penguin Group
Penguin Group (USA) Inc., 345 Hudson Street, New York, New York 10014, U.S.A.
Penguin Group (Canada), 90 Eglinton Avenue East, Suite 700, Toronto, Ontario, Canada M4P 2Y3
(a division of Pearson Penguin Canada Inc.)
Penguin Books Ltd, 80 Strand, London WC2R 0RL, England
Penguin Ireland, 25 St Stephen's Green, Dublin 2, Ireland (a division of Penguin Books Ltd)
Penguin Group (Australia), 250 Camberwell Road, Camberwell, Victoria 3124, Australia
(a division of Pearson Australia Group Pty Ltd)
Penguin Books India Pvt Ltd, 11 Community Centre, Panchsheel Park, New Delhi—110 017, India
Penguin Group (NZ), 67 Apollo Drive, Rosedale, Auckland 0632, New Zealand
(a division of Pearson New Zealand Ltd)
Penguin Books (South Africa) (Pty) Ltd, 24 Sturdee Avenue,
Rosebank, Johannesburg 2196, South Africa

Registered Offices: Penguin Books Ltd, 80 Strand, London WC2R 0RL, England

Published by Speak, an imprint of Penguin Group (USA) Inc., 2011

1 3 5 7 9 10 8 6 4 2

LIBRARY OF CONGRESS CATALOGING-IN-PUBLICATION DATA:
Osterlund, Anne.
Exile / by Anne Osterlund.
p. cm.
Summary: In exile, Princess Aurelia is free of responsibilities, able to travel the country
and meet the people of Tyralt, but when her journey erupts in a fiery conflagration
that puts the fate of the kingdom in peril, she and her companion Robert must determine
whether they have the strength and the will to complete their mission.
ISBN: 978-0-14-241739-3
[1. Princesses—Fiction. 2. Voyages and travels—Fiction. 3. Interpersonal relations—Fiction.]
I. Title
PZ7.O8454Ex 2011
[Fic]—dc22 2010009645

Speak ISBN 978-0-14-241739-3

Printed in the United States of America

For Tease, who I promised,

and Dance, who made certain I followed through.

Acknowledgments

Thank you. To Kristin Gilson for stepping in to help polish my previous book. To Amy and her team for putting on Sirens, a wonderfully inspirational conference on women in fantasy literature. To Michael Frost, Linda McCarthy, and Theresa Evangelista for their absolutely breathtaking covers. To all the people at Penguin who took yet another risk. To Maria, Dawn, Kelly, and Angelle for their outstanding support and time. To my dad, who answered three thousand questions about wagons, canvas tents, and threshing. And most of all, to the incredible readers who had faith in this story.

Exile

Chapter One
TEMPTING DANGER

HOOFBEATS THUNDERED FROM BEHIND. IMMINENT. Aurelia flung herself farther forward, low against the neck of her mare. *Go, Bianca!* she urged. The muscles beneath her shifted into a smooth firing of movement, and the gray horse burst into a more rapid pace, soaring over the stones and sand. The spring air turned cold as it sheeted across the exposed section of Aurelia's face, and the thinning fir trees along the road blurred into solid walls of forest green as the sounds of Bianca's hooves blended to a single continuous roar.

But the other hoofbeats did not stop. Nor did they fade or mingle with Bianca's. Instead, they pounded the road's surface at an even faster rate, closer and closer. Aurelia knew she could not outrun them. They would reel her in, pull her down, overtake her. There was nothing she could do to stop the inevitable, only close her eyes, hang on, and refuse to give her pursuer the chance to breathe. Her heart pounded at the same pace as the hooves of her mount, and for one long spectacular moment she saw nothing.

Then the hand touched her shoulder.

She forced down the scream conjured by memory and reached for the reins.

Bianca resisted, pulling for release, then obeyed, and the roar of hoofbeats splintered to individual steps. Aurelia sucked in the fresh air and let her chest rise off the horse's neck. Her eyes blinked away the tears formed by speed, and she smiled at the thrill of the ride.

Then she turned to her pursuer.

Robert did not smile. His hand held tight to the reins of his mount as Horizon reared, the muscles of the bay's powerful chest rising. The stallion kicked out impatiently with deadly hooves, and Robert clung to Horizon's back, legs gripping tight, torso tilted forward to maintain balance. He did nothing to battle the horse's unbreakable will, just waited out the stubborn display until the stallion dropped once again to the ground. Not one bead of sweat shimmered on the magnificent red-brown coat.

"Satisfied?" Robert said, running a hand through the waves of his dark brown hair.

Aurelia raised her face to the sun and let herself glory in the moment: sunlight, horses, adventure. *Yes,* for this one moment, she could describe herself as satisfied. Almost.

Her gaze returned to the young man before her. Robert's face was drawn, and its typically animated lines had gone sharp. His hand slid to his recently wounded shoulder, and she felt a twinge of guilt for forgetting he might not yet be up to a full-blown race. She considered an apology, but his deep blue eyes ignored her, instead scanning the haphazard firs and barren patches of the dwindling Kryshan Forest, where there was positively nothing, Aurelia thought, worthy of appreciating those eyes.

"You realize we might have more than an hour's ride back to the expedition party," he continued.

"And wouldn't that be tragic?" she teased, sweeping the loose strands of her brown hair out of her face. "A whole hour without the company of six guards." Not to mention a horseman and two wagon drivers. The pride of her escape filled her chest. Not that she did not appreciate the expedition. It was her dream—had been her dream since she was a small girl: to travel and see all the people and places she had heard about from the poets, playwrights, and tale-spinners who came to court. And at last she had the freedom to make that dream a reality.

But freedom was relative. A week the expedition party had been on the road, and not once had she and Robert been alone together. Until now.

Horizon jerked his head, and Robert tugged on the stallion's reins. "I have responsibilities, and so do you."

Responsibilities? Now that was humorous. "For what?" she replied, unable to suppress the self-satisfied tone in her voice. "I don't have to marry an old vulture stuffed in his Anthonian wedding garb. I don't have to swelter in silence through another state speech. And I don't have to attend a single royal function. What possible responsibilities could I have in exile?"

"Staying alive," he said. And the blue eyes finally settled on hers, their depths piercing her confidence. He reached for the reins of her horse.

Aurelia swerved away. Why couldn't he just enjoy the expedition instead of bringing up problems she wanted to forget? She did not want to think about her sister's failed attempts to assassinate her. Or her father's failure to acknowledge the crime. "I am perfectly *alive,* Robert. And I have no intention of spending this entire trip under the supervision of the royal guards. If you miss their company so much, why don't you just hurry back to all those armed men? I'm sure they couldn't possibly make their way down this road without you."

Again the blue eyes fled, this time inspecting the opposite side of the road, as if a couple of gorgeous lady's maids might materialize in the distance to rescue Robert from her dull company. A chill wave of disappointment skittered down her chest. Two weeks ago, he had been just as happy to spend time alone with her as she was with him. What had she done wrong?

The answer to her question seared her mind: *I need you at my side*. She should never have told him that—back at the palace when she had asked him to come along as her expedition guide. Though he had said *yes,* and foolishly, she had interpreted that as meaning something more.

After all, *he* was the one who had kissed *her*.

But that had been before.

I need you. The phrase taunted her again. She did not need him. Of course not.

"You did not have to come after me!" she snapped, urging the mare forward in the opposite direction of the expedition party.

Robert blocked her path, and for a moment, she anticipated the challenge of a worthy retort. At least now she had his full attention. But before he opened his mouth, the sound of approaching hoofbeats interfered.

A tall horseman rode into view, the rider's silver bandanna glistening in the sunlight, a ruby red stud decorating his left ear. He wore a black vest over a crimson shirt, and an eagle feather sliced brazenly through his hatband. A wide grin creased his dark face as he pulled up alongside Aurelia. "Nice day for a ride, Your Highness."

She shot him a look that could have warped iron.

"Drew." Robert acknowledged the horseman, then rode past him, heading back the way they had come.

Aurelia felt the heat of her disobedient temper storm through her face as she watched Robert pull away.

"I take it the ride didn't go as well as planned." Drew chuckled.

Her temper snapped. "You couldn't handle a few hours without us," she accused.

He held his palms up in mock innocence. "Hey, this wasn't my idea. He's the one who told me to come."

"And you're taking orders from Robert now?"

The horseman had the wisdom to let that comment fall. Everyone on the expedition had started looking to Robert for advice: where to camp, when to stop, when to head out. Not that Aurelia wanted to control every mundane aspect of the trip. It was fine with her if they wanted to organize their lives around his suggestions. But that did not mean she had to.

She wanted to go north, to travel at least as far as the desert, and to see and learn everything she could on the way there. She did not want to live as though she were still at court, with every moment of her life planned by someone else. "If he wanted you to escort me back," she said, "why didn't he just send you instead of coming himself?"

Drew raised an eyebrow. "I'm thinking because he knew he had the only mount fast enough to catch Bianca, as you're well aware, Your Highness."

She set her jaw.

The horseman grinned. "Don't be too hard on him, lass. Sometimes a lad needs a little help interpreting the lay of the land."

She bristled at the innuendo and whirled Bianca around. "He doesn't want my help. Apparently, he doesn't even want to talk to me."

Drew's large hand came down on her shoulder. She flinched, and the horseman pulled away. "He's scared."

"Of me?" she scoffed.

"*For* you." Drew's voice was low, scolding. "We've had no word that policies have changed at the palace. Which means there is still a threat—"

She did not want to hear about the palace. "I went. For a ride. It's not. A crime."

His head turned as he made one swift scan of the area. "You went off for a ride . . . alone, less than a day outside of Sterling, the second-largest city in the country and the closest to the capital. Anyone seeing us leave Tyralt City would know where you were headed next. Which makes Sterling the most obvious place for another assassination attempt."

Aurelia refused to allow Drew's warning to spoil her anticipation as she rode into the Central Valley at dawn the next morning. True, word would have spread, passed along by travelers heading in either direction. The people would know she was coming. But surely the benefits outweighed the risks. And at last Aurelia would have others with whom she could share her enthusiasm.

As she dipped deeper into the valley, however, her confidence faltered.

Eyes watched her. From behind pitchfork tines and around morning glory trellises, through the gnarled apple trees, and under the long, crisscrossed shadows of orchards that would soon bear the cherries, plums, peaches, and nectarines of the coming season. She tried smiling at the onlookers, but they ducked beneath their leafy screens and sank to darker slate-gray depths. She bit her lip, kicked her heels, and urged Bianca on down the road. Perhaps the imminent welcome would come as she neared the city.

But she could feel the anxiety heighten in the six guards around her. Their swords came out of their scabbards and turned upright in their hands, surrounding her like the points of a fence. Why was the feeling around her so hostile?

She longed to ask for an explanation, but Drew had ridden ahead to arrange lodging. And Robert was riding just far enough away to avoid conversation. His sword remained in its scabbard, but the muscles in his left arm stood out in tense cords, and his hand clenched in a fist. His profile shifted as he swept his gaze along the periphery.

Taking in all those eyes.

They were growing in number.

As the deep reds and oranges faded in the eastern sky, the empty fruit stands lining the road were replaced by wooden shacks, then houses: first in twos and threes, now fours and fives. The powerful odor of horse manure emanated from a roadside livery, and the clang of a blacksmith's forge announced the transition from farmland to city outskirts. Up ahead, a stone structure soared into the air and curved over the roadway. The Southern Arch. Aurelia felt her heart speed up. *Sterling.* The first test of her journey.

If she could not succeed here, only a week's ride from the capital, perhaps her entire expedition would fail.

Around her the onlookers had grown more brazen, no longer hiding but staring openly. And when she looked back, they did not flinch.

They did not smile either.

At last she understood that her expectations had been flawed. There would be no cheers and shouts of excitement. In fairness, she could not blame these people for their lack of zeal. After all, she had never done anything for them. She had not transformed their modest village into a thriving trade center. They had done that themselves, without king or command. Sterling's inns and taverns, now usurping the roadside houses, had sprinted past the Southern Arch that marked the site of the town's ancient stone wall. The people had torn down their boundary, defying Tyralian tradition.

As did the barren flagpole on the closest establishment. The royal standard was not flying, a detail that dug into her mind like a hook and began to work its way back and forth in her brain. The citizens of Sterling, now lining the highway in solid rows, had a right to be wary. She would not bet their future on the strength of her father's decisions. And she, herself, had nothing to offer them. Nothing but questions and curiosity and the support of someone with no real power.

Was the purpose of her expedition really to earn accolades?

No. The real purpose was to know her country. And her people.

But then why was she riding above them? Coming into their city under the auspice of being crown princess? With a fence of armed guards around her? She was not here to represent the palace. She did not speak for the throne. She would not and could not make any promises to these people beyond her own desire to understand them: their hopes, their plans, their dreams.

The buildings blurred around her as she crossed through the shadows of the Southern Arch and entered the city's heart. She could not see the streets, only the crowd: beneath her, behind her, stretching out away from the road, and up ahead, filling the central plaza in a shifting throng.

Of tension.

She could not stay as she was.

She had no right. She would not enter that plaza as the crown princess.

Her hands tightened on the reins, pulling slack. Fingers brushed her arm. Robert's. When had he gotten so close? But she did not have time to explain to him. She had to do this now, while it was right, while she was still setting the stage for this expedition and who she would be during it: a citizen of Tyralt.

She wrapped the reins around her saddle horn.

Swung her leg over Bianca's back.

And descended into the crowd.

Chapter Two
A PUBLIC DISAGREEMENT

ROBERT COULD HAVE KILLED HER. WHAT HAD SHE been thinking, endangering her life by dismounting into that crowd? All day he had to keep his mouth shut as she worked her magic on the stubborn tradesmen, wealthy financiers, and common laborers of the city. He listened to her debate the merit of city tariffs, support the call for improved roads, and decry the practice of child labor without the benefit of an education or skilled apprenticeship.

Anyone would think she had expressly chosen to honor Sterling as her first public stop, instead of simply stating that the expedition should head north, leaving all the arrangements—for lodging, meals, navigating—to him, either to achieve on his own or to delegate. He would have preferred to avoid Sterling altogether, but it was the country's crossroads. He had had no choice.

When at last the expedition party arrived at the inn serving as their quarters for the duration of their stay, he marched up the stairs, ignoring the smell of roast lamb from the common room, dropped off his pack, and hurried across the hall. There he disregarded all manner of good convention and barged through Aurelia's open door. "Are you insane?!" he demanded.

She gave him a cool gaze, her eyebrows rising in perfect arcs over her brown eyes, matching cheekbones, and smooth jawline. Then her fingers continued unbuttoning the printed sleeve of her travel jacket. "Not that I am aware," she replied, "but I am not certain one would be aware of such a thing if one was insane."

He could have pummeled her. It was such a wretchedly rational answer for the young woman who had ignored all rationality that morning. "You could have died," he said, wrestling his voice under control.

"Well, there's something new." She removed her cotton jacket and placed it on the back of the walnut chair at her side.

Sarcasm. At least that sounded like her. He tried logic. "Aurelia, that crowd could have swallowed you. One shout, one trace of panic, and there would have been nothing any of us could have done to pull you out. You've been trained for royal processions. You know you never dismount."

She stepped forward and closed the door to the hall—something he should not have let her do, but then he had no influence over her.

"I'm not royal," she said, again in that strange, calm voice.

"Oh, is that why all those people are swarming outside the courtyard?"

"I'm not inheriting anything, Robert." She unlatched the brass catch of a trunk. "I gave my father the right to name another heir when I refused to marry the king of Anthone. We both know that."

"You're still the crown princess, Aurelia."

"In public."

"Which is where we are. And where you were this morning when you climbed off your horse and . . . disappeared . . . into that crowd."

She pushed back the rounded lid of the trunk, peering down. "I'm not going to pretend to be anything other than what I am to the people of this country, Robert. I thought you would understand that."

He could see her point of view. In some odd, self-deprecating way, this was her attempt to strip off the past: her own loss, her sister's hatred, her father's betrayal. In the last week, so much of her life had come apart. He understood her reluctance to see beyond the expedition—to plot out any route after the desert or make plans for a return. In fact, he admired her desire to explore. She did not need to plan out her entire future.

But he had no patience for her failure to ensure that she had one. "An assassin could have picked you off in that crowd without lifting a knife," he said.

She did face him now, her dark eyes glittering. "I thought you were done trying to protect me."

Trying. The word plunged into him, taunting his ineptitude.

"I obviously didn't have a chance this morning," he managed to reply.

She turned and unraveled a long blue ribbon from her trunk. "There's no motive," she said.

"What?" He tried to follow her leap in the conversation.

She wound the blue silk around a bedpost. "There's no reason for Melony"—her voice caught as she said her half-sister's name—"to have me murdered now."

He cringed at the denial. If she had risked her life today under a foolish assumption, he had to tell her the truth, no matter how brutal. "Your sister has just as much reason to murder you now as she did a week ago."

Aurelia's cinnamon skin paled, and the ribbon cascaded to the floor.

He did not wait for her to speak. "Your father has yet to publicly, or, as far as we know, legally, renounce you as heir to the throne. As long as you remain the public face of the future queen, your sister will see you as a threat. And there is no reason—none—to believe she does not."

Color now rushed up Aurelia's cheeks. "I'm not living in fear."

Useless. Absolutely useless. He had hurt her with the truth for nothing. Robert's patience split. "Then use a little common sense," he snapped.

"Just go away, Robert!" Her voice rose. "You've been avoiding me all week. Why don't you take advantage of this opportunity?"

"I thought you wanted someone on this expedition you could trust to tell you when you're being a fool!" He reached for the door latch and backed into the hall.

"I wanted a *friend!"* She slammed the door in his face.

The parting comment cut into his gut. He had thought he could be her friend, had promised himself when he had agreed to guide her expedition that their relationship would be nothing more. He had learned that lesson, in the pool of his own cousin's blood. If Robert had not allowed his feelings for Aurelia to interfere with his investigation of the assassination plot, Chris, on Melony's behalf, would never have been able to use Robert to place Aurelia in danger. *I will not make that mistake again.* Her life depended on it.

Half a dozen servants ducked behind doors as he turned around, and Drew's mocking chuckle greeted him from across the hallway. "You realize," said the horseman, his long arms crossed over his chest, "that news of this argument is going to be all over the city by nightfall. Across the kingdom by week's end. Nothing in this country travels faster than rumor."

"I'm right." Robert swept past the horseman into their shared room. His pack was already on the floor next to a high table bearing a basin and a pitcher of water. "You know I'm right. She could have killed herself dismounting into that crowd."

The older man's face turned serious. "I'd wager you were on the ground about two seconds after she dismounted." Drew gestured at Robert's sword.

"A lot of good a sword would have done in the middle of

all those people." Robert avoided looking at his weapon as he unbuckled the scabbard and hung it on the wall. He could not view the sword without also seeing Chris's chest heaving in pain above the metal shaft. "I ordered the guards to stand down. You think any of us could have protected her in the face of that throng?"

The horseman raised an eyebrow. "*You* ordered the guards?"

Robert brushed aside the comment. It had been more of a silent gesture than an order. He poured water into the basin, then dipped his hands into the icy liquid and shuddered. "She won't listen to me. Yesterday, I told her to stay close to the wagons, and not twenty minutes later, she took off alone on Bianca."

Drew grinned. "I recall."

"It's *not* funny."

The grin only widened.

Robert continued, "An assassin could have killed her anywhere along that road."

"And you think if you keep ignoring her, she'll live longer." Drew propped a boot on the rung of a chair. "I don't suppose it's occurred to you that she wouldn't need chasing if you would just talk to her."

What was that supposed to mean? "I talk to her."

"My crooked elbow you do. When?"

"Just now."

"Oh yes, that sounded like a very friendly conversation."

Well, Robert had a problem with watching her risk her life.

He could not help that, or erase the memory of sprinting across the field in the palace arena, knowing he could do nothing to stop the assassin already running her down. He could never forget the crumpled body on the dirt of the racetrack and the knowledge that that body could have been hers, that he could have lost her. He could not accept that, no matter how much distance he tried to place between them.

Drew was studying him. "You know it's possible," the horseman said, removing his foot from the chair, "that maybe the reason you're angry with her is that she was successful today."

Robert clenched his teeth.

"I may not have been there, lad, but I saw enough of that crowd. Those people weren't out to greet Her Highness this morning. They were curious, aye, but defensive—hostile even. And that's not the case tonight. All you have to do is look out to see it." Drew turned around and pushed open the large hinged window.

A cool gust rushed into the room along with the sharp snapping sound of the royal standard whipping in the wind, not one, but hundreds of flags, their golden crowns on purple backgrounds, clinging to every spire and rooftop in view. "Every buyer and beggar in Sterling is talking about her," Drew continued. "She's *their* princess now. In the course of one day."

Robert moved to shut the window.

But the horseman stopped his arm. "You may have spent the past four years on the frontier, lad, but you were raised at court. You know how rare that ability to win over a crowd is." Slowly

Drew allowed the framed glass to swing shut. "She was born to rule." He moved toward the doorway, then paused. "And don't tell me you really want her father to name her sister in her place. If you do, you're not half the man I thought you were."

Robert closed his eyes and heard the door click shut. He leaned back against the wall, the horseman's words penetrating his mind. Did he want Melony to rule Tyralt? A murderess and a manipulator without the faintest understanding of this country or its people? On some deep, inner level of his conscience, he could not.

But if it meant Aurelia would be free—free to live the rest of her life without danger; free to travel the kingdom, decide her own future, and one day choose whom she would marry . . .

No. He slammed the wall with his fist.

Melony could not become queen.

Chapter Three
CONFLAGRATION

A WEEK LATER, FEAR WOKE ROBERT IN THE COLD chill before dawn. His body tensed, leg and arm muscles tightening. His eyes swept the black inside of the tent. A figure moved in the darkness—an unnatural hump looming overhead. Boots shuffled in the dirt. A hand. And from the hand a long snakelike shape, curving left, then right. A rope.

Robert shot to his feet.

The humped figure stumbled back, hit the canvas wall, and tumbled to the ground onto a pile of rough maps. "Horses and hounds, lad, you scared the oats out of me!" Drew's voice.

Robert squinted at the fallen figure. The horseman grappled with something: the straps of his pack, Robert realized. "What are you doing?" he asked, holding out a hand to his tent-mate.

Taking the offered hand, Drew rose awkwardly to his feet. He hunched over to fit both the pack and his tall frame beneath the six-foot-high ceiling. "Time to head out."

It was definitely not time. Not even close. Robert lifted the tent flap and peered into the silence. Faint stars still shone over the valley, though the blackness of deep night had shifted to subtle gray. A thin cloud of ash drifted from the doused campfire, but nothing else moved, not even an ill-tied flap on one of the other five canvas shelters. The horses, of course, might be awake, but they had been tethered to the apple trees on the other side of Robert and Drew's tent. The horseman's idea.

Robert's gaze whipped back inside. The entire left half of the tent was barren. Drew had not only shouldered his pack but tied up his bedroll with the rope. "Told Her Highness I'd take her up on her offer to live off royal coin for a week, and I've already doubled that," said the horseman.

Robert dropped to his knees and scrambled for his boots.

"You don't have to see me off." Drew chuckled.

"You can't leave now."

"Course I can. Had a bit of business to finish up in Sterling—let my contacts know I wouldn't be in the area for a while—but that's done, and I've no interest in dragging my boot heels through every burg from here to Transcontina. Nay, I'm for the sands of the Geordian. I'll leave the pleasures of politickin' to you and Her Highness. You can think of me seeing all that legendary desert horseflesh while you're negotiating with your twenty-fifth innkeeper."

Robert knotted his second boot and snagged his jacket. He

could not deny his own desire to see the Geordian Desert—to test the story of his stallion's sire against the knowledge of the tribes, and learn if Horizon was, in fact, descended from those famous northern herds. But the lure of the desert did not validate Drew's sudden departure. "You can't leave without telling her good-bye."

The horseman caught him by the elbow. "Now, lad, you aren't going to wake her for that."

"I'd rather not!" Robert had yet to hold a civil conversation with Aurelia since their fight at the inn. He saw no point in wasting his breath if she was just going to ignore him.

Drew lifted his bedroll, bent his knees to duck beneath the low tent flap, then stepped outside and rose to his full height. He tramped toward the corner pole, no doubt heading straight for the horses.

Robert shot a futile glance at Aurelia's tent on the opposite side of camp. Too late. By the time he managed to warn her, the horseman would be gone. Leaving Robert to explain. At a time of day when Aurelia was *not* at her best.

He followed Drew, protesting, "You can't leave me to be the one to tell her you've gone."

"Ah, yes." The horseman spread a saddle blanket over the wide bronze back of his sorrel mount. "With me out of the way, you and Her Highness will have to talk to each other."

"You know she's hoping you'll stay longer."

"Maybe." Drew lifted his saddle over the diamond-patterned blanket, then buckled the strap.

"You owe her a departure in person."

"You're going to have to talk to her, lad. I've been talking too much for the both of you." Drew tied his belongings to the back of his saddle. "Unhook that tether, would you?"

Robert reluctantly retrieved the stake and handed over the rope.

"Coward," he said, aware that he was describing himself as much as Drew.

The horseman swung up into his seat and rummaged in his pack, procuring his hat with the eagle feather. He settled it on his head, adjusting the feather's slant, and pressed his heels to the sides of his mount. Then he turned and winked. "I'll owe you one."

Robert watched the other man's departure without actually seeing the figure fade along the road between the outstretched limbs of competing apple orchards. All he could picture was Aurelia's face when she found out Drew was gone without a word. The blood that would darken her skin. The lines that would sharpen her forehead and jaw. The flames that would shoot from her eyes. Whatever Drew owed him, it was not enough.

"He's gone?" Panic rushed to Aurelia's throat as she repeated the words for the third time. Beneath her, Bianca shuffled her feet, no doubt sensing her rider's distress.

Robert looked annoyed. He steered his mount away from the mare's hooves. "You knew he would be leaving."

She had, but today? On their first full day out of Sterling? With Robert still not speaking to her? Why did Drew have to leave now? And without saying good-bye? No, that wasn't true. He had said good-bye. To Robert. She took her frustration out on him. "You knew, didn't you? Why didn't you wake me?"

He raised his gaze toward the backs of the guards, already heading out along the road. "There wasn't time."

"Oh, I'm sure you had more pressing things to do at that hour of the morning."

He bit his lower lip, slapped his horse's reins and urged Horizon forward, leaving her with the magnificent view of his stallion's hind end.

She could have screamed. Throughout the week in Sterling, she had managed to distract herself from Robert's blatant silence, but on the road it was different.

And now Drew was gone. Drew, who she had been counting on to fill Robert's place until Robert decided to forgive her. For what, she was not certain. It did not seem fair that he could be mad at her for risking her own life, but apparently he was. More than mad. Though she was starting to think something else lay behind his strained behavior. Something darker. And less easy to forgive.

A fierce pressure built up behind her temples as the day crawled on. The ill-maintained Northern Road seemed bent on testing her patience, and she could not quite allow her mind to wander, though Bianca was doing an admirable job picking her way around jagged stones and crevices.

The sun fought a losing battle with the clouds, and the shadows of isolation spoiled the approach to the Asyan Forest—the largest forest in the kingdom, stretching over an eighth of Tyralt. Aurelia longed to ask about the mysterious blue-green tinge shrouding the horizon. There were folktales about the Asyan, whispered by palace servants and shared in the open by street performers and puppeteers in Tyralt City: about people entering the forest and not coming out for a thousand years, poachers turning into wolves and mountain lions, trees swallowing the souls of outlaws who tried to find shelter under cover of branches.

"What do you think, Bianca?" Aurelia whispered in her mare's ear. "What lies amidst those trees?"

The magic, of course, was false, but the danger? There must be some reason for generations to repeat such frightening tales to their children. A tingle of forbidden allure rippled through Aurelia's skin. She wondered what Robert would say—

Stop thinking about him! She buried her face in Bianca's mane and tried to push away the memories of all the friends who had drifted, one by one, out of her life, too uncomfortable with the toll of being near the crown princess.

At least she still had Bianca. The mare was more than a friend, the type Aurelia could count on and tell secrets to with absolutely no fear of disclosure. She bent down and wrapped her arms around the horse's soft gray neck. "You'll never stop talking to me, will you, Bianca?"

The mare nickered in response.

It did not occur to Aurelia until that evening that there were eight other humans, their presence forced upon her, that she had not considered befriending. It was galling that after her father had failed to prosecute her sister, he still had the authority to assign his eldest daughter a protective guard. Though somewhere in her mind, she knew this was not the guards' fault.

They had selected the campsite, probably with Robert's advice, though she had not witnessed the conversation. Dusk had settled its cold fingers over the swath of blue-green trees surrounding the tent-lined clearing, and everyone had gathered close to the crackling flames of the fire. Robert, seated on the opposite side of the drifting smoke, was crouched forward, his hands loosely linked, eyes cast down, avoiding hers.

Painfully conscious of that restricted gaze, Aurelia tried to focus elsewhere. The smell of roast venison permeated the sharp smoke, and several of the men were inching closer to a burly, well-muscled guard turning the roast on a spit. "Back off," he growled at them. "T'aint no royal banquet."

"'Fraid not," replied a thin blond wagon driver with bony arms and shoulders. "We'd need the wine." He raised an invisible glass. "Only question is what kind."

The burly man pulled the stick off the fire and tested the meat with his knife. "Heard Valshone is the best," he said grudgingly. "Those farmers in the mountains don't have anything better to do than grow their grapes." He propped up the spit, then began carving away the roast.

Eager trenchers stretched at once in his direction, but he pushed them away and deposited the first slice onto Aurelia's plate, then gave her a wink.

She glanced at Robert, who was still studiously avoiding her gaze.

Determined not to let him spoil her evening, she joined the conversation. "Valshone grapes aren't grown in the mountains, just the foothills. They would freeze higher up."

A sharp *crack!* from the campfire echoed into the night as silence engulfed the party. Too late she realized she had subjugated the other speakers. "Not that I've ever tried Valshone wine."

The guard flipped his knife through the air. "Why not, Your Highness? Rumor has it there's a whole crate of fancy wine back there on the wagons."

There *was* a crate, she remembered, stowed away for improving national relations, packed up by palace staff who had assumed she would be meeting with various aristocrats along her journey. She had not known the guards were aware of the wine's existence. But come to think of it, improving relations was just what she needed. "Maybe we should open it for a tasting?" she suggested.

Robert's linked hands tightened.

And cheers sounded around the campfire.

She stood up. Robert rose at the same moment. For an instant, their eyes met over the crackling flames. Intense disapproval flared at her from his deep blue gaze, and a flicker of triumph pulsed through her veins. But he flinched, setting down his empty plate and vanishing into the shadows of his tent. Fine then, she did not need his silent presence dampening her spirits anyway.

"Can't hold his liquor," the burly guard joked, and the other men's laughter rippled a bit too loudly into the dimming light. Two guards rose beside Aurelia, offering to help with the crate. She raised her chin, spared one last glance toward Robert's tent, and led the way to the stash of expensive spirits.

Her return to the campfire was greeted by raucous applause.

The two men deposited the crate on the ground, and the burly guard hefted a large log over to the fire beside the crate. "Your throne, Highness," he said, motioning toward the log.

"Aurelia," she said, shoving the log back and seating herself on the ground. "I would prefer it if you would all call me Aurelia."

She retrieved the first unopened bottle and held it out, just beyond the burly man's reach, as she waited for him to say her name.

"That's a bargain, Aurelia." He stretched for the bottle, popped the cork with his knife, and then motioned for her to take the first drink. She wrapped her fingers around the smooth stem, then tipped it back. The sticky sweet taste did nothing for her, but the roar of approval from around the flames warmed her soul. She handed back the bottle, and he took a large swig.

As the wine began to flow, the fire caught the rough bark of the larger logs and licked into the higher echelons of the gathered pile. Light glowed a seductive orange, its warmth pulsing amid the night's embrace, and the men glided closer, ignoring the sultry threat of smoke as they coaxed her to open one bottle after another, always insisting she be the first to savor the contents and not sully her lips. She did not care for the flavors, sweet or bitter, but after several tries, a tingly feeling ran into her head, and the taste no longer bothered her.

She let herself drift amid the conversation. Meandering tales and cavalier jokes slid along the outskirts of her mind like water over glass, and the laughter enveloped her in its undulating current. Providing her with what she needed. Distraction. And sanctuary from isolation.

Until the last bottle had been opened.

Then one by one the men shuffled off into the darkness. As the final guard doused the flames, Aurelia had no choice but to rise from the ground and stumble across the clearing to her tent. She struggled to untie her boots, then gave up, sank down on her cushioned pallet, stretched out her limbs, and let her weary body give way to sleep.

But the nightmares she had hoped to hold at bay leaped forth to strangle her. Images torn from memory.

Her sister hurling bitterness about Chris's death.

The king ordering Aurelia to marry Edward of Anthone.

The body of Marcus Gregory. Her assassin. Crumpled, battered limbs useless in the dirt.

Battered by her. Crumpled by her. Dead because of her.

Aurelia woke up gasping, unable to clear that final image

from her mind. She had been the one riding Horizon. She had been the one to order the stallion to attack Gregory. She had done so knowingly. Knowing she would kill him. Knowing if she didn't, he would kill her. Knowing …

Knowledge was not all it was given credit for. She had never thought of herself as capable of killing anyone. Now she knew different. And she was not yet sure she could live with who she had become. Could anyone?

Her father, her sister, and her stepmother had all rejected her, placing status and power above her welfare. Her mother had left, perhaps with good reason, after learning that her husband had fathered another woman's child, but still—in the fourteen years since then, had Aurelia's mother ever contacted her own daughter? No.

And now Robert.

The tears came without permission, and Aurelia doubled over, crushing her stomach against her fist. It had been like this every night since that day in the arena, when she had killed the man who was trying to kill her. Every night the nightmares came. And every night she tried to push away the hurt and guilt and pretend she was all right. To remind herself she was now free. That the home she had thought she had and the family she had thought she loved were a delusion. They had never existed, and she was well rid of them.

She was living her dream, free to travel where she wanted, to see and meet the people she had always wanted to see. To explore the kingdom … that was no longer hers.

No! She pushed back the thought. It was still her kingdom. As much as it belonged to any of the citizens of Tyralt. She had a right to see her country. She had always wanted this. It wasn't pointless. It wasn't.

But after dark, it was harder to believe. With the cold chill seeping into her bones and the silence illuminating the emptiness around her—inside her—there was nothing that could stop the pain from ripping through her chest and draining her mind.

Only tonight something was different.

She stood, took a half dozen steps to the tent opening, and lifted the flap. A chill wind rushed in to battle her hair.

You're drunk, she told herself.

Of course she was, and despite others' claims about the effects of alcohol, she was neither happy nor out of her head. Only hurting. And sad. And unwilling to put up with it when one of the solutions to her problems was only a matter of courage.

What courage? came her taunting conscience. *You're running away.*

She was running. She knew that. And she ought to feel bad about giving up her right to the throne and with it the promise that one day she would be able to help her people, but Aurelia had learned that that promise was a sham. She had never been in line to inherit that type of power. She had been expected to marry according to her father's wishes and to one day let her husband take on the real power. The future of Tyralt had never been within her grasp.

And she was too wounded and too tired to fight that stark reality. She wanted a future. She wanted love. And those, she was quite certain, had nothing to do with political power.

But they had everything to do with the young man in the tent less than fifty feet away.

She looked, Robert thought, like he felt. Her hair was tangled and . . . damp, for some reason, the strands in the front clinging to her face. Her cheeks and nose were red in the candlelight, and her clothes, the same she had been wearing all day, were crumpled and creased. Which meant that she, unlike he, might have slept, though clearly she was not rested. She stood, clinging to the sides of the tent flap as if she might collapse.

"Why?" she demanded, the hoarseness of her voice matching her disheveled appearance. "Why won't you talk to me?"

He moved toward her, but she sliced out with her hand as if thrusting him away.

"Why are you ignoring me, Robert? Not just this week, but before that. I *know* I've done something, but—why?" Her fingers slid off the canvas, and she slipped down.

He caught her elbow, but she pushed him back, standing up on her own.

Her breath reeked of alcohol.

"Aurelia"—he started to tell her she was drunk and should not be there.

But she interrupted him. "I'm sorry." She was choking now, falling once again, this time to her knees.

An apology? He had not expected that. Not when he had been the one to start the fight, and he had been the one sulking like a child for the past week. Her next words flattened him like a violent wind.

"I killed him. I know you can't forgive me because I killed him."

What? His heart wrapped around a tent pole and wrung itself dry. Was that what she thought? That he blamed her for defending herself against an assassin? It was himself he blamed, his fault she had had to defend herself.

"You didn't kill anyone." He sank to his knees and reached for her shoulders.

But she lashed out at him. "I did!" She choked, and only now did he realize the wetness on her face was caused by tears. "I chose . . . I *chose* to kill Gregory. I saw him with the gun, and I chose."

He could have kicked himself for his own stupidity. He should have guessed—should have known she was coming apart inside. Especially tonight when she had suggested drinking, and he had been so certain she was testing him to see if he would try to stop her. She had a right to fall apart after all she'd been through.

"You had no choice," Robert told her. "He would have killed you."

"You can't—you can't—"

"I know," Robert said, not even sure what words she had been grasping for but still understanding. "It's not like in the stories where the villain dies by his own sword, or the hero walks away in triumph, certain he vanquished evil for the greater good."

Recognition flashed in her eyes. "I keep seeing it," she whispered. "Every night when I close my eyes, I see his face and wonder what would have happened if I had made another choice."

Robert nodded. "How many times do you think I've refought that duel with Chris?"

"I . . . I'm sorry"—she was apologizing again.

"Why are you sorry? It's my fault you were in that arena. My fault Gregory came near you at all."

"But Chris . . ."

Robert drew closer, gently circling her upper arms with his hands. "What about Chris?"

"You would never have had to kill him if it weren't for me."

The incongruity of her statement took a moment to sink in. At first he had no idea what she meant. Then slowly Robert realized she had been suffering behind the same wall of self-guilt that he had for the past two weeks, blaming herself for the nightmarish events in the arena. The only difference was that she had already forgiven him for his failures. At least, she had told him it was not his fault, back in the garden, on the day of the assassination attempt.

It had never occurred to him to offer her the same kindness.

Instead, she had assumed that he was growing more distant from her because he blamed her for the events of that day. "Aurelia"—his hands slid up toward her shoulders—"none of this is your fault."

"Chris—," she said.

"It was Chris's choice...." Robert choked over the words even as he said them, knowing they were the truth but struggling with his own sense of guilt. "It was his choice to die as he did, helping Melony."

Aurelia nodded slowly, then dropped her head to his shoulder. Her hair brushed his face, and he could feel the remnants of her tears on his skin. So much for his promise not to feel any more for her than friendship. Her pulse was still pounding, but her breath slowed as he cradled her in his arms.

"You can sleep here tonight," he whispered. He kissed her hair, then lifted her gently onto his pallet. It was not as if he was going to use it tonight. Instead, he blew out the candle and sat beside her, smoothing the tears from her face and covering her hand with his. When was he going to get past appearances and remember that beneath her temper and bravado lay real fear? And hurt. For a while, he was not certain she would ever be calm enough to sleep; but then her body relaxed, and her head sank into the cushion.

She had been right, back at the inn. She had not needed him to tell her about the danger to her life. She had been dealing with that the only way she knew how, by ignoring it. What she had needed from him was understanding.

Why had he not thought she might be facing the same guilt that haunted him? It had occurred to him once when she had first described her defensive actions to her father. Why had Robert never seen her need to discuss it?

She had seen the need in him that very first day.

He lowered his head, resting his forehead beside her hand. Was it any wonder she thought everything was her fault? Hadn't all the people who mattered in her life betrayed or abandoned her? "I'm not leaving," he whispered into the darkness, promising her sleeping figure. "I'm not leaving you alone."

The derisive voice of a coastal jay mocked him from a distance. *Strange.* He had not known the birds came this far inland. Sitting up, he smoothed a strand of dried hair back from Aurelia's face and took a deep, shuddery breath.

It was then he smelled the smoke.

The sudden intense odor cleared his head and made him whip around. Shadows danced on the canvas flap, shadows that could not have formed without light. A strange, eerie light that should not have been there.

Robert unfolded his legs and stumbled as sharp spikes shot through his veins. Forced to pause, he breathed in the smoke-ridden air, then staggered to the tent flap.

Boots pounded past. One pair. Two.

His chest tightened as he peered out into the night.

Two figures sprinted across the campsite and joined a ring of dark silhouettes.

Around a tower of wild flame.

Orange tongues wove upward, tracing separate paths on canvas, then coalescing, brilliant sparks spraying the darkened sky. At the tower's center, there were no logs or branches, but the clear form of a tent. *Aurelia's.*

Robert's gut urged him forward, but something held him back: his father's voice, the same voice that had echoed in his head since childhood. *Never rush into a situation without first surveying the scene.*

Robert counted the silhouettes. *One, two . . . six.* Two more shifted into view. *Eight.* Each of the guards and wagon drivers. How had they all woken to the presence of the fire before he had even noticed it?

And something else was odd. Above each figure, though hard to spot against the background of orange flame, a smaller light glowed. *Torches.* Robert inhaled the meaning with the thickening smoke. The campsite off the main road—one of the men had suggested it. The wine—to dull her senses. *They're not fighting the blaze. They're feeding it.*

A sharp scream ripped through the air.

And for one awful second, Robert thought it was Aurelia—that he had only dreamed of her presence behind him, and the blazing inferno was her reality.

Then the scream cut through the clearing again, and he recognized the high-pitched voice of Horizon's fury. The horses were on the far side of the blaze. Panicked. Torches shifted, their wielders reacting to the same incredible scream.

And something clutched Robert's arm. Fingers. *Her fingers.*

He spun around.

To see the reflection of murder in Aurelia's eyes.

Curse it! Hadn't she seen enough without this? He shoved her away from the tent flap.

She resisted.

"Stop it, Aurelia." His voice was low but commanding. He had to get her to the horses before those torches swung in this direction. How long before the murderers came after him, or questioned the missing odor of burning flesh or the princess's failure to cry out? "We have to hurry."

He tugged her to the back of the tent and, bending down, ripped a stake from the ground to lift the canvas. "Go!"

She obeyed.

He grabbed his pack and thrust it through the opening. Aurelia grabbed it from the other side. He should have been grateful for her help, but those torches could arrive at any second. "Head for the trees!" he hissed, then rushed back toward his pallet, wrenched a blanket from the bed, and thrust it through the gap. Again, she yanked the object from his hands.

"Aurelia, go!" he ordered.

This time she argued back. "I'm not moving one step without you, Robert."

They did not have time for this. His eyes scrambled over the tent's remaining contents: his flintlock, maps, saddle, saddlebags, bridle, and ammunition. There was no time to gather them all. *Just get her out of here,* his conscience demanded, but something made him snatch one last item—the one object in the tent he would have preferred never to see again.

But the sword was his father's, or had been before Mr. Vantauge had given it to his only son. And Robert could not erase that memory. Any more than he could erase the blood that had tainted the weapon in his own mind since the day of his cousin's death.

Sounds came from the clearing. Voices.

Robert thrust the scabbard through the gap and this time went with it.

Aurelia was still there, her body a shadowy outline. He tugged her into the trees, buckled the scabbard around his waist, then snatched the pack from her arms; she must have stuffed the blanket inside.

"Where—," she breathed.

Crack! Something snapped in the distance.

"Don't speak," his lips whispered in her ear as his arms wrapped around her. He strained to listen. *Footsteps*. Then a new waft of burning fabric. He could feel Aurelia shudder as a second swath of flames lit the sky, and he wanted nothing more than to protect her from witnessing the hatred unfolding before them.

With the caution of the hunted, he eased her deeper into the spruce trunks and draping branches. Movement was vital but terrifying. Every snapped twig, brushed branch, or uneven footfall amplified in Robert's ears. Without a moon, he had no choice but to use the violent glow of the fires as his directional guide.

We have to reach those horses. If daylight came, and she was still here, any tracker worth his salt would follow the path from the second burned tent. Even Robert could have done it, but he could not disguise the tracks on his own. Not at night in an unknown environment with the princess at his side. He needed his mount, and he and Aurelia had to reach water.

Follow it far enough to lose anyone hunting them. And then?

In Tyralt's name, where can I take her?

He thrust the question away and tried to focus on the present. They must have reached the southern edge of their camp. The orange glow had shifted.

Whose orders were behind that deadly light? Or rather, whose were not?

Her sister, her stepmother, even her father had a motive after his eldest daughter's threat to reveal the truth about the assassination plot. Aurelia's words from the last day at the palace came back to Robert. *You*, she had said, *are the only person I can trust.*

Only now did he realize the shattering truth behind that statement.

At his side, Aurelia staggered, wrenching him from the shadows of his thoughts. Instinctively he reached for her arm. She pulled back, but his hand came away sticky. With blood. He froze, then broke his own moratorium on speech. "You're bleeding."

"It's a scratch," came her hushed words of explanation.

He tried to believe her. There was nothing he could do if the injury was severe.

Again Horizon screamed, and a chill ran through Robert's body. Why was the stallion still distraught? The orange glow was fading now, not growing stronger.

Just get her there, Robert told himself.

The glow had changed position again. They must be close.

Horizon's next call confirmed the thought. Though still high-pitched, the sound was a whistle of recognition.

Robert swept his gaze over the trees. His eyes were used to the dark now, but the tangle of branches made it almost impossible to tell what lay in front of him.

The horse, though, did not need to see in order to sense his rider's approach. Thrashing hooves pounded nearby, and as Robert crept toward the sound, Aurelia at his back, a tail swished into view.

The furious stallion had wrenched his rope high up along the tree trunk to which it was tied and was kicking not only air and ground but the trunk as well.

Waving at Aurelia to stay back, Robert moved swiftly to place his hand on the horse's side. The dangerous hooves pounded once more against the trunk, then dropped to the earth. They pawed the ground, and the stallion swung his head. Robert ducked as a pair of equine teeth snapped in his direction. Horizon's entire body quivered.

"Shh," Robert whispered as he edged toward the halter rope. "You know it's me."

His fingers found the knot. Tight. Impossibly tight. He snatched the knife from his pack and, in seconds, cut the rope.

The stallion broke free—

To reveal the mare behind him: *Bianca,* her body flat upon her side, a horrid slit at the base of her throat, blood emptied onto the ground.

Robert whirled toward Aurelia, but he was too late. She had seen her mare, and opened her own mouth to scream.

Chapter Four
SURVIVAL

AURELIA'S CHEST RIPPED APART AT THE SIGHT OF Bianca. Her friend. Her confidant. The loyal, trusting mare who had given love with no expectation save her rider's own heart.

Now broken. Aurelia wanted to scream and scream, but she could not because Robert had muffled her mouth against his chest with the demand that she *not make any noise.*

Then the world fragmented.

Terror defined the flight from the blood. Darkness, pain, and the piercing cold of drenching mist. Grasping tree limbs that tore at her and threatened to thrust her from the stallion's back or rip her to pieces in the attempt. Then icy sheets of black creek water that seemed to wind forever beneath Horizon. And always the scalding flames that had stabbed their way beneath her skin, threading through the corridors of her mind, obliterating thought, hope, and reason until the only thing keeping her moving was the constant pressure. . . .

A hand on her back. A grip around her waist. A pull, push, or tug.

The thin line between nightmare and reality had blurred within her. There were visions: her sister injecting venom through fingernails at Aurelia's throat, the guards turning her own charred body on a spit, Bianca's neck gushing and gushing and gushing blood. Another death. One more life on her conscience. Who else would have to die as the cost for her friendship?

Him.

She tried to push away the thought, but it dripped down into the crevices of her sanity.

"Aurelia?"

She was stiff, like solid stone.

"Aurelia?" There was an urgency in the voice now. What gave *him* the right to talk?

Pressure on her shoulder. She jerked awake . . . to a gray, impenetrable mist. The tree limbs of nightmare surrounded her, now in sober stillness, their needles weighted down with the morning's oppression. A black horsetail swished between two solemn tree trunks, then vanished in the vaporous shroud. The underbrush held back, keeping a subtle distance, but Robert, kneeling beside her on the hard ground, lacked the same common sense.

She did not want him here. Did not want him to witness her in this shattered state.

His hand reached for her wrist.

She jerked away, her shoulders burning as the wool blanket slid down past the red scratches marring her skin. Her sleeves hung in tatters, and she shuddered.

Concern etched the lines of Robert's face. "Are you all right?"

The flames within her head escaped, a white orange wreath forming around the nearest tree trunk, then licking its way up the scaly bark. Burning. She could not speak.

Robert pressed a canteen into her hand. She swallowed the cold water, trying to douse the fire. It smoldered, leaving her in shivers.

The concern on Robert's face deepened. He lifted the blanket back to her shoulders, setting off fresh pain. "I'm sorry we can't light a campfire this morning."

Because the guards might see it.

"Maybe tonight after we've covered more ground," he added. "I've been thinking, and I believe we should keep heading north."

Which way was north? She had never felt so lost.

"We can't go back to Sterling," Robert continued. "The guards will expect it, and there's too much open ground."

Open ground. As if she were prey to be hunted. The smoldering tree trunk began to burn again.

"And we can't take the Northern Road to Transcontina as planned. They could spread out along it."

Lying in wait at every village. She *was* prey.

"We will have to forge our own path through the forest, though it is really too dense for decent riding." His gaze shot to the scratches on her skin. "There's food in the pack."

Not enough. The careful way he had said it made that much clear. His hand clenched the hilt of his sword, then let go as he continued, "I don't have my rifle, but I can fish and set snares, or maybe make a bow. . . ."

Her mind was falling farther and farther behind the trail of words. The flames were once more scaling the nearby tree trunk. She knew he could not see them. Only she could see them.

Oblivious to the smoke writhing around his ankles, he crouched down over an array of items spread out on the ground beside the open pack.

She squinted through the haze, trying to identify the objects.

Something round and black. With writing. A compass.

String.

Folded parchment.

A handful of silver. Some of it battered.

Rope. She did not linger there. It conjured darker images.

Hooks with sharp spikes.

A knife. *Blood spilling from Bianca's throat.*

Flint and steel.

I can not *scream.*

Another drink. The flames subsided, ash drifting down.

Pressure on her hand. Robert was still talking. "I know it's not much, but . . ." She lost the thread of his voice as she stared at what he had given her. Red. Dark. *Not blood.* Dried berries. She raised them to her tongue and swallowed.

He slid the knife into his boot, packed away all of the items except for the compass, and disappeared into the smoke. She wanted to stop him, but her throat was seared shut. The flames spread, and the black fumes grew thicker and thicker, making her eyes sting.

Then Robert emerged, leading Horizon. The stallion swept forward, chest high, ears cocked. He tossed his mane, sending the long black strands flying in and out of the flames.

She reached again for the canteen, but this time the water did not help.

Robert's lips were moving. He gestured for her to come. "Walk." He wanted her to walk.

Yes, of course.

The fire followed, insidious flames creeping along invasive vines. When she slowed, the flames crawled; when she stopped, they crackled; when she hurried, they shot forward. The vines were the conduit, enabling the fire to spread from one tree trunk to the next. More and more orange wreaths spiraled up the bark to inflame moss and needles.

Her steps drifted into minutes, minutes into hours, her feet blistering along with her mind. Her riding boots had not been designed for endless walking, and her left ankle was rubbed raw. She could no longer track time. Had she been walking two hours or six?

The smoke intensified until she could make out little in the miasma, except the flames and the dark red coat of the stallion beside her—the stallion whose every move reminded her of Bianca's corpse.

Dead.

Dead.

Dead.

Then the fire began to spread from one branch to the next, burning around her in a shifting ring. She tried to keep walking, but the needles above her inflamed, hailing ash. She covered her face with her arm.

Pressure drew down her hand. She winced from the contact, but Robert did not release his grip. Instead, he moved in front of her, closer. For the first time in hours, the flames shrank back.

"You're limping, Aurelia." He nodded at a fallen log that was charred but not burning. "Please sit down."

Her searing ankle complied.

He released her hand, bent low, and unthreaded her boot laces. She bit her lip as he tugged off the torturous leather. Then gently he removed her stockings, his fingers lightly touching her bare ankle.

His eyes moved to hers. *Blue.* She had forgotten. *So blue.* If she stared into those eyes forever, she might remember who she was.

Then without warning, cold water splashed over her injury. And she screamed, her voice slamming through the trees and shadows of the forest. It ricocheted off earth and bark and the battered walls of her mind. She could not stop—did not want to stop. She wanted to keep on screaming until all the pain and blood, frustration and fury, let her go. She screamed until her tonsils burned and her throat was raw and her eyes watered. Until...

The flames went out.

Her scream invaded Robert's veins. He had been wrong. He had thought nothing could be worse than her death, but losing her like this, right in front of him—this was death and agony and loss compounded together in living form.

He had tried so hard to convince himself he could save her. If he took one step at a time and focused on the details for bringing her north. If he blocked out what had happened, ignored the way his words drifted past her, the fact that she would not speak, the terror in her eyes that never left. If he planned for any event, checked for every danger, avoided all mistakes.

But his own hand—the simple act of trying to cleanse her bleeding skin with the water from the canteen—had ripped apart what was left of her sanity and unleashed a void.

He did not want to face this, did not want to see the young woman he had cherished since childhood disintegrate in front of him. He would rather just vanish in this tangled sliver of Tyralt, with her. Burying his head in his hands, he lived the scream.

A soft, fragile whisper brought him back. "Robert?"

Was he imagining what he wanted to hear—the sound of his own name once more from her lips? Had he succeeded in losing his own mind?

"Robert, look at me, please." *She was speaking.*

He searched her dark brown gaze and, for the first time since the attack nearly ten hours before, found . . . her. *Thank Tyralt.* He tried to reach for her, to enfold her in his arms and prove to himself that she was there—whole—in front of him.

But she pulled away, fear shuddering behind her pupils.

"You were right about Melony," she said, a ragged breath exiting her body. "Back in Sterling, when you said she still had every reason to kill me."

Yes, he had been right. That did not make him feel any better. He did not want to talk about the attack. If she tore apart again, he might never get her back. As if she were his. As if she had ever belonged to him.

There was something beyond the attack's basic horror that disturbed him, something he had not taken the time to rip from the hollows of his mind. And he did not want to. He had tried before to unravel the meaning behind the attempts to assassinate her, and only loss had come from the effort. He did not want to understand the kind of hatred that lay behind this most recent attack.

Did not want to see it.

Did not want to remember it.

Did not want to think about it. Ever again.

For four interminable weeks, Aurelia battled her way through the Asyan and the forest of her own mind. Even the tall spruce, bent ferns, slick moss, and poison oak failed to compare to the mental tangle. Her thoughts had detached themselves from the sticky web of flame, but the scars left her struggling. Her strength, her pride, everything she had known about herself had incinerated in the recent maelstrom of hatred.

Her feelings toward Robert were a snarled mass: awe, guilt, envy, gratitude. And fear—this wild, misshapen fear that caught on any number of snags. Her talks with him were stilted, limited to the moment. He would not discuss the past, and she would not speak of the future.

He knew so much: how to use a compass, set snares, read tracks, build shelters, find water—all skills he must have learned on the frontier. And yet she had not known about any of them. She had chosen him as her guide based on emotion. *An emotion that had almost gotten him killed.*

By the end of the second fortnight, her world had narrowed down to whatever patch of forest floor lay ahead of her. And because of that, she was the first to spot the sharp silver glint in the afternoon shadows of the underbrush. She paused, sensing danger, then crouched, snagged a loose branch from the forest floor, and stripped aside the leafy vines. To reveal a large steel trap.

"Robert!" she called, eyes fixed on the deadly object.

The rustle of footsteps told her he was at her side. He bent down, asked Aurelia for the branch, and shifted more of the vines. His intense stare focused on the ground, but the branch unveiled nothing.

Her mind reeled with the significance of the trap. Someone must have been here, which meant she and Robert were not alone. At least not as alone as they had been for the past four weeks, never encountering any sight, sound, or smell indicating that another human being had ever traversed the same ground.

"Let's go." Robert stood, jostling her.

"What?" She caught herself with her hand, then rose to her feet.

He motioned her away from the glinting steel. "There is at least another hour of daylight."

"But shouldn't we stay? Won't someone return here to check the trap for game?"

He took her by the arm. "It's already been sprung, Aurelia."

Oh. She looked down, this time noting the tight clench of silver teeth. But that did not mean the trap had been abandoned. "It's not rusted. Shouldn't we wait at least a day?"

"No." He was walking now, pulling her along. Was she imagining it, or was he moving at a faster pace than he had been before? Her breath began to swish in and out.

Perhaps the trap was a sign they were nearing the forest's edge. Perhaps Robert was right, and stopping would only prolong the time the two of them remained in the Asyan. Isolated from civilization. And its clutches.

I should not think that way. She dropped her gaze once again to the foliage in front of her.

What was left of the day rushed past in a blur. The morning mist had burned off at noon, but her skin felt damp, the hurried pace and late afternoon heat making her sweat between her shoulder blades. She felt dirty and disheveled and as tattered as her riding skirt. Her ankle had healed, but her hem had paid the toll in the service of bandages. By the time she and Robert stopped to set up camp, Aurelia was worn out. And the monotonous chore of collecting firewood loomed before her.

Robert, meanwhile, picked up his already rapid pace. He cleared away brush, cut two piles of spruce boughs, and set up a campfire ring before she had managed to gather three decent pieces of fuel.

Then he reached for his bow, a smooth shaft he had carved and shaped from a fallen hazel sapling he had found by a creek.

A queer tightness settled in her stomach. "Robert, it's near dark."

"Dusk is the best time for hunting." He did not look at her.

His averted eyes and frenzied pace made her think something was wrong—had been wrong ever since the trap. "Not tonight," she said.

He removed his self-made quiver from the pack, then dropped the bag at her feet. "Tonight."

"If you would stay here and teach me how to shoot, we could catch twice as much game," she pointed out logically.

" We don't have time for that."

"Why not?" She dropped a third piece of wood on the pile.

"Aurelia, it takes more than one lesson to master a bow. There are a million ways for you to be more helpful." He eyed her paltry stack of firewood.

"Well, if you would take the time to teach me some of them, I might learn," she snapped.

"Aurelia"—he hooked the bow over his shoulder—"this is a matter of survival."

Her frustration boiled into bluntness. "Whose survival? I'm the one everyone wants to kill. Why shouldn't I be able to defend myself?"

Something shifted behind Robert's eyes. His hand flexed on his sword hilt. A habit. One he always seemed to use these days before ducking out of a conversation. "The ability to shoot is not self-defense."

She flicked a hand at him. "Look at you! You've been trained to fight since you were born. You have a weapon for everything. A knife to slit a rabbit's throat. An arrow to bring down a deer. Goodness knows what you can hit with a rifle! And you can use a sword to—"

"Kill my best friend."

Silence reigned.

Too late she recognized the emotion behind his eyes as pain.

Robert tugged the knife from his boot and flung the blade into the earth in front of her. "Have it," he said. "But if you think I'm going to train you to kill someone, Aurelia, you could not be more wrong."

She did not know him. The thought stabbed through her as he tossed the sheath beside the hilt, then spun and left the clearing. Who was this young man who had almost single-handedly brought her out of the flames and back from the edge of insanity?

And who was she? Before the attacks, she had thought of

herself as intelligent, confident, caring. Had all these traits been reduced to ash?

She had not meant to hurt him just now. Aurelia retrieved the knife from the ground and stared at the sharp edges. She had meant to say that he could use his sword to save lives. He had done so—saved her and the king—by defeating Chris. But she had failed to fully comprehend what that act had meant to Robert. Perhaps she could not. Perhaps that was what he had just tried to tell her: that she couldn't understand that type of guilt because she had never wielded the weapon that had killed someone she loved.

Her eyes scrambled after his figure slipping away into the dusk. *Yes,* her thoughts argued. Yes, she could understand guilt. Safety was an illusion. And she trusted the instincts that said he should not be out there alone. Not tonight. She would never forgive herself if something happened to him because she had chased him away.

Returning the knife to its sheath and tucking the weapon under her skirt band, Aurelia shot a quick glance at Horizon, decided the stallion could take care of himself, and set off after Robert. At first she tried to hang back thirty or forty paces. She knew better than to announce her presence, not wanting to hear his refusals. She just . . . needed to know he was safe.

The forest was different at dusk, the palette of greens and browns fading to gray. Scurrying footsteps and the flash of a furry tail indicated that nature's creatures had come out from their hiding places. The air itself had changed. It felt clean, clear, easier to move through than the mist-heavy dawn and the weary stretch of afternoon heat trapped beneath the spruce canopy. She had not even considered walking at night since the terror of her escape, but to Aurelia's surprise, the feeling beneath her speeding pulse was not fear.

Thrill. The startling, forgotten joy of taking a risk.

And Robert was there ahead of her.

Then he was not. Her heart thudded in her ears as she hurried forward to the spruce trunk where she had last seen him. It occurred to her then, and only then, that she could not find her way back to the campsite. She had no compass, and her inexpert eyes were useless in tracking a path through the foliage, especially in the dimming light.

The sleeve of a buckskin jacket appeared again in her line of vision, and she exhaled. *Fool,* her conscience scolded. *What will you do when night truly falls, and you can no longer see him?*

She put off the dilemma and followed closer, determined to pay heed to her surroundings. They were not all foreign. That clearing there, with the large boulder—Robert had thought about using it for a campsite. And the bird's nest over there—he had snagged feathers from it for his arrows. *He's retracing our steps from this afternoon. Why?*

The answer came as the grays of dusk shifted to a darker spectrum. Robert paused beside a stream, crouching for a minute over a patch of earth. Aurelia waited, impatiently rubbing her thumb along the knife sheath tucked in her waistband, then crept forward, doubtful she would be able to read whatever sign had held his attention. But the earth here was damp, and the track formed in the mud was astoundingly clear. Five perfect curves of a paw, and matching V-like formations. *The claws of a cat.*

A chill started in Aurelia's feet, climbed her legs and spine, and crawled over her shoulders to raise the flesh on her arms. This must be the reason Robert had hurried her away from the trap. But why was he following the tracks now? Why would he go after a mountain lion? The meat could not be worth the danger.

Still trying to protect me. Can't he see it's his presence that does that?

Her pulse galloped. The latter thought had come without intent, but as soon as it formed, she acknowledged its validity. Not once in the past month had he gone to sleep before she had or woken after her. Even in the middle of the night when she had jolted awake, he seemed to sense her distress from across the clearing and to wake as well. Not once had he questioned his place at her side. Not once had he mentioned that his life also had been in peril that night of the deadly flames. Could he possibly be foolish enough to risk himself now, when she needed him on the most basic level?

She did need him.

Aurelia inhaled the truth just as he slipped through a wall of thick brush and sank out of sight into the darkness. She hurried forward, stumbled over a branch that was stretched out oddly on the ground, then launched forth again. She had to stop him from this insane hunt and explain her own fears. He had been so adamant about wanting to protect her. Surely, he could understand her need to have him safe.

She reached the wall of brush and peered down a small slope into a thicket, a soft bed of needles surrounded by dense spruce. It took a moment to make out Robert's figure amid the shadows, his arrow drawn.

A sound rustled. Aurelia's mind spiraled in panic as a deadly mountain lion burst from the trees, its form a stunning blaze of speed and muscle. The arrow from Robert's bow plunged into the golden chest, but the cat did not die. Then a loud gunshot ripped through the air. A wild cry rent the dusk, and the cat twisted in mid-flight, then fell to its side. A second shot, from another direction, ensured the creature no further agony.

And a sword blade flashed at the thicket's edge, then settled, shimmering and silver, into the hollow at Robert's throat.

Chapter Five
THE FORTRESS

HE HEARD THE SCRAPE OF STEEL—THE ROUGH *SWISH* of warning. Close enough and loud enough for him to draw his own sword in defense. But his fingers failed to react.

His mind refused to lift the blade.

An instant later the choice seemed never to have existed. The sharp tip of an enemy sword pricked his throat. "Poaching," snarled a thin, masculine voice, "is a criminal offense." Then long fingers dug into Robert's shoulder, yanking him to his feet, and a circle of raised muskets emerged from the brush. All pointed at him.

"No!" a sharp female voice rang through the clearing.

What was *she* doing here?

Aurelia emerged from the trees, her face smeared with dirt, hair tangled, bare arms exposed by ragged sleeves. Nothing remained to attest to her title, save the anger firing from her dark eyes.

"Release him," she ordered.

Every man in the thicket flinched. Regret coursed its way through Robert's thoughts. Why would a band of armed men be traveling without the insignia of a local lord? Unless they were outlaws? He had seen the strangers' tracks that afternoon by the trap and known what they were hunting. But he had not told Aurelia because he had not wished to raise her hopes for rescue . . . until he could ensure that the hunters were no threat. Naturally his plans had ended in disaster.

A round of murmurs shifted through the clearing.

The clawlike grip on Robert's shoulder tightened. "Ye're trespassing," the sword-bearer's thin voice accused.

"We are not," she snapped.

Even if she weren't the crown princess, I suspect we'd have as much legal right here as you. Robert tried to speak, but as soon as he opened his mouth, a hilt clubbed him in the head.

The forest spun, and hands ripped Robert's scabbard from his waist. A strange lightness flooded his veins, as though a poison held too close had been removed from his soul.

By the time he regained his vision, a large broad-shouldered man with a sprinkling of pox scars on his jaw had stepped toward Aurelia. He wore no crest or uniform to distinguish himself from the other rough-clad men, but his stance identified him as their leader. He held one palm out to the side in a gesture of cessation. "Ye're in the forest, aren't ye?" he addressed her.

Her eyes were on Robert, something strange in their dark depths.

She lifted her chin and turned to the pock-faced leader. "We request," she said, without a hint of petition in her tone, "your hospitality."

"Ha!" smirked the lanky sword-bearer. "Ye don't think ye'll get off that easy."

"Hold yer tongue, Jeynolds," the leader glowered, then turned to the rest of his men. His deep voice penetrated the darkness. "We'll make camp, then take them both to the Fortress."

The fog of confusion followed Robert into the night. His head continued to throb, and he found himself unable to sort through Jeynolds's high-pitched snarl, the leader's brusque orders, and Aurelia's commanding tone. At last, upon the hard ground and without intention, he slept.

Then, at dawn, came the familiar whistle of his stallion. It made no sense that Horizon should be there, but when Robert tried to ask for an explanation, Jeynolds's sword demanded he prepare to march. Aurelia, gripping the stallion's lead rope, sent a forced smile across the campsite. No further explanation was necessary. Somehow she must have convinced the outlaws to help her track Horizon, though judging by the way they were all keeping their distance from the sharp hooves, none of them was much of a horseman.

An instant later, those hooves were in the air, the stallion's scream shredding Robert's eardrums as two outlaws, bearing the corpse of the dead mountain lion swinging from a branch upon their shoulders, stepped into the clearing.

Fools! Robert lurched forward.

Only to find Jeynolds's blade at his throat.

Aurelia had let the rope slide through her fingers as the stallion reared, and now she took a step away from the thrashing hooves. "Put the corpse down!" she shouted.

"No." The leader's firm voice took over. "It's coming with us. Take the cat out of the clearing, and carry it ahead of us downwind."

The men obeyed at once, and the stallion's screams subsided.

The scarred leader frowned, though his eyes were low, making it impossible to tell which of the incident's participants were the objects of his fury. "Formation," he growled at the forest floor.

Like ghosts, the remaining band members shuffled around the captives. Two to their left. Two to their right. One up ahead a little ways, with three more beyond view. Though all had drifted so far into the trees that if Robert had not seen the dispersal, he would have been pressed to spot any of the men. No wonder he had had such a hard time tracking them the night before. They moved without sound.

Of all the outlaws, only Jeynolds remained in the clearing, his blade still out.

Robert's hand reached reflexively for his own sword hilt and closed on empty air.

Jeynolds shoved him forward with unnecessary force.

Robert moved. His head had cleared from the clubbing, and he had no desire to incur a second one. The forest floor shifted beneath his feet, and time began to stretch. *Focus,* he ordered himself. *Prepare yourself for whatever is coming.*

He peered more intently through the trees at the silent men. All armed. All except Jeynolds with a rifle in hand. At first, those were the only observations Robert could note, but as the journey lengthened, his eyes began to pry further details from the shadows. The weapons were all held in the same position. The men moved at the same pace. When they paused, they stood with their feet apart. In the same stance. *At rest.* Like the palace guard.

No. These were not the same men who had tried to murder Aurelia. They could not be members of the royal guard, or she would have recognized them. And hired assassins would not be out hunting mountain lions.

Though Horizon did not seem impressed by this fact. The stallion had slowed his pace and was walking with an uneven gait, lifting his hooves high and kicking at the underbrush. Aurelia moved up close to the horse's neck.

Just then a second cluster of outlaws drifted out of the trees. Also armed.

A stocky, mid-size man stepped forward as if to exchange greetings. But the pock-faced leader shook his head, lifting his chin in the direction of the bay stallion pawing the earth at Aurelia's feet. The newcomer looked, his face muscles stiffening, then his head turned back to the scarred man, and a long gaze transpired between them. No gestures were made. No hands shaken. The second band of men dissipated into the forest, leaving only the same eerie quiet broken by the remnants of Horizon's distress.

So there were more than a dozen outlaws. That should not be a surprise, but the control exhibited by each band's leader to hold the other men to silence—there was nothing normal about that. It required training. *Intense organized training.* Not the kind found among criminals.

His senses now alert, Robert kept an eye on the stallion as the party proceeded. He was more prepared for—and disturbed by—the appearance of a third band of men. Then a fourth.

Patrolling.

And then the houses began to appear. Small timber constructs gathered together along worn footpaths and eventually an actual road with wagon tracks. Women bustled forth, carrying wood. Most of them paid no heed to the party at all, but their children rushed up to the armed men, words of horror and excitement sweeping from young mouths to ask about the mountain lion's corpse that had already passed their way. The stern expressions on some of the band members' faces creased into smiles, and one man laughed as he ran a hand through the ruddy curls of a young boy whose features matched his own.

These people lived here, then, amid the forest. Though none of the maps Robert had studied revealed any villages in the depths of the Asyan. Perhaps these men were a valid city guard. But no—even a local guard was required to identify itself. And no village could afford to hire the number of men he had seen this morning.

There was something just beyond his grasp.

And then the answer materialized. Ahead, the forest gave way to a giant man-made structure. Walls of thick, solid spruce rose from the earth, their massive strength as intimidating as any stone barrier or gated portcullis. The roof arched in a steep slanted V, then stretched out behind and to the sides, covering not only the main building but what appeared to be stables as large as those at Midbury. And in front of the entire complex stretched a field, carved in the heart of the forest....

And crawling with soldiers. Not a city guard. Not outlaws. *A private army.* More than a thousand men.

Someone had gathered them here, trained them, and given them a reason to stay.

What would the king think if he knew how many men stood here, weapons in hand, three hundred miles from the capital? There were laws—clear, strict laws limiting private guards to specific charges. And numbers. Lest any one lord gain too much power over another, much less the crown.

Robert's gaze flew to Aurelia, and he wondered if the same thoughts had crossed her mind.

He could see her eyes flick from soldier to soldier. Counting.

As the party approached the crowded field, a tall man with dark hair and a rigid countenance came forward, then made a sharp gesture to his right at a boy in a brown vest who hurried forth to reach for Horizon's reins.

The stallion reared, and Robert felt Jeynolds's sword return to his throat before he even had a chance to intercede.

Aurelia stepped between the boy and the sharp hooves. "He's temperamental," she said.

The dark-haired soldier gave no response to her words, just gestured again toward the boy, who eased forward once more and stretched out his hand for Horizon to smell. The stallion snorted, stamped his feet, then turned away as though bored.

Aurelia's gaze slid toward Robert, a question in her eyes.

Of course he would have preferred to keep watch over the stallion, but the sword now easing toward his back made that impossible. He gave a slight nod, and she released the reins.

Stallion and boy headed toward the stables. *One confrontation avoided.*

But the dark-haired soldier's first comment severed any chance of respite. His tone stern, his words clipped, he turned his gaze from the prisoners to the scarred leader and said, "His Lordship wishes to see them."

Robert felt his thoughts whirl as minutes later he stepped under the beams of the Fortress entryway, his eyes resting on the brown skin of Aurelia's neck where it met her squared shoulders. Was it possible the head of this place was a genuine lord? A man with the authority to enforce law over the Asyan?

But a deep warning cut through Robert's thoughts.

A man who had gathered his own army in defiance of the crown. For whom no one, short of the king, would be less welcome than the crown princess.

Blood pulsed in Robert's eardrums. What he would not give for a minute—thirty seconds—to speak to her alone and warn her to remain silent. To maintain her anonymity.

But there was no privacy. And no time.

A thickset woman in brown housekeeper's garb bustled forward, her sharp gaze sweeping over the soldiers and landing on Robert and Aurelia. "The man first," came the woman's brisk command. "In the great hall. His Lordship is prepared for judgment."

Jeynolds shoved Robert forward.

Aurelia's protest rang behind him. "You have no right—"

Don't! he thought desperately. *Don't tell them who you are.*

Her voice faded behind a closed door, and Robert moved at sword-point down a long barren corridor and through an open entryway.

Into a giant space of light and unrestrained voices. Tables surrounded with men crowded the room. Serving-women bearing pitchers of beer and platters of food squeezed their way around dangling feet and swinging elbows, and the scent of roast pork sent a knife through Robert's stomach. Then a brutal shove thrust him out into the hall's center aisle. Alone.

A man at the front table stood up.

All sound halted. And all eyes turned toward His Lordship. The man's fiery red mane draped past his bulky shoulders and down from his chin. In one hand, he wielded a glass of ruby wine, in the other, a knife bearing a giant hunk of meat. The rich food could explain his wide girth, but the muscles in his large arms belied all labels of the sedentary aristocracy.

The man's own gaze drilled into Robert's. "Approach." The lord pounded his wine glass down on the table. Crimson liquid splashed out.

It could be worse, Robert told himself, as he stepped past the crowd of onlookers. *I could be asking to court his daughter.*

"Your name," the lord ordered.

Robert held his tongue. There was no telling what detail, no matter how minor, might betray Aurelia's identity. And though Robert's first name was not nearly as well known as his last, there were bound to be rumors: about the missing princess; her journey; and, as much as he had tried to deny it, her relationship with him.

The lord waited, then took a bite of his meat, chewed, and swallowed. "You have been charged with hunting on my land. Is this true?"

There was no point in denial. Surely one of the men from the band of captors had already told about the events of the previous night. "Yes, Your Lordship," Robert replied.

"And are you guilty?"

Lies came too easily and cost too much. "Yes."

The man lowered his knife, allowing the now barren blade to dangle outward as he strolled around the table, his eyes on everyone in the room except for Robert. "I don't suppose," he said as though sharing a joke with his audience, "you would care to elaborate." He completed the half-circuit and stopped five feet away.

Robert's thoughts scrambled for an explanation, one that would bear the ring of truth without betraying *her.* He could not find one. "No, Your Lordship."

"Do you know who I am, *boy?*"

No. And . . . *yes.* There was only one man with a real title to the Asyan. Robert had not thought of him before because the lord's indolent reputation held next to nothing in common with this muscular figure. But then . . . a man plotting treason would not survive an accurate reputation. "Yes, Your Lordship." Robert could not suppress the edge in his voice.

The knife plunged into the crease of the circuited table. "And do you doubt that I could have you killed this instant with the full support of the law?"

This titled man with his treasonous army chose to invoke the name of the law? Robert's sarcasm was now heavy. "No, *Your Lordship.*"

A half dozen soldiers, swords raised, launched from the sides of the room.

And Aurelia's voice rang over the vast hall. "Release him in the name of the crown."

Honestly! she thought, sweeping down the center aisle in her tattered riding clothes. *Couldn't their host see that Robert was trying to protect her?* It had become clear to Aurelia, moments before when she had been offered a silk dress to change into, that the person in charge knew who she was.

"Your hospitality is rather lacking, Lord Lester," she said, stepping past Robert and coming to a halt in front of the red-haired man she had never met before.

The large man arched an eyebrow and gave an ironic bow. "We can hardly be blamed for not being prepared for your visit, Your Highness, as there was no warning. Though it is, nonetheless, an honor to have you at our estate. The crown excluded, of course."

She raised her chin.

Robert's hand gripped hers from behind. *Why did he always know when she was bluffing?*

"I have long missed out on meeting you at court, Your Lordship," she replied, a caustic bite to her tone.

Lord Lester chuckled. "I am much more at comfort here, Your Highness, where all the weapons are clearly displayed."

She allowed her gaze to circle the audience, taking in the vast number of armed men, all prepared to arrest her at the slightest gesture from their leader. "I am impressed," she said, "by the committed group you appear to have gathered."

Robert's grip tightened on her hand, and she pulled away, taking one more step forward. If this lord was an enemy, she would cede him no authority.

"That I have." Lord Lester's chest rose in pride. "I daresay you'll not find an equal example of loyalty in the kingdom." The crowd erupted in a brief cheer of support.

Aurelia blinked. "On the contrary, I believe the young man you have threatened just now is at least as fine an example. Would you not say his refusal to betray my identity or lie to you at peril of his own life can compare to any *form* of loyalty?"

The raised swords at His Lordship's side eased toward the ground, and there was a brief silence.

Lord Lester grinned, a glimmer in his eyes. "Not sure *loyal* is the term I would use. But then who am I"—he chuckled—"to question a man for taking a risk to protect a woman of your particular bloodline."

Her bloodline?

"I hope you will not judge my men too harshly, Your Highness." He gestured at Jeynolds, who still held his sword to Robert's back. "After all, they may have recognized your face, but they could not be certain of who you were."

What did that mean?

Again he chuckled, this time the light in his eyes stretching across his ruddy cheekbones. "But I am indulging my sense of humor at your expense. My wife"—he paused and his voice gentled—"will not approve."

Then he stepped aside and gestured backward at a portrait.

Of a woman. Seated. Thin arms clasped, false light haloing the face and dark features.

My hair. My skin. My eyes.

Aurelia felt her heart explode at the sight of her mother. *Her portrait.* In this buried-away fortress in the depths of Tyralt, in a great hall filled with gawking soldiers. On display here, when it was never, ever displayed in the royal palace.

Yet there was something even more disturbing about the image: the hollowed cheekbones, the indentations of the woman's temples, the lines in the skin along her eyes. Age.

Lord Lester's statement finally penetrated. *My wife will not approve.*

His wife?

Aurelia wanted to scream or cry or fight. Her mother was here? In this fortress? Now? But even so, the former queen was absent.

Nothing.

Aurelia had never had any defense against nothing. She whirled and flung herself from the room.

Chapter Six
THE BLUE ROOM

THE SWORD WAS STILL AT ROBERT'S BACK, BUT HE could not have followed her anyway. He had seen the look on her face. A look that forbade contact.

Far better that than her empty gaze from the forest. Though this man—this *lord*—had risked plunging her into that abyss with his tactless revelation. "Is that what you were hoping for?" Robert accused. "Treating her *life* as if it were your entertainment."

The array of weapons lifted again.

But His Lordship did not bother to reply. Instead he gestured toward a woman at the door, the housekeeper from the entrance. "Find her." Lester's voice rang across the room.

The woman nodded and bustled away.

The large man's chest rose and fell several times. Then he gave a sharp gesture to a soldier on his left. "Clear the room."

At once the serving-women and the men from the tables withdrew, filing out with such speed the hall emptied in a matter of minutes. Steel remained at Robert's back, and the aura of danger swelled within the vacant space. No one else remained save for Jeynolds, the row of soldiers beside Lord Lester, and the man who had hired them.

His Lordship began to pace, staring at the floor as he pounded back and forth. "What brought you here?" he demanded from Robert.

"Your men."

Lester spun, color splattering his face. "Why? Why are you here?"

Robert replied coolly. And slowly. "Because your men brought us here."

The pacing stopped. "If you will not provide answers, you have no place on the premises."

Robert bridled. "I'm not going until I am certain Her Highness is all right."

A fierce, almost animal-like growl exited from the man's throat. Then he turned and stalked around the table and all the way to the portrait at the front of the room. The red head tilted back as Robert waited for the next pronouncement.

At last it came, the words directed to the soldiers. "Take him below," His Lordship ordered.

The ivy on the guest room tapestry invaded Aurelia's mind as she sat, still in her rags, on the hard wooden floor. Waiting. Her back was against the bed, her eyes tracing and retracing the deceptive heart-shaped leaves and long deathly vines that strangled everything they touched. Like love.

Her mother had not come.

At least three hours had passed since the housekeeper had shown Aurelia here, offering her the room as a place of solitude. It had remained solitary—leaving Aurelia facing the empty dark cavity within herself, the sting of rejection. And futility. Her mind had detached from the present to traverse the wasteland of time. So few memories. A gentle embrace, the smell of lilacs, a beautiful laugh that could in no way be mistaken for that of her stepmother, Elise.

But it was Aurelia's *mother* who had abandoned her daughter. Fourteen years ago. Without a word. And still after all those years, like a naïve child, Aurelia had thought her mother would come. And what? Apologize for the minutes, months, and years of not being present? That was never going to happen.

A faint rap came at the door.

"Hello?" said a soft female voice. Too familiar. The door caught upon the latch. "It's me, Daria."

Emotion slipped. In the midst of all that had happened, Aurelia had failed to connect her arrival on this estate with the presence of her best friend. *Of course Daria is here. Her husband is Lord Lester's courier.* Aurelia scrambled up, tripping on the green bedding she had pulled down to the floor. She crossed in front of the hanging ivy, removed the lock—a measure of control enacted to deny she had none—and opened the door.

A figure in gold muslin stood in the hall, her once-thin cheeks filled out beneath upswept raven hair and her black eyes glittering with concern.

Is it that obvious I am damaged?

Then warm arms reached across the space and wrapped Aurelia in a fierce hug.

Daria—who had rescued Aurelia from boredom during endless hours of etiquette training. Who had stood guard and made up stories to excuse her best friend's escapes from the palace. Who had laughed at the ancient royal suitors and dared Aurelia to find someone who moved her heart instead.

None of that mattered now.

"Is it true?" Aurelia murmured. "Is my mother actually here?"

The hug tightened, then released. "Yes."

Then you knew. The bitter thought replaced the warmth. How could one's closest friend harbor a secret like this?

Daria must have read the anguish in Aurelia's eyes, because explanation spilled forth. "I only found out when Thomas brought me here, upon my arrival. And I was sworn to secrecy. It's a condition for living on the estate."

A true friend would never take that oath.

"Of course, that is no excuse for not telling *you*."

The admission cut a rift in Aurelia's turmoil.

"But I did not dare write!" Daria declared. "I did not want your stepmother to intercept the message. Or your father."

Aurelia took a step back toward the barren hearth. There was so much her father *had* known and not told her. She had feared that her mother's location might be another fact he had chosen to withhold. "Then my father doesn't know my mother is here?"

Daria blinked, stretching out her fingers toward her friend. "No, of course not. Why do you think Lord Lester never returns to the palace? And why else would he hire this many men to defend his estate? It's all for your mother's protection."

Protection?

Daria's empty hand dropped, along with her gaze. "It's hard to know how your father would react. There might be . . . well, there might be repercussions."

Aurelia staggered back, her side grazing the sharp corner of the mantel. It had never occurred to her that her mother might be in danger, having left the palace, or that she might have been in danger living there when her husband clearly preferred another woman.

But if the assassination plot had taught Aurelia anything, it was that the palace was unsafe. Even if her father had no intention of harming her mother, he could not be relied upon to protect her. Daria was right.

"She hasn't come," Aurelia said.

"Lady Margaret never comes."

Margaret? Her mother's name was Marguerite. "What?"

"She never leaves her quarters."

That made no sense. Surely Daria was exaggerating, trying to defend her best friend from reality. Aurelia had no interest in excuses. "Of course she does."

"No." Daria shook her head. "Lady Margaret has a single space at the end of the hall on the third floor, one flight up, her own private residence known as the Blue Room." *Private. Meaning no one is allowed to enter without permission.* "She never leaves. Ever."

Aurelia struggled to take in the implications. But how could she? If the past three hours had proven anything, it was that she knew nothing about the woman upstairs. "She has not sent for me."

Daria's voice wavered. "It must have been a shock. Your arrival. I do not really know her . . . but I know she has been like a talisman to the people here. They would defend her with their lives."

The people have always loved my mother. But she has never loved me. Aurelia backed away until the hollow of her spine hit the edge of a glass table along the wall. Her elbow jostled a vase of dead flowers.

Porcelain tumbled, and white shards sprayed across gray stones.

Daria pulled her friend away from the shattered pieces. "I know it's not fair, but if you wish to see her, then *you* must go to her."

"I can't."

"Why not?"

Because I am a coward. Because I'm not who I was before the forest. Or maybe I am. Maybe that dark cavity inside me was always there. "She left me, Daria. Not just my father—*me*. And I don't . . . I don't understand why."

Her friend's voice remained calm. "Then why don't you *ask* her?"

As if it were that simple.

Aurelia sank down and buried her head in her hands, reaching for the strength within herself. But there was none there. She had been avoiding the thought of her mother for so long, nothing had ever filled the gap. Perhaps that was the weakness, the flaw in her own design, that had allowed Aurelia to lose herself in the forest.

All this time—her entire life—she had blamed her mother for leaving. And for much more. For the failure to be there, to teach her daughter *how* to become queen, and to answer her questions. Yet now, when Aurelia had the chance to alter that reality, she had chosen to lock the door.

Hiding was her father's technique. And her mother's.

I cannot—I will not *be my parents,* she thought.

She gathered the threads in her soul, pulling them tight. If the cavity within herself was due to her mother, then confronting her was the only way out of the mental vines and tangles that had clutched at Aurelia ever since the morning after the fire.

Slowly her body unfurled, and she stepped toward the door. Her chest contracted, and her breath ran shallow. Her friend's hand threaded through her fingers, but she shook it off. This was not something Daria could do for her. Nor Robert. Nor anyone else in the length and breadth of the kingdom. *It is* my *task.*

Without looking back, Aurelia forced herself beyond the threshold and down the corridor. The rising circular staircase swallowed her whole. Antler horns sprouted out from the walls above her, their sharp points threatening like spears. The wood-grain wall ran from reds to blacks, and the steps, though perfectly constructed, seemed to narrow as she climbed.

Toward her greatest fear. She could not help but feel that ignorance would be easier. Then there could be no misunderstandings. Or brutal truths. Was the chasm in her heart not better than her mother's open hatred? Were fragile memories not better than broken ones? And was it not all better—the hurt, the emptiness, the anger—than the agonizing flutter of hope?

At the top of the stair, she saw only the blue door, a bright unavoidable color that pulled her all the way to the end of the hall. Her hand reached for the latch, fingers refusing to curl into a polite knock. To do so would permit refusal or allow time for retreat. *This is my choice.* I *must make it.*

The barrier swung at her touch.

Sky blue walls opened around her. Ocean-colored fabric graced pillows and cushions. Robin's egg curtains fluttered at an open window. And dozens and dozens of fresh bluebells filled the room. A woman, her back to the door, was arranging a handful in a vase on the windowsill.

There could be no doubt about her identity. Dark brown wisps drifted down her neck, and her brown skin mirrored her daughter's. But the woman did not turn.

"Mother?" Aurelia whispered to the only person who had ever held that title in her heart.

The woman froze, shoulders stiffening like a statue's, thin arms with bent elbows pressing tightly into her sides, fingers strangling the flowers in her hand. Her face, profile, gaze—withheld.

As they had been forever.

Doubt assailed, a deluge of emotion sweeping through Aurelia. She was again a three-year-old child without strategy or defense. Everything she had built up, every verbal and logical weapon, fell useless, sucked into the swirling whirlpool of the carpet. And she could do nothing but stammer the truth. "I . . . I know you do not wish to speak to me, but . . ."

The statue did not turn.

She forced herself to continue. "I need to know why." There, the words were out. And now—*bother!* The tears were coming, stripping her of her dignity. There was no winning in this situation, no stopping the sick hollow feeling in her stomach.

The woman remained frozen.

"Why?" Aurelia demanded. She wiped the salty smear from her face. "Why won't you look at me? Or talk to me? Why don't you want to *know* me?"

The statue began to tremble. Its entire frame, though the same height as Aurelia, seemed as slight as a child's. The shoulders came down. The flowers dripped from shaking fingers. Only now did her mother turn, tears flowing freely down her face. The beautiful dusky skin was thin and blotchy, and the matching dark eyes were red and ringed in shadows. "Because," came the ragged whisper, "I didn't know if I could survive ever having to say good-bye."

Then her mother had never wished to leave? At least had never wished to leave *her*? Could that be possible? Could it be enough?

The anger that had propelled Aurelia through so many confrontations deserted her as she struggled to reconcile the emptiness in her head with the shaking, desperate figure before her now. Her mother was so thin—the bones in her arms and face protruding more than they had in the portrait in the hall. Intricate lace graced her throat. And embroidery with the same pattern trailed down the folds of her skirt to the hem.

What must this lady think of the bedraggled figure now claiming to be her daughter?

The thin woman gave no insight into such questions. Instead, she retreated to the fallen bluebells and the empty vase.

At this, Aurelia swept forward to retrieve the flowers, then offered them up. To her mother.

But the stranger moved to the other side of the vase.

Chapter Seven
SANCTUARY

"DON'T WORRY, I WON'T KILL HIM," SAID A WRY, masculine voice.

Robert woke to those auspicious words and the bleak view of a gray-stone basement room. No windows. No hearth. No curtains, cushions, or tapestries. Only the bed, a side table, and a solitary wooden chair upon the bare stone floor. After a month of struggling to survive in the Asyan—of waking at every *snap* and *crack* in the forest in order to protect Aurelia—he had fallen asleep. In the traitor's lair.

Robert could not even summon the energy for regret. At least here, no one but himself would pay for his lapse in vigilance.

A female voice, not Aurelia's, responded to the earlier comment. "But Your Lordship—"

"I am the head of this estate, am I not, Mrs. Solier?"

Solier? Robert had heard that name before. He lifted his chest. "Daria?"

The black-haired girl he had rescued from swarming bees when he and she were both seven hurried toward him. Her hair was still dark, and her eyes still glittered; but despite the fact that he had seen her less than two months ago, she looked somehow older and more complete.

Her gaze dropped at once to his shoulder.

Too late he realized the scar was showing through his loosened shirt. Immediately he tied the laces at his neckline.

"Chris's sword?" she whispered.

Robert winced. His cousin had been her friend as well.

"It's not a safe occupation, is it?" she murmured. "To protect a princess."

He had never managed to protect Aurelia.

And he could not discuss this with Daria.

Especially not with Lord Lester's bulky chest blocking the doorframe, his large arms crossed over the hilt of the confiscated Vantauge sword.

"Where is she?" Robert could not help asking.

There was no hesitation in Daria's response. "Upstairs with her mother."

"In truth?" He knew Aurelia's feelings toward her mother were far from warm.

"Indeed." Lord Lester uncrossed his arms and drew closer, then slowly propped the naked weapon against the wall. "You may wait outside, Mrs. Solier," he stated in a clear command, his gaze scanning Robert with deliberation. The lord's muscle-bound arms furled again.

Robert did not have the mental stamina for political cat and mouse. "What is it you want to know?"

His Lordship's green eyes narrowed. "It's a matter of need, not want. I need to know what the two of you were doing in the forest. Alone."

Was this man accusing Robert of running off with the crown princess? "You should ask *her*. It's not my place to answer for Her Royal Highness." The title flew off his tongue like a weapon.

Lester's red beard twitched at an odd angle, then actually broke into a grin. "I've heard the gossip. It bears no credence."

That was good, because Robert had not heard the gossip and did not care to defend himself against any rumors that were flying around, though he had an uncomfortable feeling he knew what they might be.

The grin faded, and Lord Lester continued, "But my wife is upstairs, speaking with her daughter for the first time in fourteen years." He paused as though struggling with deep emotion. "And for my wife . . . that is everything. I will not allow it to end in carnage."

For his wife? She was the one who had abandoned her daughter. If someone had the right to fear emotional carnage, it was Aurelia.

"I know about the assassination plot," Lord Lester went on, "and I am fully aware that His Majesty did not release adequate details. So I'm telling you I not only want details, I need them.

If I am going to house both the former queen and the crown princess under my roof, I need to know the truth to avoid bloodshed."

Bloodshed. Then the carnage this man spoke of was literal. And he might well be correct. If the king found this place—if he sent his men hunting for his daughter and discovered, in the process, an entire army, as well as the woman who had humiliated him—the meeting might well end in slaughter.

Robert closed his eyes. Was there nowhere he could take Aurelia? Nowhere she could be safe from the threats that kept piling, one upon the other, like bodies from a massacre?

But this man *had* kept someone safe for over a decade. And he was offering to protect Aurelia as well.

Robert told him the unvarnished truth. "The guards assigned to the expedition tried to kill her."

There was no response from His Lordship.

"We escaped with our lives. But I did not dare take her back to the road, in case the guards might ambush us. They could have staked out any town between Sterling and—"

"Transcontina," Lord Lester finished for him. The city at the northern edge of the Asyan. "That's less than three days' ride. I'll send several men to investigate. If palace guards have been in the city, there are those who will know."

"And if the guards are there now?" Robert had no desire to see conflict erupt.

"Then my men will watch them and send word when they

head back toward the capital. You are to remain here until we receive that confirmation."

I'm under Her Highness's authority. Not yours.

But Robert did not dispute the order.

His Lordship nodded brusquely and turned, then at the doorway came to a sudden halt. "I've spoken with my courier." He cleared his throat. "He and his wife have agreed to offer you more *suitable* lodging."

He walked out.

Robert felt his jaw clench. The meaning behind the message stung. He was not of the correct class. He had no power, no title, no status. No right to even share a roof with Aurelia. No right to think of her as anything more than his future monarch.

But that could not alter the truth that had plunged into him when she had stormed down the center of the hall, her chin upraised, eyes flashing, voice confident. Recklessly risking her life to defend him. Slaying all threats that stood in her way.

He loved her.

And there was nothing he, or anyone else, could do to change that.

Her mother would not touch her.

Not on that first visit. Or the next. Or the next.

Each morning when Aurelia came to the Blue Room, Lady Margaret—as she was now called—sat alone at her window in her solitary wicker chair, where she could avoid meeting her daughter's eyes by staring at the flower gardens below.

She was like a set of porcelain shards pieced together. Anything Aurelia said might cause her to crack. No topic was safe: the palace, the king, the politics of Tyralt. At every reference the former queen's hands clutched her windowsill with such force that her knuckles went white. And after a brief mention of the Vantauge family caused a powerful silence, Aurelia dared not even talk about Robert. Or the expedition, a choice which—she tried to convince herself—had nothing to do with her own reluctance to think about the future.

The past could not be broached, not without any foundation or common ground. Even minor topics felt like chasms for her to plunge into. Her attempts to speak to her mother's interests only revealed Aurelia's ignorance. She knew next to nothing about gardens, embroidery, or painting. Every broken conversation served as evidence of her own inadequacy.

She longed to quit. To forego the awkward silences and the frightening reflection of her own weakness. But if she gave up, the cavity within her would claim dominion.

Desperate for something to break the silence, she forced herself past the final image of Bianca and dared the topic of horses. Surely here, at least, the former queen was not the expert.

But Lady Margaret's skin turned as pale as Daria's. The hands again clutched the windowsill. And the silence thrust Aurelia away.

The next day the blue door was locked.

Aurelia wanted to scream, to pound down the door and destroy forever any hope of reconciling with the stranger on the other side. But something would not allow her to do it—the stark hollow terror within her. And that illogical inner thread that still craved her mother's love.

Stupidity. She should run down to the Soliers' cottage right now and forget the woman in the Blue Room. But if Aurelia arrived at the cottage this early, her best friend would not allow her to forget. Daria would ask questions. As she had about the assassination plot. Questions that seemed to chase Robert away to his new job at the stables. And questions Aurelia did not want to answer.

Instead, she left the Fortress for the village interwoven among the shadowy canopy of dense trees. She sought distraction, but found herself swept up in genuine curiosity. Here, beyond the knowledge of the king, the people had just as many plans as those in Tyralt City. They were building a school. And over a dozen houses were in construction amid the foliage. She met butchers and builders, seamstresses and weavers, teachers and leaders, all of whom spoke well of Lady Margaret, though none had actually met her.

How could these people feel a connection to the woman her own daughter did not understand? Every morning that week, before returning to the village, Aurelia silently tested the blue door, and every morning it remained locked.

At last, after seven days of being exiled from her mother's residence, she gathered enough humility to approach the one person who might be able to help. She braved the cacophony of the great hall at suppertime.

"Your Highness." The red-bearded man who was technically her stepfather offered up a knowing grin and pulled out a vacant chair at his right.

She could not help but feel as though he were mocking her. But she bit her tongue and did her best to remain civil as he introduced her to the soldiers at his side, all hired in defiance of her father. The task was not as hard as she had expected. The conversation, to her surprise, centered more on the welfare of the village people than on hunting or training techniques. And she regretted the moment when at last Lord Lester dismissed the other participants from the table, though she had come to complete a mission.

"Your Lordship." She used his title, not as a means to mock him, but as a boundary. She already had a father, and she could not quite forgive this man for his dreadful treatment of Robert upon their arrival. But no one else could provide her with the insight she needed. "I wish to ask your advice."

"Patience," he replied, tilting a bottle of red wine over his glass and raising his arm so that the crimson stream stretched higher and higher.

She silenced herself, thinking he was telling her to wait before she spoke.

He chuckled. "My advice, with regards to your mother, is always patience. I courted her for ten years under this very roof before she agreed to marry me. And believe me when I say I've been locked out of that room for far longer than you are ever likely to be." The bottle thudded down.

Aurelia blinked. This man, whom she had assessed as rude and brash, had waited ten years for her mother to marry him? And according to the locals, he had felled half an acre of forest for the gardens so that she might have fresh blossoms in her room. And he *had* raised an entire army to protect her. Perhaps he did not, entirely, deserve Aurelia's disdain. "I think I upset her when I mentioned horses."

"Ah." Lord Lester tilted the wine in her direction.

The scent twisted her insides and darkened her thoughts. She tried not to inhale, pushing the bottle away.

He corralled it in the crook of his arm, then stated, "Your mother has never recovered from your brother's death. Horses remind her of the accident."

Was her entire family always to remain captive to that moment fourteen years ago, when Aurelia's brother had been trampled by her father's mount? Nothing could undo that slicing imprint. And she well knew, based on her experience with the king, that she could never measure up to her brother's place in her parents' eyes. "I see." Aurelia rose to go.

"She isn't punishing you."

Of course she is.

"She's only afraid."

Of what? The former queen had not once tried to initiate conversation—had taken no risks at all. "She's made no attempt to get to know me."

"She has let no one else into that room without my presence in fourteen years."

Could that be true? Had her mother taken a risk simply by allowing her daughter over the threshold? And what folly to learn that now!

Aurelia took a half dozen steps away, then paused. It was not this man's fault her mother was scarred. "Thank you," she whispered.

"You're welcome."

The next day the door was unlocked. Aurelia hovered on the threshold.

Her mother was sitting in her chair beside a large basket of delphiniums, gazing out the window.

"I'm sorry I'm late," whispered Aurelia, as if she had not been barred from this azure refuge for the past seven days. "I was assisting a family that is moving into their new home in the village." The words tumbled over one another. "They have ten children, and I was helping the little ones find their way."

Her mother turned so that the midmorning sunlight shone on half of her face. "The Rienthur family."

Aurelia was astonished to hear the name from the former queen's lips. She had come to think her mother's interests were restricted to the minutiae of her surroundings: the paintings on the wall, the fabric, the flowers.

Lady Margaret's slender fingers reached down to the overflowing basket and removed one of the long stalks of cobalt blossoms. On a small table at her side lay a pair of shears and a ball of twine. *For drying flowers.*

Again her mother spoke. "A great many families have come to the estate this year. That is why the new school is so important."

"You know of the school?" Aurelia edged into the room.

"I sponsored it." Her mother clipped the stem.

Aurelia caught herself at the curved end of the bedpost, startled. The idea made sense. The former queen had been well known for her passion for education, but that had been . . . before.

Lady Margaret tied the twine around the severed stem and retrieved another strand of blossoms. Then the shears wavered in the air, and her voice faltered. "Did . . . did you like the room?"

"What?" asked Aurelia, unable to follow the sudden shift in the conversation.

"The room that the Rienthurs vacated."

Until today, the family Aurelia had helped move had been living in a large corner room on the second floor of the Fortress. An open, airy space with buttercup walls and yellow coverlets, the aura far superior to her own dark, vine-covered quarters. "Y-yes." She furrowed her brow, uncertain why her mother had changed the conversation.

Still the shears wavered. "I thought . . . you might prefer it."

"Oh! Yes! It's . . . beautiful!"

A faint, but genuine smile appeared on her mother's lips. "Of course, we would have given you the room earlier, but His Lordship did not wish to displace an entire family."

Bolstered by the smile, Aurelia allowed herself to approach the overflowing basket, crouch down, and inhale the delicate, sweet scent.

Her mother edged away, compelling her daughter to retreat back to the bedpost.

"The . . . the Fortress is entirely full, isn't it?" Aurelia queried.

"I believe so," said Lady Margaret, then reached hesitantly for the twine. "The room you have occupied was the only one available upon your arrival, except for the basement, which is not fit for guests, as the rooms have no hearths. His Lordship offers every space he can to newcomers to the estate, those who do not yet have the means to provide for their own lodging."

"But where do all these people come from? And how can there be so many who even know about this place? Enough to keep this entire Fortress full as they wait for new homes to be built?"

The knot Lady Margaret was trying to tie came apart. "Many are family to those already here."

But that was only half an answer. "Why do they come in the first place?"

There was a long pause. And for a moment Aurelia feared they had reached another unknown precipice. Again the knot came undone, and her mother's hands shook as they wrestled with the twine. "His Lordship . . . forgives all debts . . . all former crimes. He asks only for loyalty and service. . . . None of the young are bound to pay for their parents' failures. . . ." Lady Margaret looked up, gazing once more out the window. "All are welcome, and all have the chance to stay if they respect His Lordship's wishes."

And if they do not? Aurelia suspected Lord Lester's justice was swift and final. But clearly the man's offer to forgive past wrongs held appeal.

"All these people are fugitives or family members of those who have broken the law?"

Another long pause. Lady Margaret lowered her head, and her response came in a soft whisper. "The king's law."

And only then did Aurelia realize her mother had included herself in her daughter's assessment. That perhaps she, as Lord Lester had implied, had spent the past weeks dreading her visitor's judgment. "Then this place—the entire village—is . . ." Aurelia thought about all the people she had met: the townspeople, the Rienthur family, even the soldiers at His Lordship's table. "A sanctuary."

Her mother's eyes fluttered up, meeting her daughter's gaze, their brown depths filled with . . . *relief.*

Lord Lester's offer to provide Aurelia with a place at the Fortress haunted Robert for five weeks. Like a gray blanket that gave off the impression of solace and then split in half and twisted itself into a rope to strangle him.

Because he knew he would have to leave her.

She was safe here. *Safe.* Her stepfather's contacts in Transcontina had sent word that a group of His Majesty's guards were, in fact, in the city. *Lying in wait.* But here she was shrouded in secrecy. Surrounded by armed men who were free from her stepsister's influence. And she had her mother.

A figure who had reigned just below the highest position of Tyralian power and foremost in the hearts of the kingdom's people but had, somehow, forgone that love. And the love of her own daughter. Robert knew it would be good for Aurelia if she could find it in her heart to forgive that betrayal and heal its damage.

Though it hurt to know he would lose her to this shadow of a queen.

In truth, the loss had already begun. Initially, after he had been transferred from the Fortress to Daria and Thomas's modest cottage, Aurelia had visited often, but he had not known how to talk to her—to tell her, first, that he loved her, and second, that he had informed her stepfather about her situation.

What could Robert say? That despite what he felt for her, which had somehow strengthened in the midst of all the arguments, trauma, and danger they had been through, his feelings did not matter? Because in the end, there remained three facts: She was a princess, her life was in danger, and he could not protect her.

Instead, he hid behind Daria, pretending his silence might allow the two friends time to talk. But Daria had too many questions, and the visits from Aurelia had grown more rare. At one point, he had gone to see her and had been informed, by a Fortress guard, that he needed an appointment. An appointment!

It had become an excuse. A reason to keep himself from seeing her. Because doing so hurt too much. It was easier to bury himself in work, down by the stables or helping Thomas, than to witness her dark brown eyes struggling with his silence, and to know that any day, any minute, he might receive word from Transcontina that the guards had vacated the city, leaving Robert free to return to the frontier and a future he could not envision. In which he would never see her again.

He knew the Fortress's sanctuary could not be his own. He could not bear to stay here, isolated from his country. And from her. Watching her from a distance.

Though he would never be free of her eyes. They haunted him, even as he bent low in the dimness of the estate's stables to inspect the health of Horizon's hooves.

"What are you doing?" Thomas Solier appeared over the rim of the stall.

Robert jumped, though he knew by now that Daria's husband tended to move like smoke, silent and subtle.

The stallion gave a swift kick, and Robert dodged into a corner. "Risking my life, I suppose, checking Horizon's hooves."

"Why?"

After more than a month under this man's roof, Robert knew better than to obfuscate and receive a second *why*. "For when I need to leave."

Thomas arched an eyebrow. He had the perfect look and demeanor for a spy. Nondescript hair. Vacant gray eyes. Voice, expressionless. Robert did not doubt that this man's role as Lord Lester's liaison to the palace had involved far more than the tasks of a simple courier.

"I have a wheel that needs setting on a cart," said Daria's husband. "Could you lend a hand?"

Robert nodded, gave the stallion a slap on the rump as a caution for the recent kick, and exited the stall to the sound of a powerful hoof thudding against the back wall.

Thomas led the way down the stable's central aisle to the far end where the scent of horse manure faded under the pungency of pork grease. A cart with a light body of splintered and worn wood sat tilted at an irregular angle, the left axle, its spindle already greased, propped up on a dusty barrel. A clutter of nails, tools, and semibroken objects graced the nearby shadows, but a sturdy, twelve-spoked wheel with a brand new frame rested against the end stall.

Robert headed for the wheel.

The other man's hand stopped him, taking his wrist, then placing a thin scrap of paper into his palm. "From His Lordship," said Thomas. The man's face was buried in shadow.

Robert flipped over the scrap and moved his hand into a thin stream of light by a crack in the stable wall.

His Majesty's guards have vacated the city.

A fierce, hard knot tied itself in Robert's gut. Time then. Tonight.

"I haven't heard anything about Her Highness wishing to renew her expedition." Thomas reached for the propped wheel and began to roll it to the cart. *Was that it then?* No discussion of what the man knew or didn't know.

"Neither have I," Robert replied, too fiercely.

"You're planning on heading out alone then?"

Ah. So there was to be a discussion. Robert set his grip on the side of the wheel. He did not bother to reply—did not trust himself.

"And you haven't yet told Her Highness." Thomas secured his own grip. "Do you think that is wise?"

"She doesn't need me." Robert strained to lift the wheel.

"That's disputable." The other side lifted as well.

It tilted wildly. "She seems happy here," Robert lied as he fought to regain balance. Happiness was too much to expect after what she had been through, but she *did* seem to be returning to a semblance of a normal life. Based on the frenzied talk he had heard about her visits to the village, which seemed to have grown longer and more frequent over the past weeks, she was gaining the same awe and respect she had garnered in Sterling. And Tyralt City.

The wheel steadied.

"She's found her mother and is building a relationship with her," Thomas said, guiding the large hub toward the inclined end of the axle. "That takes time."

The wheel had gone too far in the wrong direction. "I'm glad for her." Robert shifted his grip and pulled.

"My." Thomas tugged back. "Such enthusiasm."

How is it a man with no expression can master sarcasm? Robert's arms strained. "Either help me with this or lose the help!" he snapped.

Finally the wheel scraped into place. Thomas did not react

to the sharp comment. Instead, he slid a thin metal ring over the end of the spindle and then slowly twisted the nut onto the threaded bolt. The silence was painful.

"She's safe here," Robert said at last, giving the one reason that surpassed all argument.

"I suppose." The other man straightened. For the first time, those gray eyes settled on Robert—clear, nothing vacant in them now. "As safe as any of us are in this kingdom."

The back of Robert's mind churned. Since when had Thomas become a voice of politics?

Though he was right. As Drew had been back in Sterling. None of them would truly be safe if Melony took the throne. But Robert could not shake the memory of the smoke, the dense clogging odor that had filled the air around the rising ashes of Aurelia's burning tent.

"Risking her life on an expedition won't save Tyralt," he said.

Thomas tested the wheel. It spun with a swift, smooth turn, the sanded grains of the new frame blurring together. "It seems to me she made that choice."

That had been before—before the smoke, before the scream in the forest that had ripped Robert apart and brought her back to him. He found himself staring into the clutter-filled shadows.

"She knew it was not safe to defy her father's wishes," Thomas continued.

"She doesn't care about being safe."

"Ah. Then it's *you* who wants her to stay here."

No, he definitely did not. But *he* could not protect her. Her stepfather could. "This is best."

"*The end of the crown* it is."

Robert's eyes widened at the foul language.

"She should finish the expedition," Thomas said. "You know it, and I know it. You've lived on the frontier, Robert. You know the divisions that have been building. From what I hear, there's talk the north does not even need a monarch. I can't believe you rode all the way back to the palace without at least some thought of saving this country."

Robert pulled away. This was not about politics. He headed toward the stalls.

"You should tell her how you feel." The voice stopped him. "Tell her what you want, Robert. If you don't, you'll regret it."

He closed his eyes, leaning up against the corner of the end stall. He could not tell her. What he wanted was selfish and unsafe and not the best thing for either her or Tyralt. He flexed his hand. The scrap of paper must have fallen when he lifted the wheel, but the written words still burned in his head. The ashes of reality settled upon him.

There had been men, for well over a month, waiting in that town to kill her.

And there had been no word, as far as he knew, about any search parties or efforts on the part of the palace to find her. Even if the king believed rumors that she had run off on a romantic whim, surely, at the very least, he should have made an effort to investigate. Unless he, like her sister, now desired her death.

"Robert!" The female voice slammed into his thoughts so forcefully that for a moment, he thought she had risen up from his own imagination to scold him for accusing her father. But the figure speeding down the stable aisle in a green blur was no illusion. Though the fury on her face fit the image well enough.

"Yes?" Robert glanced behind him. There was no sign of Daria's husband.

"You told Lord Lester about the assassination plot and the attack in the forest," Aurelia accused.

Robert sighed. So she had found out. Even this he was not to be spared. "He already knew there was more to the plot than what your father had claimed to the public."

She froze in her tracks. Gone were the rags from her journey, in their place an elegant forest green gown, the gown of a lady. Clearly, she had not planned on this trip to the stables. "Do you think Daria told him what she knew?"

"Perhaps." *Daria or Thomas.* Robert shrugged.

Aurelia's head was shaking, and her hands were trembling.

It would not be fair to thrust his own guilt on Daria. "I made the choice to tell your stepfather about the attack in the forest," he admitted.

"Why?" Aurelia sank down onto a wooden crate, showing little regard for her gown's trailing hem. The green fabric folded itself into the dirt.

Robert quelled a sudden urge to draw closer. "He is your

stepfather, Aurelia. He wanted to protect you, and he has taken a great risk housing both you and your mother here."

She let her head fall back against a stall door, her dark hair drifting past her shoulders. *Soft.* He longed to touch it. One last time. Her hair, the changeable contours of her face, her arms. The desire to hold her once—just once—without the aura of tragedy stalking them both, gripped his chest so fiercely he had to fight for breath.

"But it was my story to tell," she said. "Not yours."

"I think . . ." Robert knew if he so much as stepped toward her, he might lose the will to let her go—that he would beg her to come with him, condemning her in the process. "I think your stepfather was trying to spare you that trauma." It took a lot for Robert to admit, but Daria and Thomas claimed that His Lordship would do anything to spare his wife, and by extension his stepdaughter, pain.

"He's trying to protect you," Robert said. "I certainly failed at that."

"What?" Her back suddenly arched.

"I'm sorry."

"You are what?"

"Sorry." His control began to slip. "I am sorry for what you went through in the forest, Aurelia." He could not help but tell her, though he knew it was his own selfish need for closure that propelled him to mention the dark memory.

She stood up. "*You're* sorry?" Her face flared alive, that vivid shift of line and color that he knew would chase him down no matter how far he fled. "You're sorry for being the only person on the expedition who didn't want to murder me? For keeping me alive? For bringing a spoiled, thankless princess across the Asyan on foot?! I'm the one who's sorry. Robert, I've been trying to thank you, but every time I see you, you seem so distant I—"

"I'm sorry."

"Ahh!" She stormed from the stables.

He stared after her. Unable to take in what had just happened. All he knew was that she had come in, angry with him for doing something wrong, and left, furious with him for apologizing. And his pulse raced with the contradiction.

"Yes," Thomas Solier's emotionless voice drifted out of the shadows. "I see how much she doesn't need you."

Chapter Eight
THE PRICE OF DESTINY

He WAS SORRY! AURELIA RUSHED UP THE HILL toward the Fortress. It was her stepfather who should be sorry, drilling Robert about the danger to *her* life. She should have questioned Lord Lester further about the messenger from Transcontina. But His Lordship had been well into a bottle of heavy red wine, and—she might as well face it—when Robert's name had come up, she had leaped at the excuse to confront her expedition guide instead.

After all, he had buried himself in his work at the stables. She had scarcely seen him these past weeks. The argument, just now, had been ludicrous, but even more bizarre was the way it made her feel. Humming with the interaction. Her pulse rushed, and her lungs struggled for air within her corset. *This dratted dress!*

She filled her fists with the heavy fabric and tugged the long skirts above her ankles as she swept through the dirt field of her stepfather's courtyard. She should never have put on her mother's gown in the first place. But Aurelia had thought if she accepted the gift, it might somehow strengthen their relationship. Though no number of dresses would heal the cavity within her chest.

It was time, she thought, as she entered the Fortress and climbed the stairs. *Time to ask the harder questions.*

She tapped gently on the door, then entered the Blue Room. Her observations were now far sharper than they had been on her first visit. She saw not only the sky blue of the walls but the subtle shift from black to navy along the head of the swallow in the painting beside the window. And the way slate blended to midnight blue on the dramatic wing of the heron soaring in the opposing portrait. She noted the thin white crack along the arched neck of the cerulean flower vase and the blue-gray embroidery of a dolphin's fin among the indigo waves of a nearby tapestry.

Her mother was embroidering now. An emerald V along the throat of a mountain canary. For a moment Aurelia gazed down at the minute stitching with awe. Four different shades of green had already gone into that single V-shaped element. She could never have borne such exactitude.

Nervously, she seated herself on the chair at the left side of the window, across from her mother. Aurelia knew the continued silence upon her entrance was not rejection. After all, there were now two wicker chairs where before there had been only one. But she was about to break an unspoken rule. "Mother," she said softly. She always found it hard to speak in her regular voice in this room. "Why did you change your name?"

Lady Margaret looked up at the personal question, blinking in the late afternoon sunlight, then dropped her gaze once again to the embroidery. "I didn't want to be Marguerite anymore." The answer came out even softer than the question. "Marguerite was a name chosen for me. Margaret feels less . . . destined."

Aurelia knew well the flaws of having one's life defined by birth, but her mother had not been born royal. "How were you destined?"

The needle froze. "I was Marguerite of Valshone."

And what did that explain? "I don't understand."

A strange, grim smile appeared on her mother's face. "Well, then, perhaps some good came from my marriage's end after all." *Her marriage.* To Aurelia's father. It was the first time her mother had broached the topic. The needle plunged back into the throat of the canary. "Have you never heard of the Right of Valshone?"

Aurelia racked her memory.

Her mother took another stitch. "I see. Your education must have been controlled in this matter."

With ignorance. Yes, Aurelia's father had been very good at that type of control. "What is it, then— the Right of Valshone?"

"Tradition." Her mother began to stitch more quickly. "Dating back to Tyralt's first real test in power. There was an attack to the southwest—"

"The attack of the Gisalts."

"Yes, well, your learning has not been too dismal then. It was the first and last time Tyralt was ever attacked on the southern coast. No one has tried since."

"Because the mountains are so treacherous."

"Because the people who live in the mountains are treacherous." Her mother looked up, then down, without slowing the rapid stitches. "The Valshone are trained fighters. Their defense of the southwest border is key to Tyralt's ability to protect itself. At the time of the attack, the king of Tyralt realized this, and he and the Lord of Valshone made an agreement, an oral contract, which means even more to the people of the mountains than a written one. It stated that the heir of Tyralt, instead of wedding royalty from another kingdom, would marry within, a member of the Valshone." The needle paused, then lifted again very slowly. "Upon my birth, I was chosen for this Right."

Aurelia struggled to understand. Perhaps it was unfair to blame her father for her own ignorance. She had always been reluctant to study the region of her mother's birth. "But if the child of the Lord of Valshone is always chosen to marry the heir of Tyralt, wouldn't that mean my father should be your cousin?"

"No. Because the lordship of Valshone is not inherited, but earned."

Earned? Aurelia had heard of titles being given for great feats, but to do so from generation to generation? The idea was startling.

"My father earned his place," her mother continued. "He knew and admired the lord before him, but they were not related; and my father was not required to select his own child for the Right. It was his choice." Her thread had grown short, the loops smaller with each stitch. "Of all the Valshone people, I was the only one to have a destiny selected for me." She paused. "I was taught that this was a great honor, and I believed it. I believed it when I married your father. And when I gave birth to you and James." The needle came to a sudden halt. "I think I believed it right up until your brother's death."

A slate-gray shroud covered her mother's face. What had it cost her to mention James? And what did it say about the change in her relationship with her daughter?

"And then you left," Aurelia whispered, "when you found out about Melony." She knew her mother would never broach the topic of the king's indiscretion herself.

Lady Margaret reached for the thread scissors on the window and fumbled, knocking them to the ground. "I cried first," she said, bending to pick them up. "And then I yelled, which served no purpose. Your father denied any responsibility for his actions."

Aurelia's stomach churned.

"I realized then that I wasn't safe." Her mother clipped the thread. "I knew your stepmother, Elise, not closely, but well enough. I knew if the king would not renounce her, that sooner or later, she would find a way to usurp me. There were rumors . . . about her husband's death."

Another death. Aurelia had known, of course, that Elise's husband had died right after Melony's birth. Why had it not occurred to her to question the cause?

"I threatened the king," her mother said, trying to rethread her needle. "Like an animal in a corner, I threatened him, and then I ran."

"But . . . how?" Aurelia asked. "How did you know to come here?"

The thread dropped, and her mother's barren needle plucked at the fabric. "His Lordship was not, at the time, so disinclined to come to court. Though, due to the vast distance, his visits were . . . notable."

Aurelia's eyebrows rose. Notable how? Had Lord Lester made romantic advances toward the queen?

The idea was not, when she thought about it, all that absurd. His Lordship was boisterous, opinionated, and sometimes rash. He seemed to care little for the rules and strictures of society, though this relaxed perspective did not apply, in any way, to his view of his wife's safety. If there was one thing Aurelia could not doubt about her stepfather, it was that he truly loved her mother. And he had done all he could to protect her. Even, Aurelia realized now, from his knowledge of the threats to her own daughter's life. Lord Lester might keep careful watch, through covert means, on the nation's politics, but Lady Margaret was clearly oblivious.

"Tyralt owes the Lester family a great deal," Aurelia's mother continued. "All the land between the northern Asyan and the Geordian Desert was once theirs, you know. It was His Lordship's father who made the decision to forego much of the title and open his lands for settlement."

Aurelia nodded. She had studied the history of the frontier *very* well. "Yes, I know."

"Lord Lester had come to your brother's funeral. At the time, he offered his estate as a place of solace if I ever required it." Her mother's eyes peered out the window, past the garden, and into the tangled trees. "It was as far from the palace as I could hire a carriage to take me.... As far away," her mother whispered, "as I could hide." The needle lay still.

Now was the time for the hardest question, the one Aurelia had avoided. "But I was only a child. Why didn't you take me with you?" She closed her eyes, afraid of seeing the emptiness remain on her mother's face.

"I was afraid. I didn't know anything about this place ... or if I would be able to stay here. I knew I couldn't go home to the Valshone. By leaving my position, I had disgraced my father. I only had a vague idea that I *must* flee. I could not take you with me. I didn't know if *I* would survive."

A stark image painted itself in Aurelia's mind, her mother riding through the shadows of the Asyan, her fingers gripping the side of her carriage, lest anyone ask it to stop—such as the king's guards, waiting to execute her on the road.

Flinching, Aurelia opened her eyes. There was no point in

pursuing the topic, questioning if her mother had ever been concerned for her daughter's safety at the palace. Or why that concern was any less valid than the rest. Aurelia already knew the answer: *fear.* Her mother was driven by, defined by, and living in fear.

Lady Margaret again lifted the needle, though there was no thread on it. "Even after I was here, I could not trust anyone." She took a stitch. "At times . . . at times, I wanted to end my life. I had failed at everything I was raised to do, and I didn't have any dreams beyond that."

Again Aurelia's stomach turned. The story was too familiar. The upbringing to become queen. The disillusionment. Lack of power. Flight.

Her mother's hand shook, and she pierced her own skin with the needle. "I can't ever feel safe again." Blood welled between her ring and middle finger.

Aurelia reached toward the injured hand. Was this what lay ahead for herself? This abject terror of everything beyond the Fortress? Or even a single room? "Lord Lester—" Aurelia whispered, "do you love him?" Because maybe if her mother had love here, then her life was not entirely desolate.

"I don't know." Lady Margaret pulled her hand beyond her daughter's reach. The blood continued to swell. She could easily have wiped it off, but instead she waited, letting the bead fall and spread in a bright red stain upon the embroidered bird's throat. "He loves me. Isn't that enough?"

No, Aurelia thought as she descended the stairs, the sick feeling plunging deeper in her stomach with every step. She hurried down the hallway to the yellow room, thrust in the latch, and shoved open the door.

To see Daria, standing like a dark omen, already there.

"I—I'm sorry," Daria stuttered. "I didn't mean to intrude."

She was always intruding. Always pushing boundaries. Aurelia had not been to the cottage for days, maybe a week, for that exact reason. When had Daria become so assertive?

Silence filled the room.

"But this is urgent," Daria said, thrusting a bundle of cloth at her. "They're . . . they're my old riding clothes. I know yours were ruined."

Ruined? There was nothing urgent about riding clothes. Aurelia had not ridden since . . . Bianca. The brutal last image of her bleeding horse jabbed Aurelia in her gut. "Please go." She felt the bile rising in her throat. She was about to be ill. "Just go, Daria."

The other girl stood, stubbornly. "Robert is leaving."

Aurelia threw up, right onto that borrowed green dress.

Her chest felt like it was about to explode. She gagged, and her eyes watered. She tried, futilely, to undo the gown. The buttons were down the back.

Then Daria was there, releasing the buttons, ripping at the laces of the corset, helping her friend step free of the yards of reeking fabric, then wrapping up the entire pile and depositing it outside the door.

In her shift, Aurelia stumbled to the washbasin.

And Daria was there too, pouring a glass, and holding the basin while Aurelia flushed the sickness from her mouth and spit out the remnants.

Finally there was air. She could almost breathe. Enough to say, "No."

Her friend smoothed back her hair.

Aurelia tugged away.

"No," she repeated. "Robert can't be leaving. I saw him"—she glanced out at the darkening sky—"only a few hours ago." She had been up in her mother's room far longer than she had realized.

"Yes. I know." Daria held out the riding skirt, then helped her put it on. "Thomas overheard your conversation with Robert."

Aurelia blinked. She ought to react to that, but how could she? There was too much to comprehend.

Her friend's hand closed upon hers. "Robert is leaving the estate, Aurelia. Tonight. After dark."

Reality emptied as Aurelia's stomach already had. "No," she found herself saying, without logic. "He didn't say—"

"He discussed it with Thomas."

Thomas?! She flung away Daria's hand. "He hasn't discussed it with *me*."

Her friend didn't flinch, instead holding out the smock to go with the skirt. "It should not come as a terrific surprise."

Perhaps not. The cold realization gusted through Aurelia as she dressed. Over the past five weeks, Robert had become more and more distant. That was why she had gone running down to the stables today. She had needed the excuse in order to see him.

But how could he think of leaving without telling me? She tried to say the words aloud, and they came out, "How could he leave without me?"

"Do you want to go?"

"Yes." Well, there it was. The truth.

"Then go." Daria crossed the room and opened the wardrobe. "Just"—she paused—"don't hurt him, Aurelia."

Hurt *him*? Aurelia felt numb. "What do you mean?"

Her friend returned from the wardrobe with wool stockings and Aurelia's battered riding boots. She did not release them. "You must know."

Know what? "Daria." Aurelia's tone was threatening.

"He's in love with you."

The world stopped. For one long, outrageous moment, Aurelia let herself consider the statement. He had *kissed* her. Once. And saved her life. More than once.

But the idea that he could be in love with her did not—could not be true. "That's nonsense." She had tried to let Robert know she wanted to spend time alone with him on the way to Sterling. And he had rejected her. He was *still* rejecting her.

Daria handed her the stockings. "Honestly, Aurelia. There's nothing wrong with being in love."

Aurelia was not at all certain of that. What had love ever done for the people she knew? She thought of Lord Lester's unrequited devotion to a woman who never left her room. The king's blind attraction to Elise, a woman who might have murdered her first husband. And Melony's twisted passion, which had turned Chris into a killer. And a corpse.

"I don't expect love, Daria. It's not in my destiny."

"Why not?" Her friend crouched down as though to help put on the boots. "You chose to leave the palace," she pointed out. "You refused to marry the man your father wanted. Why can't you marry for love?"

For a ridiculous half-moment, Aurelia let herself picture the image her friend had just suggested: a life in a cabin on the frontier with a husband, their children running around them, wheat fields in the background, the sunlight glowing. The vision was so thin, Aurelia could see through it.

She snatched the boots and jammed them onto her feet.

Marriage was not happily ever after. Even Daria's. Aurelia was no fool. She knew that Thomas's real role at the palace had been to inform upon her own status, and that of the king, to Lord Lester. What must it have been like for Daria to realize that her husband had initially been interested in her only as a means for reconnaissance? And how must Daria have felt when she arrived at her husband's home and learned he had been keeping so many secrets?

"If not for love, then why do you want to go?" Daria asked.

Aurelia tightened the laces of her boots. "It's *my* expedition."

"I don't think the expedition is that important," her friend replied.

It *was* though. Aurelia faced the reality she had been avoiding for the past five weeks. And yet even without speaking about her broken dream, the need for the expedition and its true purpose—to learn more about her people—had only become more obvious. She had known nothing about the inhabitants of the Asyan and very little to match her mother's description of the Valshone. And those were only two regions of Tyralt. She needed to complete this journey.

But she did not have time to explain that to her friend. Now was the time to say good-bye.

"Thank you . . . Daria." Aurelia's eyes clouded. "Thank you for coming here tonight and telling me. I'm sorry things haven't been . . . easier between us."

Her friend's fingers threaded through her own. "I know. But you have been through so much in the past two months, more, I'm sure, than I know. How could I have expected you to stay the same?"

Aurelia blinked. They had both changed.

"You are so strong," her friend continued.

How could she have noticed the change and still think Aurelia was strong?

Daria swung her friend's hands. "Try not to be too hard on Robert tonight," she said. "You know he honestly thinks he is making the best choice to protect you."

"He doesn't love me, Daria. If he did, he wouldn't be planning on leaving me now."

"If he didn't, he would have left for the frontier two months ago." Daria enfolded her in an embrace. *She was still a true friend,* Aurelia realized. The type to challenge a crown princess who had just received the shock of her life. Or to enter a room without permission so that her friend would not be irreparably injured by someone else's disappearance. Aurelia returned the embrace.

And before she had the chance to wipe the tears from her eyes, Daria was gone.

The light outside the window was failing, and Aurelia could not bear another good-bye.

But was it fair, she asked herself, to leave her mother like this?

She thought about the woman up in the Blue Room. The woman who had locked herself off from her entire past and had built an almost sacred refuge to keep it away, but then, piece by fragile piece, had allowed Aurelia in. Yet, in all that time between them, there had been no laughter. No touch. No tears, except for that first heart-wrenching day.

I didn't know if I could survive ever having to say good-bye.

Yes, Aurelia realized. In fact, this was the only way, for either of them.

Nothing could be gained by a return to that room. She had already learned everything she could from this encounter, and her mother was too fragile to withstand such a personal departure. There would be no warm embrace between them, no true relationship, no future. Because her mother was never going to leave that room. And Aurelia *was.* She had survived. And somehow, in the process, the chasm within her own chest had healed, if not filled. Her mother's emptiness and fear were not her daughter's fault. And they held no power over her.

Robert found Aurelia, fast asleep, on the back of his horse. *Impossible.* At first, he thought she was an illusion, conjured by his own exhausted mind and the shudder of the lantern's glow against the stables' pitch-colored night. It was late. Hours and hours later than he would have chosen to leave—hours of agonizing over whether he was making the right choice, whether, after all the extra time, he would have the strength. But Thomas had insisted Robert wait until word of his departure had cleared the chain of command—a delay that had taken an eternity. And most of his sanity. So it did not seem all that strange that now he was having delusions.

You promised, the vision seemed to say.

"She's safe here," he tried to argue. But he *had* promised, before the flames that night, promised her he would not leave her. And it didn't matter that she had been asleep, as the vision was now, resting with her arms dangling along his stallion's neck and shoulders, her cheek pressed into his mane, her left knee cocked, her boot wedged just enough to be caught in the stirrup.

Robert's mind tried to make sense of that detail.

He had not saddled and bridled Horizon. It was the task he had been dreading, the final task. Because, somehow, to tighten that cinch, to strap on his supplies—the pack, the canvas

Thomas had given him, the extra sack Daria had thrust into Robert's hands at the last minute—to go through those final mundane actions, was to sever the greatest bond in his life.

I can't do it. Robert sank back against the wall and lost himself in the darkness. Even if he left tonight, if he managed to force himself out onto the path or the Northern Road or even across the Gate to the frontier, it would lead to the same thing. A night, a week, a month from now, he would have to turn around. And come back for her.

Relief washed through him.

But when he lifted his head, the vision remained: that of his stubborn horse tolerating a sleeping passenger.

Impossible.

But Robert drew closer. He reached out and felt the sticky texture of the saddle's leather. Could one envision touch? Could he have imagined that crease, so fine, running along the curve of her neck? Could he conjure movement, the oh-so-subtle rise and fall of her chest and stomach as she breathed?

"Aurelia." He reached out gently. A strand of her hair tumbled at his touch. His breath caught, and he pulled back, then reached again. Her shoulder was warm beneath his hand. "Aurelia." He pressed down lightly.

She looked up at him, her eyes peering through sleep, straight into his.

He fell back for an instant. It was *her.* No illusion.

Impossible.

"How are you here?" he whispered.

She eased her head up along the stallion's neck, her sleep-blurred words running together. "You're not leaving me behind."

He closed his eyes. The feeling that rioted through his chest and gut had no right to be there.

"This is my expedition, Robert." A long, soft yawn interrupted her speech. "I intend to finish it." She buried her face back in the stallion's neck. His stallion. His ornery, disloyal, docile stallion.

You know, Thomas's final, expressionless words came back to Robert, *you can always borrow that old roan at the end of the stables if that stallion of yours can't handle all your personal effects.*

The crown princess of Tyralt: a personal effect.

His gaze shot back toward the pile of supplies by the stall's entry. No wonder Thomas had insisted on the canvas tent, even though Robert had stated he could sleep rough. And no wonder Daria had waited until he was halfway out the door to thrust that extra pack in his hands, when he was too tired of waiting to take the time to inspect it. And the delay? Had Thomas been stalling to ensure that Her Royal Highness would be able to leave the estate, alone with Robert?

Impossible.

But he found himself exiting the stall, walking down to the end of the aisle, and pulling the sturdy spotted mare out of her sleep. Found himself tugging her back in the direction he had come and strapping on both packs, the canvas, and a saddle he knew would not bear a rider tonight. Found himself arguing all manner of logic in his head.

He should wait until morning and discuss this with her stepfather. But in the end, she would either win or run off anyway.

There should be an escort. A new set of armed men. But they would only attract attention and destroy any advantage gained by waiting for the palace guards to leave Transcontina. Those guards *must* continue to believe Aurelia was dead. Which meant she could not travel as herself. She would have to be a commoner.

Impossible.

Robert allowed his gaze to return to the sleeping figure on the back of his half-wild stallion.

There was nothing common about her.

And though she had proven she could blend in with any level of society on the streets of Tyralt City, that meant nothing across the gateway to the frontier. And she had no concept of that.

Though neither did many of the people making their way north for the first time.

Perhaps it would work. If he helped her. If she would listen to him.

Impossible.

Robert attached a lead rope from the halter of the roan to the saddle of his own horse. And retrieved Horizon's reins. Then, gently, he eased her drowsy figure forward, mounted behind her, and clicked his tongue against the back of his teeth, urging the stallion into motion.

Aurelia shifted, gave a soft, sleepy-headed sigh, and folded herself into Robert's arms.

Impossible.

But she *was* impossible.

Chapter Nine
INTO THE LION'S JAWS

AURELIA AWOKE IN ROBERT'S ARMS. SHE HAD NO idea how she had come to be there, but it felt nice. Warm. Like her entire soul had been healed. And she did not want to move in case she might lose that wonderful sensation. Or her balance. It felt like she was on horseback, though she had not ridden since—

She did not want to think about that cold night. She just wanted to remain here. Awake. Free from the nightmare, where Daria had told her . . . told her what?

Robert's chest shifted, and Aurelia snuggled deeper into it. The Daria in the dream must have been crazy. Because Robert would never leave without saying good-bye. And he could not possibly be in love—

The thought jolted Aurelia from her lulled state, and her

eyes flew open. The arms were real. And the chest. And those blue, blue eyes. For the first time in ten years, she almost fell off a walking horse.

She would have fallen if Robert had not grabbed her shoulder and hauled her back into his embrace. Which she had no reason—none—to accept.

She reached up and slapped him.

The grip on her shoulder released. And she dropped down of her own free will.

Onto a road. A trail, really. Through this same cursed forest, its branches, limbs, and heavy foliage pushing in around her. Her feet launched into a rapid walk. Right. Left. Right. Left. She had no idea where she was going, and she did not care. She just needed to escape the young man behind her and unravel her tangled memories of the previous night.

What had happened?

How had she gotten here?

Her ankle threatened to turn on a wheel rut, and she hopped forward, biting her lip, then forced herself on, into the memories. She remembered now the horrible discussion with Daria. And being ill. And the hurried good-bye letter she had written to her mother and stepfather. Then going down to the darkness of the stables and waiting beside Horizon, rehearsing over and over what she would say to Robert when he came. But he had never arrived.

And she had longed to fall asleep but did not dare. So she

had saddled and bridled Horizon and climbed onto the stallion's back.

Where she must have slept anyway. Because that was the last thing she could remember. Until waking up in Robert's arms. Which made no sense.

"Aurelia." The voice behind her was too low to the ground for him to be mounted. The sound of his steps drew nearer to her own.

"Why?" she said, staring at the needle-covered trail and cursing her voice for its trembling. "Why would you leave me without a word?"

The answer did not come. Only silence, probably Robert gathering himself mentally, thinking through what he was going to say. She hated that about him—that unfair amount of patience.

"Why?" she insisted.

His voice was almost sad. "I couldn't."

She stumbled. "But you intended to."

His hand clutched at her elbow. "Aurelia, I want you to be safe."

That stupid word again! She yanked away and continued walking. Always, always with Robert it was the same thing!

He grabbed her elbow once more, spinning her toward him, then held her by the shoulders. "We've been through this before, Aurelia. It's time we face it. I know you don't want to believe that your safety is a good enough reason for making a decision. But it is to me." Those blue eyes were intense. "I need you to understand that."

The air scraped through her chest. She knew how foolish it must seem for her to be mad at him for trying to protect her, but since when did that protection mean abandoning her? Didn't he know what her life would be like?

"I could never stay at the Fortress, Robert, locked away from the world like my mother. I was . . . afraid after the last attack. I am . . . afraid."

The grip on her shoulders softened.

"But I can't . . ." She struggled to voice the fear that had stalked her ever since she had first entered the Blue Room—a fear that had not fully revealed itself until her last discussion in that virulent refuge. "I can't become her."

"Aurelia"—his right hand moved to the side of her face—"you are nothing like your mother." The words were so calm. So certain.

"How can you say that?" she asked. "When I look exactly like—"

"You confronted Lord Lester's men in the forest. And then His Lordship. You went into the village and talked to the people there face to face. And last night you climbed up on Horizon's back and fell asleep."

Was that last part meant as a critique? But his tone had sounded more like pride. And he was right. She *had* done all those things, after the attack. Confusion swept through her chest. Which side of the argument was Robert on?

"I could never live my life without purpose," she said, trying to clarify her own viewpoint. "The expedition is important. I need *you,*" she repeated his earlier words, "to understand that."

"I have always believed in the expedition."

Had he? *Yes.* He had told her she should travel to the frontier.

"But I can't protect the crown princess," he said.

"The expedition was never about the people seeing the crown princess, Robert," she tried to explain. "It was about me learning about them."

"I know," he replied, his fingers still on her cheek. "But I can't take you north—"

"Robert, we have to go north. I have to see the frontier and the desert. I can't deny half my country."

His hands locked on her shoulders. "I was going to say I can't take you north unless—"

"I have to pretend to be someone else." That had been the plan, the one she had prepared to share with him last night.

"Yes." His sudden agreement startled her. "You'll be Daria. And I'll be Thomas. It's safer if we invent as little as possible."

She stared at him, wide-eyed. He had thought this out already.

"But, Aurelia, if we do this," he continued, "there are things that we need to settle first. This territory—it's different than the capital and central Tyralt. It's harder. Raw. And mistakes have repercussions that you won't be able to see. You asked me to be your guide, and I need you to let me do that. To trust my judgment. Can you?"

Now he asked her this? After last night?

And yet she could not quite bring herself to say no. "Will you promise not to leave me?" she said. "Even for my protection? At least not without telling me?"

His hand dropped from her cheek. His eyes closed, the vein on his forehead pulsing, and his fingers formed into a fist. "I swear it," he said, with a tone of fealty. When his eyes opened, they were wet.

She reached out toward those glistening eyes. "I trust you, Robert."

"Good," he said, taking her hand. "Because we can't detour around Transcontina. We have to walk straight into the Lion's Den."

Robert felt no regrets. The floating sensation in his chest was closer to euphoria. They traveled east for three days, and he told himself he had no time for looking back. Or for second thoughts. Instead, he drilled Aurelia on the answers she would give if asked about her identity.

But one of her questions caught *him* unawares.

"Have you ever heard of the Right of Valshone?" she asked on the final morning in the forest.

His hand jerked, and the stallion snorted, kicking at the trail. "Your father terminated it," Robert said, referring to the marriage treaty that would have made his own feelings for Aurelia even more illogical. "A decision I fully support."

Wait! Had he said that last part aloud?

Her cheeks had gone a dark red, and her focus was intense as she prodded the elderly roan.

Robert tried to cover the awkward moment. "I've always assumed you approved of his choice as well."

"I never knew of the Right until four days ago."

How was that possible? The Right of Valshone had everything to do with Aurelia. But then again, it never had, because her father's edict had come so shortly after her brother's death. And until that time, her brother would have been the one bound by the law.

"Where did you learn about it?" she said, leaning forward as if that would transform her slow mount into a racer. "Not in school?"

No, he guessed not. "My father . . ." Though now that she mentioned it, his father had discouraged Robert from ever discussing the topic with her. "I think, perhaps, people were afraid it might disturb you, hearing how the king changed the law because of your mother." He watched closely to see how she would react to his mention of the woman she had left behind.

There came a pause of acknowledgment, and the mare stopped walking altogether. But Aurelia did not allow either to halt the conversation. She dismounted and began checking the mare's hooves. "I can't imagine the Valshone were pleased with the change in my father's policy."

"Maybe not." Robert circled back on Horizon. This was dangerous territory, retracing the past. "But since one of their own ended the law in practice"—he referred obliquely to her mother's flight from the capital—"before your father did it in writing, I guess they had no choice but to accept. Though it's hard to know, since the only person the Valshone send to court is the Heir to the Right."

Aurelia lifted one of the roan's hind hooves. "Did my father ever send liaisons to ease the change?"

Robert shrugged.

She frowned, switching to the mare's foreleg. "Your father—did he say anything about whether the Valshone intended to maintain their side of the treaty?"

She was worried about the repercussions, Robert realized. Here, hundreds of miles north of the Valshone Mountains, and nearly two decades after the Right of Valshone had been brought to an end.

How could he help but love her? "There haven't been any threats of attack on the southern border," he said in an attempt to comfort her. "We seem to be safe."

As safe as any of us are in this kingdom, Thomas's skeptical words taunted back in Robert's head.

Aurelia plucked a stone from the upraised hoof. "And if the people in the south never send anyone to court, how would we know if there *were* an attack? One would think if the inhabitants of the mountains were once important enough for the former kings of Tyralt to make this treaty, then the Valshone must be just as vital to this country today."

"Yes," Robert replied, and for the second time, he opened his mouth and said something he had not planned to vocalize.

"But your father, and the rest of the court, have never been particularly interested in the people at the far reaches of Tyralian society." *What am I doing talking politics?*

"My father cares about Tyralt." Aurelia flung the stone into the trees. "He may have been willing to marry me off to save his own reputation, but he wanted to do it at the greatest benefit he could manage for this country."

Robert cringed, unable to accept her defense of the king's shortsighted attempt to barter her off. "Your father cares about Tyralt's power. I'm not so sure he cares about the needs of the people living here."

She did not flare back, as he had anticipated, but she did not grant him the point either. Instead, she moved to the front of the roan and pulled lightly on the reins. "I think . . ." Her eyes studied the horse's gait. "I think he cares, but he's too afraid of change; and he's surrounded by people, those already at the center of power, who want to use Tyralt's resources for themselves."

"Like the queen." Robert dismounted, leaving the stallion between them.

Aurelia did not bother to argue. "She's never had any interest in people outside the aristocracy."

"Maybe that's why the Treaty of Valshone was made." Robert's focus blurred on the path as he thought aloud. "Not to protect the southern border, but to ensure that another voice was always heard at the palace. After all, the Battle of Gisalt would never have been a surprise if the Tyralian king had had regular correspondence with the Valshone. And the Valshone would never have lost so many warriors if they had asked for support from the Tyralian military." *In the name of the crown, I'm still talking politics!*

Something swatted him on the head.

Aurelia, who had somehow remounted the roan without his notice, was leaning over his temperamental stallion, her pack crushed upon his saddle, the strap dangling loosely from her hands. "So you think I should marry a member of the Valshone after all?" she said, teasing him for the first time since the night of the burning tent.

A warmth he had not thought he would ever feel again washed through his body. "No, of course not," he rallied. "Marriage to you? That might destroy all hope for peace in this country!"

She swatted him again. And his stubborn, half-wild stallion just let her do it.

Aurelia's first impression of Transcontina, when she stepped out from the shadows of the Asyan to peer down into the open river basin, was of sheer magnitude. The sun's high-noon rays powered down onto hundreds and hundreds of white sails. Not ships but wagons. Heavy, curved wagon boxes with white canvas hoods. On every last section of cleared land between the basin's bowl-shaped walls and the deceptively calm waters of the mighty Fallchutes. Not a city, she thought, as she witnessed those wagons. A fleet.

"That's Transcontina." Robert motioned toward a small, insignificant structure at the center of the wagons. Four log walls with sharpened ends pointing toward the sky, their intended aura of strength dwarfed by the mass around them.

"If *that* is Transcontina, then what is this?" She gestured at the fleet below them.

"People who want to settle the frontier."

"All of them?" she gasped.

"Yes." He turned around and headed back into the shadows of the forest, guiding both horses.

Was it possible so many people could crave adventure? She sent another stunned gaze down into the basin, then hurried after him. "Robert, what are you doing?" It had taken her two months to get out of this wretched forest. She wanted to stay out.

He wrapped Horizon's reins around the saddle horn and attached a lead rope. "I'm hitching the horses here. Horizon is too conspicuous, and he doesn't lie when asked to identify himself."

The words drew her concern. She knew how much Robert valued his horse. If he was willing to leave Horizon behind, the danger below must be grave. "But the palace guards left the city, didn't they?" she asked, moving to help hitch the roan.

"Yes, but they will have asked questions, and word will have spread about your disappearance."

"Questions about Horizon?"

"Aurelia, they won't just be looking for you."

Fear shot through her. Of course, she had endangered Robert as well.

"Come on." He took her hand, guiding her through the trees, and together they strode forward into the basin. As they descended, sounds from below began to rise up: the harsh cracks of gunpowder, the thuds of an ax, the *thunk* of shovels hitting rock. And then everything. Baaing, moaning, squealing, baying, barking, clucking, and crowing. Bawling infants. Screaming youth. The rattle of buckets and pans. The spitting sizzle of campfires in the already fierce midday heat. And the unbroken squall of human voices, crossing from one tone to the next without constraint from walls or barriers.

She held her hands to her ears, aware that the noise was as much an inner cacophony as an outer one, the sharp reaction caused by her long absence from so much sound. "All these people are camping here, on top of each other?" she asked as her sensitive ears began to adjust. "Why?"

"They have no choice." Robert circled around a cooking fire. "They're waiting for a pass."

"A pass?" She followed him and almost ran into a small girl.

Aurelia bent down to apologize, then peered closer. The toddler was half naked, her ribs showing beneath her torn garment, her heel planted heedlessly in fresh bird dung. Aurelia turned to the child's mother, but the woman looked worn, her hand barely moving as she stirred a pan over the fire, sweat dripping from her forehead.

This was not adventure.

Reluctantly, Aurelia left the toddler behind. "A pass?" she repeated to Robert.

"Yes, no one can cross the Gate without one."

Then she remembered hearing that there was a monthly limit on the number of people allowed on the narrow mountain path. "You mean we'll have to wait for all these people to receive a pass and cross over the Gate first?"

"No, Aurelia." There was something bitter in Robert's tone. "We aren't going to have to wait."

Doubt threaded through her mind. Did that mean he was going to use her name in exchange for the pass? She pushed away the thought. *He asked you to trust him.*

She would have liked to know more, but they had neared the narrow entrance in the log walls around the actual city, and a crowd of people had gathered. "Open!" a loud voice from somewhere up ahead called out, just as Aurelia and Robert had reached the group's center. And suddenly she found herself in the midst of a pressing swarm. The close bodies shoved against her, tighter and tighter, the scents of sweat, soil, and urine ramming into her nostrils.

And then she was through, the crush dispersing into a cramped marketplace. Stalls clustered one upon the other, their surfaces teaming with furs, guns, raw meat, and tools. The ring of the blacksmith's forge clashed against the pounding of the carpenter's hammer. And the vendors' voices battled for customers, despite already exhaustive lines.

Robert made no move toward any of them, instead steering her along the edge of the walls until he and Aurelia had neared the back of the market. "There," he said, pointing her toward a dark wooden building. The words OFFICE OF LAW were carved into the sign beside the door. "That's where I'm going for the pass. I need you to wait here."

"No, I'm coming as well." She did not like the trepidation in his voice.

"That's not a good idea. The man in there—they call him the Lion."

The cryptic comment from three days before came back to her. Obviously it had held more significance than she had realized. She started toward the building.

"I need you to let me deal with him," Robert said.

She nodded.

Still he refused to relinquish the issue. "I'm serious, Aurelia. I need you to stay silent."

She glared back. *Enough.* She was not letting him go into the Lion's Den alone.

Robert cringed inwardly as he led her into the room of pilfered spoils. Crimson, silver, and speckled pelts overflowed the far corner beside an empty jail cell. A pile of gold rings, a diamond brooch, and a jeweled shell-shaped watch rested on the surface of a nearby chest. A rack of specialty rifles lined the same wall, and a half dozen pistols, all with fancy inlay, were scattered on the dirt floor to the left of the entrance. Though none of the weapons matched the engraved ivory-gripped flintlock on the desk of the Lion.

A thick, swarthy-faced man leaned back in his shabby chair, the black soles of his shoes propped beside that engraved pistol. The curling hairs of his overweight chest stuck out through the open neckline of his beige hunting shirt, and the button on his trousers had been unfastened. "Name your business, or get out," he said. Robert noted the quick glance to the arched hilt of his father's sword.

He felt Aurelia stiffen at his side and willed her, desperately, to keep her mouth shut.

"We require a pass," Robert said, meeting the man's gaze. His father had taught him never to look down in the face of a bully.

"There's a wait." The man pointed his shoe toward a thick stack of parchment on the corner of his desk. "You can add your name or your mark to the list."

Robert felt Aurelia shift.

"I'm afraid that won't be convenient," he replied.

The Lion's gaze turned again, this time openly, to the arched hilt of the sword. "You have some pressing business in the north?"

"My own."

The man spit a wad of chewing tobacco into a tin. "That so? 'Fraid that reason doesn't supersede government policy."

No, of course it didn't. And neither would any reason Robert gave, though his uncle's name as the king's adviser would have done the job well enough, if Robert had dared risk it. "I'm sure we can find something that does," he said.

Again the gaze moved to the sword.

He would have loved to hand it over, to thrust from his side once more the piercing reminder of his own guilt. But it was still his father's, and the crest on the hilt would give away his last name as easily as printing it on a piece of paper. He should have left the sword behind, along with Horizon. An oversight he could not correct now.

Robert reached into his pocket and produced a gold coin.

Aurelia's grip tightened on his hand.

The man spit again. "'Fraid that won't pull you very far up the list."

No, but men the likes of this one would take as much as they thought they could get. "How far?" Robert replied.

"Hmm, maybe two, three pages."

Aurelia twisted her grip.

"Maybe more like twenty or thirty." Robert broke free.

The man bit into a hunk of beef jerky. "Maybe," he said, his mouth full.

Robert produced two more coins. He had had only four in his pack the night of the fire, and then had tried giving Thomas two of them as payment for his stay, but when Robert had reopened the pack later, he had found ten.

"Well, that'll get you about halfway there," the man chuckled.

Done. Robert palmed three more coins within his pocket, and placed them each—one, two, three—on the edge of the desk. The Lion smirked, reached into his top drawer, and pulled out a pre-signed strip of paper. "Happens I kept one back for this month," he said. "Just in case there might be an emergency." He held up the parchment. "Course that'll only get you one pass." He nodded leeringly at Aurelia. "So I reckon the little lady'll have to stay behind and keep me company. Unless you have somethin' else to offer." The gaze returned to the sword.

But Robert didn't need a second pass. He already had a permanent one, obtained back on the frontier. This man did not need to know that. Robert reached forward, his fingers grazing the parchment.

Then someone else stepped into the Lion's Den—a tall, lean man wearing a long dusty black coat. And a rope around his waist. Robert let his gaze follow the length of that rope through the open crack in the door.

And knew. Knew he had about three seconds before the crown princess of Tyralt tore the place apart. He snatched the signed pass, grabbed Aurelia by the wrist, and yanked her toward the door.

Aurelia bridled, pulling out of Robert's grasp. Was this why he had made her promise not to speak? So he could pay this horrible man called the Lion a bribe without fearing that she would interrupt? She would remember this man. She had taken in every crease and mark on his pudgy, despicable face and counted every misbegotten treasure in the room. She would have him arrested. He would pay back every toll he had ever collected, every pass he had ever withheld, and serve out the rest of his life in prison.

A tall lean man with a rope around his stomach jostled past.

She ignored the insult, eager to free herself from this den of greed. Steaming, she turned on her heel.

And it was then she saw the boy.

A child, no more than eight or nine, standing limply outside the door. Head down, his uneven, spiked hair spitting out toward her. His weight tilted on one leg, the other gingerly bent. His ragged trousers hung loose on his hips beneath scarlet chafe marks from the rope around his concave waist.

But these were nothing next to the bright red welts oozing from his stripped torso.

Horror, shock, and rage inflated Aurelia's chest. "Let him go!" She whirled to confront the man on the other end of the rope.

"Beggin' yer pardon, *ma'am*," the lean man sneered. He tipped up his stubbled jaw.

"Release that child!"

Robert's arm reached for her, but she thrust it away.

The Lion actually chuckled.

"Can't do that," the lean man replied. "He's a prisoner."

"I don't care what crime he's committed," she shrilled. "No child deserves to be beaten like that!"

"He's not a child. He's a kuro."

"A *what*?"

The man turned to the Lion. "I swear these settlers don't have the brains of a wasp."

"A kuro, gal." The Lion gave her a foul glare. "A frontier orphan who sold hisself for his keep and then rethunk. But that don't sit too well with the law."

"The law! You call this place an office of the—"

"Who do you think you are?!" the Lion roared.

An arm gripped her waist so tight that it forced the air from her diaphragm. Then Robert was literally pulling her out of that vile room. Away from those repulsive scoundrels. From their crass guffaws. And from that helpless, bleeding child.

Chapter Ten
INTENTIONS

ROBERT HARNESSED HIS FEAR AND DRAGGED HER away from the Lion's Den. She fought him. Of course she fought him. She jabbed him with her heels and battered his shins. She twisted in the circle of his arms and hammered his fingers with her fists. She dug her nails into his flesh and thwacked him straight in the eye with her elbow. Thank Tyralt she had never been trained with a sword, or she would have stripped him of his weapon and won.

Though what she would have won filled him with such dread it gave him the strength to carry her across the blasted marketplace, where every set of eyes hinged upon her. Staring. But there was no time to worry about the undesired attention. The Lion had hirelings. Minions.

Robert hauled her through the log barricade.

"Let me go!" she demanded.

"To the horses," he replied with gritted teeth.

She shoved on his arms. "Not without the boy."

"If I have to," Robert said, "I'll pack you all the way back to the Fortress."

"You haven't the strength."

He seriously doubted he could drag her another hundred feet. "Test me," he challenged, then added, "Listen, Aurelia, we'll talk about the boy, after we get to the horses."

She wrenched her torso to the side, to no avail. "All right," she snapped.

He let go. To argue further would undercut the agreement.

She stormed through the wagons, her pace so fast he had to struggle to keep up after the exertion of fighting her, but he was grateful for the speed. She cut a direct line up the hill, and his mind held the same direct route. *Get out. Get out. Get out. Before the Lion figures out who we are.*

Aurelia crested the basin, and Robert hurried after her into the trees.

Both horses were still there. "Get on Horizon," he ordered her. The stallion would move faster, even with two riders, than the roan. And if Robert needed to, he could cut the mare free.

"We're going back for that child!" She planted her feet stubbornly.

Robert unhitched the horses and tied the roan's lead to Horizon's saddle horn. "Aurelia, the palace guards knew if we were alive, we would have to go through that law office.

Through *that man.* Do you think he can't be bought for the life of a crown princess?"

She mounted, and he swung up behind her.

"Giddyap," he called, and they launched into motion. *I shouldn't have taken her in there,* he chastised himself. But something, something deep inside him, had wanted her to understand what was happening in that law office, and the impact it had over all the people struggling to make their way north.

"Who was the other man?" she asked, her back stiff.

Robert knew there might be a danger in talking, if someone came after them and overheard their voices. But there was a far greater danger in her choosing to return to the city. They had to circle the entire basin, and he had to convince her, somehow, that she could not save that child. "The man with the rope was a bounty hunter," he replied, "probably hired by someone on the other side of the Gate to track down a runaway."

"A runaway from what? They called the boy . . . I'm not sure."

"A kuro. It's something people do on the frontier." Robert tried to describe the practice as calmly as he had first heard it explained, though his gut rebelled. "It's dangerous, being orphaned on the frontier. There's nothing to fall back on. No schools or orphanages that can take in children. If a family doesn't make it, then it's up to the neighbors or acquaintances, if they are willing. An older youth, of course, can make his or her own way. Find work. But a child as young as that boy back there, if no one takes him, has basically only two choices: to starve or sell himself as a kuro."

Aurelia's fingers dug into his wrist, just above the reins. "You're telling me that boy is a slave."

Robert kept his grip firm. Yes, the boy was a slave, no matter what the law said. There was no practical difference between that boy's life and slavery. "In exchange for someone promising to provide a living for him—or her—no matter what quality of life that might be, the child offers his or her service."

"For how long?"

She was not swallowing any of this. He loved that about her. Only a handful of people Robert knew, his mother among them, reacted so strongly to the concept of kuros. There was, after all, the dreadful alternative. Starvation was a hard death.

"Legally, for the rest of his or her life." Robert gently brought his chin onto her shoulder. "Though I've never seen a kuro over fifteen years old."

"They run away." Her tone rang with justice.

He wished he could let her believe that. It would make it easier for him to keep her here, safe on Horizon. But those children deserved to have the truth told. "More often, they're sold into an apprenticeship." He lifted his chin and lowered his voice. "Or shot."

Her body shuddered.

"For stealing property," Robert rushed to explain, "or breaking a contract. Either is a legal defense. It is," he said, referring to the entire practice, "exactly as awful as you think it is."

She was choking. "Slavery." Her voice vibrated. "Tyralt has *never* allowed slavery."

He knew she was reciting one of the Rules, one of the tenets Tyralt had been built upon, taught in every classroom across the kingdom.

"My father cannot condone this." She was shaking.

"He hasn't ended it."

"Does he know about it? Do you know if he knows?!"

Why would His Majesty care about a handful of orphaned children out on the frontier? That was how Mr. Vantauge had responded to Robert's identical question; he had said it bitterly, making it clear that he thought the king should care, but that it was not reality, and his son would have to learn to live with that.

The young woman in front of Robert looked as though she had no intention whatsoever of living with it.

"It's against the law," she said, reaching for Horizon's bridle.

Robert clutched the reins with his right hand and grabbed her wrist with his other. "Not here."

"Yes, it is."

"Aurelia—"

"I'll go all the way back to the palace if I have to."

"So the guards can kill you in cold blood?" It was rough, his response, and if she hated him for it, that was fine.

She relinquished the bridle. He could see the moment when the truth hit her: that no amount of yelling or denial would save that boy's life.

But she was not like Robert's father. She did not absorb that reality and allow it to harden her.

Instead her body began to shake, as though physically

rejecting the idea. "No," she whispered. Robert knew she was not answering his question. "No, no, no, no, no."

He reached for her, but she held him back.

For a moment he doubted whether he should have told her, whether he should have brought her north, whether he knew her at all. Then her empty fingers clenched into a fist, the knuckles of her hand white as she pressed it to her forehead. "I can't . . . ," she finally said. "I can't allow slavery to exist in Tyralt. I won't."

It was what he had needed to hear, not enough, but a statement of faith: that one day she would change things.

Her shaking turned to a shudder, and Robert wrapped her in his arms as she cried.

They rode north, breaking free of the Asyan Forest and entering the Fallchutes River Valley, here a wide, grassy plain in both directions; but this, Robert knew, was seduction. The valley was a wide mouth leading into a shrinking ravine known as the Crevice, until ultimately only the steep mountain rock of the Quartian Shelf would line the dramatic plunge of the Fallchutes River into the frontier.

At first, wary of followers, he kept her to the less-traveled eastern side of the river. Then when he had no other choice, he spent his seventh gold piece, an exorbitant fee, hiring a ferry. He and Aurelia joined the flow of other travelers headed north, those fortunate enough to have escaped the claws of the Lion. This did not, however, ensure anonymity.

Her Royal Highness seemed driven to strike up as many

conversations as she could. He was stunned by the revelations she obtained from people she had barely met, people running from debt and poverty, loss and oppression. Robert found himself torn. He admired her skill and desire to learn, but he had hoped the would-be settlers would provide her with sufficient camouflage.

She betrayed that hope at every stop. At Fort Laiz, she exposed a trader for trying to sell a lame horse. This was followed by a heated discussion on water rights at the Fyonna Trading Post. And then a conflict at Kezlar Township concerning the practice of selling flawed materials to travelers.

Robert valued her need to fight injustice. But her failure to blend in terrified him.

By the time they rode up to Fort Jenkins, he longed to detour around and head straight for the Gate. However, darkness had fallen. And the high, rapid sound of a set of pipes and the spirited romp of fiddles skirled through the warm summer air, joined by the joyous shouts, stomps, and whistles of a dance in high swing.

Before Robert had even finished hitching the stallion, Aurelia had been whirled away into the festivities. She was laughing, her head thrown back, excitement rampant on her face. A far cry from the elegant, fuming princess he had witnessed less than three months ago at her sister's coming-out party.

The thought set Robert stumbling, and he seated himself on a rare open seat, the unoccupied half of a hay bale. She was so *alive.* Kicking her heels. Twirling. Not at all concerned with how people would view her.

Though here, just as everywhere else, people were drawn to

her. Not just the men, who had begun to form a line to dance with her, but the women and children as well, pulled in by the sheer joy on Aurelia's face.

She was a stunning revelation in contrasts. One day fighting mad, the next spinning in glory. It was right, he thought, that she could see both the beauty and the starkness of this region. So many people shuttered themselves from one or the other, letting the darkness embitter them or the light blind them to the flaws. Somehow she saw both.

She isn't a Falcon anymore, he realized. For years he had called her that, a nickname only he had used. And cherished. But not once on this entire journey had he felt compelled to refer to her by the old moniker. There was something royal in the name and strong, but not . . . free.

Not as free as the young woman dancing before him.

"H'llo there." A man in a blue vest and cocked hat interrupted Robert's thoughts, blocking his view. "Would ya be willin' to give up yer seat fer a grandmother?" He pointed toward a slender woman with a long white braid down her back and a catacomb of laugh lines on her face. Her foot was tapping, and her arms were swinging to the music.

"I told ya that's not needed," she said.

But Robert stood at once, and the man disappeared.

The woman did not sit down. "Sorry 'bout my grandson. He's off his head at the moment for a piece of gold petticoat."

Robert slipped into his frontier dialect. "That's all right, ma'am."

"Lad like you, what'er you doin' sittin' over here on a hay bale?" she chuckled. "Find yer own shade of petticoat."

Robert's eyes went right to Aurelia.

"Ah, she's a red one in a brown facade, isn't she, boy? Line's a mite long, though."

Robert sighed.

"Course there's a fine blue one over there"—the woman pointed at a girl with a sapphire skirt swirling up around her coffee-dark legs—"and a yellow charmer over there." She motioned toward a petite, dimpled figure spinning with her arms over her head.

Aurelia's laugh sailed out from the dance floor, and Robert's eyes instinctively returned.

"Mm-hmm," the woman chortled. "Course you could jus' join the line. Or then maybe you could try dancin' by with one those other petticoats on yer arm and see if the color yer lookin' for don't bend in yer direction."

"Might at that." Robert grinned and asked the woman her name.

"Well now, most folks refer to me these days as Grandma, but was a time when I was Stella May and a fine shade of petticoat myself."

Robert held out his palm. "May I have yer hand fer a dance, Stella May?"

She burst into her own special ring of laughter and accepted his offer, then led him straight out into the center of the fray. "And where are ya from, lad, and which way are ya headed?"

He dropped into a quick, well-rehearsed response, saying he had been a courier for a wealthy man and was intent on making his own way on the frontier. A new life.

"So this is yer first trip north then, lad?" Her eyebrows quirked at him.

He nodded.

Aurelia swirled past without glancing his way.

"Myself now," said the older woman, "I've been across the Gate four times. Spent almost a decade on the frontier."

The song stirred itself up to a high finale, then broke, but the woman's feet were still tapping, so Robert twirled her into the next tune.

Aurelia had moved on to her fourth partner.

"Ya know, lad," the woman said, "there's lots of folks as head to the frontier to start new lives. When I first went over the Gate, the talk was we'd all starve and end up trapped over there on our lonesomes, but every year there's more folks. Even talk 'bout a princess."

Robert almost ran into the man playing the pipes, an act which elicited a slur of notes and a rude shout from the musician, but the woman just laughed and continued, "'Twas all the twitter two months ago when folks were sayin' she'd run off with that boy from the palace. But then, when they started sayin' he wasn't from the palace a'tall but from the frontier, well, you know that made fer all manner of speculation. Course most folks don't think she'd have the wherewithal to make it north. They think she prob'ly run off with her frontier boy to some fancy court somewhere."

That was a good rumor. He should encourage it.

Aurelia's feet danced past once again, and Robert tried very hard not to look up. Partner number six.

"Now me," Stella continued, "I like to imagine, and I think there's a chance Her Royal Highness might head across the Gate fer the same reason as every other gal. Jus' wantin' to make a new life."

Aurelia's laughter sailed again, and Robert gave in to the compulsion to seek her out.

She was spinning on what was now the opposite side of the dance floor, just in front of the fiddlers.

Then a large man wearing a fur belt with a chain strung through it grabbed her by the arm.

Robert's spine stiffened at the forceful contact.

Stella May followed his gaze. "Reckon that was inevitable," she said, shaking her head.

"What?" Robert's steps slowed.

"Jenkins." She nodded at Aurelia's new partner. "Founder of this here fort. And used to gettin' what he wants without waitin' his turn."

Fort Jenkins. Well, that made sense.

"Don't know as how I'd let him take my petticoat out for a spin," said the woman. She elbowed Robert. "Ya might want to make this a good time t'interduce yerself."

He took a step in Aurelia's direction, then turned back. "'Twas a real pleasure, Stella May."

"And a real pleasure bein' Stella May again," she said,

"'specially talkin' to a courier like yerself from central Tyralt, with such a fine frontier accent."

Curse it!

She held onto his arm for a moment. "And jus' so ya know, lad, ya shouldn't think nothin' of my imagination. Mos' folks don't listen to the meanderin's of an old lady's mind anyhow."

No use for regret.

And no time. Jenkins had removed his hat and was holding it lower than appropriate on Aurelia's backside.

Robert plunged into a gap in the dance space and hurried through the romping figures. He had to pull up behind the wild capers of a man dancing with a jug of frontier whiskey.

Just behind Aurelia. "I don't care how many walls you've built with those hands," she was saying. "You will remove them from mine."

Jenkins chuckled. "I'm thinkin' a pretty gal like you don't have any walls. Course I'm willin' to check." His left hand reached for her skirt.

Robert grabbed the hilt of his sword.

But Aurelia spun, wrenching herself out of the man's grasp.

Jenkins tried to follow. And crashed head-on into the capering man's whiskey jug.

Glass shattered, shouts rose on all sides, and wild applause erupted from the crowd.

We will not, Robert thought, *be passing the night at Fort Jenkins.*

Chapter Eleven
THE GATE

THE SWORD IN ROBERT'S SCABBARD BURNED AGAINST his hip the next morning. He had reached for the hilt. Last night. And there had been no check within his brain. Nothing holding him back. A fact that haunted. Oozed. Penetrated his skin and seeped into his mind, mingling with the blood of former actions. He needed to go home, to return that weapon to his father and rid himself permanently of the option of ever using it again. He had known this, somewhere in the back of his mind, since Chris's death, but never before had the need felt so urgent.

"I don't see why you're in such a foul mood," Aurelia said, dragging her riding partner out of his memories and into the final stretch of what had once been the Transcontina Valley, now only a narrow strip between the steep slope of the Quartian Shelf and the churning waters of the Fallchutes. A chilly wind gusted down the Crevice, and her hands were cold where they clasped his chest as she rode behind him on Horizon.

They had left the roan behind. The old horse had little chance of making it over the Gate, so Robert had passed the mare into the hands of Stella May. His failure to return the roan to Thomas needled in Robert's gut, but the risks in sending the mare back to Transcontina with a written note were too high.

"We are almost to the Gate," Aurelia pointed out. "I would have thought you would be thrilled."

Thrilled. Her naïveté pierced through him. True, they had presented their passes to the riders blocking the trail a mile back. And done so without hindrance. But even if he could have dismissed the threat from behind—let himself forget the old woman's comments from the night before—nothing would allow him to trivialize the danger ahead.

He knew people who talked, even bragged, about the number of times they had been through the Gate. But far more swore they would never set foot on it again. Nothing he said could prepare Aurelia for the treacherous climb. Still, he should attempt to explain. "We will walk most of the way," he said. "It's steep, and the path is rough. I won't risk Horizon's soundness."

She nodded, waiting to hear more.

"The wagons only travel north," he continued. "There's no room for them to pass."

"Then what about goods coming south from the frontier?" She leaned up against his shoulder.

"Everything goes down the river and is shipped out at the

Port of Darzai. Only people, and sometimes news, come south through the Gate."

"What does it look like?"

Horizon's hooves curved around a jutting rock, and the resulting view spared Robert the effort of description. "There."

The southern entrance to the Gate rose up in front of them, a thin, gray, hideous path etched into the side of the Quartian Shelf. Rugged. Blunt. Built by weather, desire, gunpowder, and human intractability. A feat that paled against the path's soaring, jagged backdrop: the cliff. And its mirror image.

Between the two cliffs, at their base, was the powerful Fallchutes River, the only force strong enough to divide the heights of the Quartian Shelf. The river swept, not gracefully or patiently, but with waters roiling in preparation for the drop ahead. Eighteen times they would plunge downward over the course of fifty miles before emerging again, then flowing east, all the way to the ocean.

Robert turned to see Aurelia's reaction. Her teeth were clenched, the muscles in her jaw tight, her eyes locked on that trail of insanity.

She didn't gasp. Or cringe. Or shudder.

Which only meant she did not yet know what she faced.

Aurelia did not care for heights—a discovery that came at a most inopportune time, as they were less than a hundred feet up the narrow, winding path of the Gate, which, she could see, continued to climb for at least a hundred more.

She closed her eyes and willed herself forward, but her legs refused to move. In fact, they desperately wanted to bend and lower her center of balance. The path seemed somehow to have shrunk from six feet wide to three.

Robert had already moved ahead. If she didn't call out, he was liable to keep traveling without her. She whispered his name, which didn't work.

I can't do this. How am I going to tell him? "Robert!" she called and left it at that. He was bound to think something was wrong.

Something *was* wrong. She was standing on a trail at the edge of a cliff that plunged in a sheer drop down to a series of crashing waterfalls, their roar riding the wind and assaulting her on her fragile perch. This was not frightening. This was *harrowing.* "Robert!" She called his name again and plastered her backside against the jagged wall, her eyes staring out at the almost identical rock face on the opposite side of the gap. The wide, empty gap with only the river below.

"Yes?" *His voice.*

She realized then that she should have invented a logical reason she could not continue and needed to go back down. But she hadn't, and she could not think of one now because she could not think.

Robert stepped in front of her, blocking out that awful empty space. His eyes, those calm blue eyes, met hers. And then he held out his hand, as if waiting for her to take it.

Could she? Was that even possible?

She kept her left hand planted firmly on the cliff face and reached out with her right. Her fingers locked with his.

His grip was firm. Like the rest of him. And she simply didn't have the mental freedom at the moment to sort that out.

Then it occurred to her that he had the wrong hand, the one that, if he was to stay on the outer side of the path, would require her to ascend.

She tried to pull back, but Robert refused to give up his grip. "It gets better," he said.

Liar.

"It does," he continued, "once you get past the sense of climbing."

Well, that was nice of him to say, but this fear was immediate, and personal, and he could not possibly know how she would react when they went higher. She was not going higher.

"I can walk on the outer side," he said.

Yes, well, that was the plan, but for going *down.*

Though the trail *was* slightly less horrible with him standing in front of her, blocking her view of that gruesome drop. He tugged on the stallion's reins and brought Horizon around so the horse was below her, a few feet from the cliff wall, which also helped block her view.

"Now, Aurelia, you tell me when you're ready," Robert whispered. "It's the only way," he said as if he actually believed assassins might be insane enough to follow her here. "It will be all right."

Would it? Would that haunted, concerned look he kept sending over his shoulder disappear if they climbed higher?

"Are you sure?" she whispered. It was very, very important that he was sure.

"Positive."

She allowed herself to breathe.

He took a step back, which struck her as insane, but it did allow her space. Maybe she could try this, as long as he let her return to the cliff if necessary. She stared at the ground, making certain it was there, where she wanted to place her foot. Then she eased forward.

It worked. She was standing perpendicular from the jagged wall.

And Robert was there, still firmly holding her hand. Without judgment.

Though she was appalled at herself for being afraid of something as non-threatening and mundane as height. Then again, there was nothing mundane about this particular trail. And it was plenty threatening with its jagged edges and steep drop.

Maybe if she thought of the trail as her enemy, she could conquer it.

She took a step. Robert moved with her, fluidly.

She took another step, staring at the ground.

That was two, two steps on the way to conquering this trail.

Another one—three.

She fixed her eyes on the surface and set out to make it thirty.

Aurelia's terror of heights did lessen, but nothing else about the trail eased. Robert continued to glance back as if their true foe might still come from behind. She knew better. The enemy was present. It ran up and down in a series of deceitful slopes that taxed every muscle in her body. Her thighs and calves ached, and her feet felt as though they had been shredded. By early dusk on the fifth day, she wanted nothing more than to collapse.

It was then they found the abandoned wagon. Wedged into the cliff, and at an angle. How that was possible on this narrow strip between two slopes, she did not know, but she suspected it had to do with the wheel, somehow rammed into a cleft between the trail and the rock face. And the broken axle. Unsalvageable.

The vehicle blocked the entire path, the tailgate sticking out over the ravine.

Robert walked up to the side of the wagon box, untied the canvas near the back, and peered beneath it, then swore. She had never heard him swear. "They left everything in it," he said, wrestling with another tie. "We'll have to empty the wagon."

"Nooo," she groaned, her body protesting.

"I can't budge it when it's full. All the weight is coming down on the axle." He flung back the canvas, swearing again.

"What about when the people come back for their wagon?"

"It won't be here when they come back," Robert said.

"But—"

"Aurelia, it's blocking the entire path. We can't take Horizon around it. And no one else will be able to drive another wagon past it. We're going to have to push it over the edge."

She stared at him, horrified.

"And we should throw the supplies over as well, or someone is bound to wreck upon them."

He was so concrete.

"But, Robert, we can't. How will the owners of the wagon manage to begin their lives on the frontier if they lose everything?"

He gave a tight shake of his head. And then she comprehended. That the owners would not manage. They must have known the wagon's fate when they had been forced to walk away, but had not had the emotional strength to destroy the vehicle themselves.

Instead, they had left that task for him. And for her.

Robert hefted a crate and heaved it into the ravine. There was a pause, then a terrible *crack!* as the contents splintered, no doubt on some jutting rock below.

Aurelia's soul cracked as well.

But Robert gave no sign of remorse. He scrambled up into the wagon and began struggling with a plough. The seven-foot frame with its iron fittings fought against him, as if to argue its merit. Robert shoved it over. There came a thud, then another *crack!*

This time she saw his torso shudder.

And then she understood—that he, also, was appalled by what he was doing but had steeled himself for the task, refusing to leave it for someone else. He had made the harder choice.

She moved up beside the box and peered into what was left of the canvas bonnet, then lost her heart on a single object. A rocking horse, crude and unstained, its simple head in the shape of a board. But still . . .

For someone to pack such a thing—a toy—when the limited items in the wagon could determine whether a family might survive their first year on the frontier—that said something to her: that this family had thought enough of childhood to include joy. She could not see it destroyed. She scrambled up and reached for the horse.

"Aurelia."

"Just this." She looked back at Robert, pleading.

His eyes closed, but he moved to help her undo the toy's bindings. "We'll tie it on Horizon and leave it someplace where the trail is a little wider."

Nodding, she climbed back out of the wagon, then reached up. And he passed her the precious object, its light frame settling in her hands. The wood felt smooth, well sanded. Carefully she placed the horse behind her. Logic told her the action was futile, that the child in the family would never see the horse again, but somehow the attempt to save something bolstered her strength.

She moved to help Robert unload the rest of the supplies.

They worked side by side as the thin evening gray darkened, tightening its grip on the canyon below, hugging the rocks and crevices and amplifying every crack and thud of a vanquished dream. Until nothing remained, other than the rocking horse, a crate Robert had set aside, and the wagon itself.

Aurelia's limbs crumpled beneath her.

But Robert proceeded to the fallen axle.

"Let it wait until morning," she said.

He attempted to shove the crate under the broken beam. For leverage, she realized. The wagon resisted.

"Robert, it's late. The people behind us must have already camped. Just leave—"

"No!" His voice was harsh. "No, Aurelia, I have to finish this. I can't"—he pounded the frame—"I can't leave it!"

She stood up to go to him, but at that moment, the sound of hurried footsteps interrupted. Then a rustling. And to Aurelia's shock, a figure emerged from under the wagon—a man, rough-clad, with wild hair and a hard look in his eyes. His coat had caught on the edge of the wagon box.

Aurelia hastened to assist him.

"Sir," Robert said, "could you please help us?"

But the man wrenched his coat free, ignoring the rip of the fabric, then brushed past Aurelia and disappeared into the dusk.

She seethed. "How … horrible!"

But Robert just lowered his forehead in his hands, then sank back against the cliff face. "Something happened."

"What do you mean?"

"To that man. He's going the wrong way. And traveling late."

"Maybe he intended to go south."

"No, not without a horse." Robert lifted his head from his hands. "Help me?"

She moved to his side, and together they propped up the axle. Then turned. And shoved the wagon over the edge.

The wagon, and hope. The crash reverberated between the cliffs and within her very bones. She thought of the families she had met on her way here. Their stories. How they had sold everything for their dreams of a future—a future where a man could plow his own field instead of working another man's land; where a woman could work at her husband's side as an equal; and where a child could grow up free, with his or her own dreams. Aurelia stood there, silent, in the dark.

And then she realized Robert was shaking—that the horrible crash must be inside him too. And she thought of all the times he had comforted her when she had felt like her soul was injured. She could not tell him that things would be all right. To do so would denigrate the family's loss. But there must be . . . something . . . she could do. Slowly, Aurelia stepped behind him, gently wrapped her arms around his chest, burying her forehead in his shoulder, and held him. Until neither of them was shaking.

There was no more discussion that night, Aurelia facing the reality of what she had learned about the Gate and the people who crossed it. And about the young man who had ridden over it twice in the past half year, in order to help her. There was a strength within him, something she had not fathomed when he had returned to the palace. Something that had formed while he was away, confronting all this. What was it that had pulled his family this far? And what grit had allowed them to survive?

On the afternoon of the next day, she found a name etched into the side of the cliff rock—*Emily*—with dates, the final one from the day before, and the words, *Wagon over the side.* Somehow Aurelia knew those words had been carved by the man with the hard eyes. She had judged him. And had no right to judge.

Robert's hand closed on her shoulder.

"How much farther?" she asked.

"Tomorrow."

One day. She leaned forward and traced the awful etched words with her fingers. How many people had lost their dreams, and their lives, only a day from their destination?

"They shouldn't call this the Gate," she said. "It should be named the Gauntlet."

And yet there were so many people determined to cross. She remembered the crowd outside the fence at Transcontina. Thousands every year. More than ten thousand had done so successfully in the past decade.

And a little over twenty-four hours later, she was one of them.

Chapter Twelve
FRONTIER

RED-ORANGE-VIOLET FIRE DEFINED AURELIA'S FIRST view of the frontier. Not a polite, watered-down shade, but a drastic wildness flaming the upper echelons of the sky—a sky unlike any she had ever seen. No boundaries, or barriers, nothing to slice apart the spectacular curve of the vision. Not even the faintest wisp of a cloud. Only the ferocious brilliance of color over the landscape.

Raw beauty.

"Is it always like this?" she whispered.

"Never," Robert replied. "You can never know the frontier."

She did not fathom what he meant that first day, but by her fourteenth sunset, a cresting swirl of blue-green-indigo, she had begun to comprehend. That the frontier—its land and its people—resembled its skies: abrupt, unpredictable, and glorious. What appeared to be a vast landscape of rolling hills, wild grasses, and sun-ripened wheat also held meandering canyons, muddy creek basins, and even stands of lowland trees. The people—those she met at the trading post beneath the Gate and along the northbound trail—gave a limited first impression with their constant references to weather and the harvest, but she had soon come to see that their discussions were really about survival, the ability to deal with change, and the knowledge that everything on the frontier came at nature's mercy.

The more she witnessed, the more she began to understand about the young man riding behind her. Like his half-wild stallion, Robert was not all of one thing. He had the same educational background and court training that she had, but he also had all of this around her.

He, too, was of the frontier. And headed home.

Which did not explain his growing silence. She was used to the backward glances, more subtle now than they had been before the Gate. But the darkness today was different. His haunted look during the midday meal had been facing ahead, not behind. And he had spoken less than three words since then. Until now.

"Are you tired?" he asked. "Would you prefer to camp?"

Even though he had told her they could reach the Vantauge homestead this evening? "No," she replied, "unless you think your parents will be upset by our late arrival."

She felt him shift in the saddle and, when she looked back, noted his gaze staring blindly past the wild grasses to the sliced yellow stubble beyond. His hand clutched his sword hilt for the millionth time. "I don't know . . . ," he said, "how my parents—that is, I sent them a letter about the expedition, but . . ."

"You think they might not approve?" she guessed.

"I don't know how my father will react," he said abruptly, "to my cousin's death." *Oh.* This was about guilt. And parental expectation. She wished she could offer him comfort, but her experience with her own father would give her words the lie. "I didn't leave under the best circumstances," Robert added. "My father ordered me not to go and . . . I ignored him."

For *her.* He had ignored his father for her sake. Aurelia's heart hammered.

But she had no time to take in the sudden revelation because Horizon broke into a shrill whistle, then rose on his hind limbs. Aurelia crouched against the stallion's neck, fearful for the young man behind her, but his chest pressed down, his arms reaching around her back, his fingers gripping the stallion's mane just below her own. And then they were flying—she, Robert, and the magnificent bay soaring across the landscape. Warm air hurled past her face, and her blood streamed through her body as she tasted the wind.

Oh, she had missed this! Her chest pounded with exhilaration. The grasses beneath her blurred a golden brown, and the sky seemed to welcome her into its vibrant realm. She felt herself rising up over a slope, and then to her amazement the stallion no longer raced alone but against a bronze chestnut filly. Not a yearling, but a two- or three-year-old beauty. The muscles in the filly's shoulders gathered and flexed with almost the same power as her competitor, and her long neck stretched at Horizon's side, her coat rippling through a spectrum of reds and browns in cohesion with the movement.

Then a whole palette of younger horses hurtled toward the racers. The stallion and filly checked their intensity, and Aurelia felt Robert's grip shift beneath her hands. His chest lifted from her back as he tugged on the reins.

The stallion cantered to an awkward halt, and the younger horses gathered close, nickering and whinnying, sniffing both the bay and its riders. Robert petted each of the horses, dismounted, and held out his hand in a new direction.

From across the field of yellow and brown grasses approached a lithe gray mare, fine-boned, with an elegant arched neck and high, delicate steps. For an instant, Aurelia went back in time. To Bianca. Galloping across the meadow on the extended palace grounds; finding comfort in the royal stables, and setting off on the expedition. The gray horse before her now was like a ghost.

But as the mare approached, other details became clear: the extra height in those steps, threads of white amidst the gray, and thin lines along the horse's eyes. Not Bianca.

Fantasia. Bianca's dam. And Horizon's mother as well.

Aurelia's fingers stretched without permission. The sleek neck edged its way directly under her hand. *Soft.* Mist blurred her eyes, and her stomach twisted with the painful knowledge that Bianca would never again slip beneath that hand.

Then suddenly a bronze snout thrust its way forward. Aurelia blinked, her vision clearing as she found herself staring into a mischievous black eye. Smiling, she offered a second hand in order to pet both horses, but the bronze filly pushed the gray mare out of reach.

"Why you unscrupulous peacock!" Aurelia scolded.

Robert laughed, moving closer. He reached up to rub the bronze cheek. "No, not a peacock," he said, then swung up onto the filly's bare back and winked at Aurelia. "Say hello to Falcon."

The chestnut tossed her head in a show of confidence.

"Oh!" Aurelia's heart skidded as she again took in those tempestuous black eyes and the shining bronze coat, its surface glistening with the faint remnants of sweat. If he had given this stunning horse her old nickname, it was no insult.

"She's a handful," he said, "but she isn't vain—just never wants to be left out of the action. And she has her opinions."

"How old is she?" Aurelia stroked the filly's neck.

"Two."

Falcon tossed her mane. "And three months." Robert laughed.

But the laughter came to a sudden halt, his eyes flying beyond Aurelia, emotion sweeping his face. She followed his gaze past a field of partially harvested grain, a high arched barn, and a circular paddock, to a simple log cabin, unremarkable in this realm of brilliant sunsets. But just in front of the cabin's door stood a man and woman. The man remained frozen, his feet planted, with his hand over his face as if blocking out the nonexistent glare of the sun. The woman began to run, her slender figure moving swiftly and her uncovered blond hair flying back from her face.

Robert did not wait. He urged the chestnut forward and within moments swung off the filly's back and swallowed his mother in his arms. The sobbing woman's smile would have lit the trail all the way back to the Gate.

And then Robert untangled himself from his mother's clasp and turned to face his father.

Aurelia guided Horizon closer in an attempt to provide support. Not close enough to interfere but enough to see the stiffness in Robert's shoulders, the hesitation in his steps, and the familiar reach for the sword.

But for the first time since that dreadful morning in the palace arena, the blade lifted, steel scraping against its sheath, and Robert stepped forward, the bared weapon balanced on open palms. He halted, a mere three feet from the frozen figure before him, then kneeled and lowered the blade at his father's feet, relinquishing it.

And stepped back, trembling.

Aurelia knew then that the blade had become more than an item to Robert. It was blood and guilt and death in his mind. And for some reason, he had felt compelled to carry that burden here. For his father's judgment.

But Mr. Vantauge ignored the sword. Instead, he let his hand fall from his forehead and, in one unbroken movement, stepped across the naked blade and engulfed his son in a fierce embrace.

Was that real love? Aurelia wondered as she tossed under the oppressive heat in the cabin loft that night.

It had been clear from the first moment, the emotional reunion between mother and son, that Aurelia's relationship with her own mother could not bear comparison. All those weeks and weeks of struggle—the stilted conversations, the gestures of amity, the revelations of the past—all of them dissipated beneath the brilliant power of that first smile from Mrs. Vantauge.

Aurelia had known, when she had chosen to leave the Fortress, that the bond between her and her mother would never be whole or transcend acquaintance. Never be love.

But it was not the smile that kept Aurelia awake.

It was the embrace from father to son.

Again and again she envisioned that embrace. No condemnation or critique, only forgiveness.

So unlike her own father. The realization *hurt.* The king, she realized, was not the leader she had always wished him to be. But he was still her *father.* The parent who had claimed her, involved her in his council meetings, and listened to her when her stepmother refused. He had proven himself a coward—but did that mean he did not love his eldest daughter? Or that she could not love him?

Again, Aurelia rolled.

The cloying heat seemed to press down from the ceiling.

She tossed once more, this time burying her face in the straw mattress.

It smelled like Robert.

Who was probably fast asleep in the coolness of the barn.

The sudden creak of a floorboard, however, indicated that someone below was not. She lifted her head from the mattress to listen. And again heard the slow whine of wood sagging beneath weight. Then another creak, and another.

"Brian, stop agonizing," Mrs. Vantauge's sleep-filled voice carried upward. "There's nothing you can do. He's of age."

"He's acting like a child," the man said, his voice hushed but fully awake.

"He's behaving like a young man." The sleepy tone took on a note of gentle rebuke. "And that is why you are upset."

"I won't see my son turned into a subservient pawn like my brother."

Muffled laughter replied. "I'm sorry, Brian, but 'subservient'? He disobeyed *you* to go back to the palace."

"A boy is dead because of that, Mary."

The laughter was gone. "Would you rather your son had allowed that boy to kill him?"

"I would rather my son had never learned to kill."

"But that isn't something you can change—you or him. He's learned a lot, Brian. More than we know, not the least of which is that he cannot be you. And that is a hard lesson."

"I never wanted him to be like me."

"But *he* always did. You are a good man, and your son knows that. He is too intelligent not to."

"Then what is he doing with *her?*"

The unexpected point of disapproval plunged into Aurelia's chest. She shrank back, causing the mattress to rustle.

The conversation below stalled, only to be broken by an even more shocking comment from Mrs. Vantauge. "She is not the enemy."

Enemy? Why would she say such a thing?

"She's her father's daughter," Mr. Vantauge said.

"That is not fair," replied his wife.

No, it was not, and when had Robert's father developed feelings against the king?

"Are you saying that after everything," Mr. Vantauge responded, "all the effort we went through to break away from the palace, my son's purpose is to escort Her Royal Highness around the kingdom?" His derision curdled in Aurelia's chest.

"No," Mrs. Vantauge replied, "but—"

"I won't let him be sacrificed for His Majesty's reputation. Or destroyed at the whim of that man's daughter."

Destroyed? Aurelia grappled for understanding, slowly coming to grips with the knowledge that Mr. Vantauge's animosity was not about her, but about fear for his son's safety. Of course.

Mrs. Vantauge was right. Robert *had* emulated his father.

"He's trying to find himself, Brian," came her soft whisper. "You have to let him."

"Don't tell me you aren't worried. I've seen that look in your eyes, Mary. You're afraid of something as well. What is it?"

But only silence replied. Then stretched and extended until the sound of slow breathing drifted up from below, indicating sleep.

Aurelia's muscles remained tense. *He's only protecting his son,* she told herself. *Another part of that extraordinary love.*

A shiver ran through her body.

And then Mrs. Vantauge's soft female voice rippled once more into the darkness. "She'll break his heart."

No. Aurelia drowned herself in the mattress and Robert's scent. *He is far more likely to break mine.*

Something was wrong, Robert realized as he woke in the barn under the brilliant slanting rays of the sun. The cow had not been milked. Or fed. And he had slept far too late. Not that he minded the extra sleep or opposed the task of milking. It was just—the barn had always been his father's domain, and the chores were always done before sunrise, especially during harvest.

Robert scrambled from his pallet, tugged on his clothes, and hurried toward the cabin. He swung open the log door, then stared aghast. A rind of cheese, a basket of eggs, and a heap of green onions crowded the narrow sideboard. At the kitchen table, a squadron of apples awaited execution at the hands of Robert's mother, who was annihilating slabs of salted bacon.

Even though porridge was common breakfast fare. "Mother, what is this?" Robert eyed the growing mound of chopped meat.

"I am serving omelets," she said, then spun, despite the sharp knife in her hand, to check the hearth.

Omelets? Since when did his mother know how to make omelets? "Mother, no one expects a palace breakfast. Is father all right? The sun is past up, and the cow—"

"Your father can milk the cow later. I needed him to press the other apples for cider."

Cider? In midsummer?

She carried a thick skillet back over to the table, swept the massacred bacon into the pan, and then hurried over to the sideboard, still not relinquishing the knife. "I thought you should rest, but now that you are awake, can you please go outside and assist Her Royal Highness with the well?"

"She asked you to call her by her name," Robert said.

"Yes, um . . . ," his mother stammered, snatching the onions and carrying them over to the table. "I will try to remember that in her presence. Now please go help her. She wanted to wash up, so I sent her with some soap out to the well, but I'm afraid that handle might not—"

"Mother." He wanted to tell her that Aurelia did not expect to be treated like a princess.

But a male voice snarled at him. "Robert, attend to your guest."

He turned to see his father laden with a bucket. Mr. Vantauge stepped over the threshold and lowered the container with a thud. The stern expression on his face brooked no argument.

Baffled, Robert retreated out the door and around the cabin's side.

Where Aurelia, her figure bent over, face obscured, was washing her hair.

Water poured over her bare neck and down the long dark tresses, longer without their waves than he had realized. She lowered the bucket, then traced her fingers through the brown wet strands until a white lather gathered beneath her fingertips. *A frontier sky, she was beautiful.*

Desire flooded Robert's body.

Her soapy hands fumbled for the bucket, and he moved to pour the water over her unsuspecting head. She laughed.

Her laugh was even more beautiful than the rest of her.

The suds drained from her hair to the ground, and she twisted the dark clean tresses with her hands, ringing out a fraction of the water, then stood up, the long wet strands flying over her head, spraying the air, and dampening the back of her smock.

She arched her back. *More than beautiful.* Then she stretched into the sunlight. "It's so lovely here, Robert. No wonder your parents never wished to return to the palace."

Perhaps he should warn her. "Aurelia, I don't know what's wrong with them, but my parents seem—"

Her hand touched his arm. "Don't worry."

He knew that look, her you-worry-too-much look, often

followed by disaster. "I just think you should be prepared," he said.

"Your mother has been working very hard on breakfast."

"I know, but she—"

"It will be wonderful, Robert," Aurelia said.

And perhaps she had some kind of insight, because the extravagant scent of cooked egg, melted cheese, green onions, and fried bacon came floating out the window, along with his name, her title, and an invitation to breakfast.

She hurried to accept, and Robert followed, gaining ground so that they stepped into the cabin at the same time. The steaming concoction on each of the plates at the wooden table would have put the royal chef to shame.

"It smells exquisite," Aurelia murmured.

"I'm afraid we only have apples." Mrs. Vantauge stood, pouring natural cider into each mug, then gestured to her own chair at the table's end. "I'm certain you're used to fresh strawberries."

Strawberries? On the trail?

"Everything looks spectacular." Aurelia glided into the offered seat.

Robert's mother gave a faint smile, then hurried to the now almost barren sideboard and returned holding a basket draped with a blue cloth. "I'm afraid the bread is cold. I'll be certain to bake fresh—"

"Mary," Mr. Vantauge growled from his own chair, "please sit down."

She glanced back toward the sideboard, but its surface was clear, and she lowered herself onto one of the benches along the table's length. Robert waited a moment to make certain she did not spring back up, then allowed himself a seat on the opposite bench.

Mr. Vantauge immediately began to eat, and Robert followed his cue, the omelet's warm, spongy texture tumbling down his throat. *Amazing.*

His mother lifted her fork but let it hover in the air. "Your Highness . . ." She paused, then corrected herself—"Aurelia"—and turned to the young woman who appeared to be having as much trouble as Robert not inhaling the entire omelet in a matter of seconds. "Our son informed us of your expedition. Is it near completion?"

"Oh." Aurelia's fork stilled in mid-bite, then lowered. "We haven't seen the western coast or the Valshone Mountains or—"

"And do you intend to visit all those places?" Mrs. Vantauge's eyes moved to Robert.

His own focus turned to Aurelia.

Until this moment, she had never mentioned any goals beyond the desert. Which had seemed, at the outset, so distant.

"W-we . . . I hope . . . to see as much as I can," she stammered. He noted the switch from plural to singular. Was she doubting if he would come with her, now that they had reached his home?

"We're traveling to the Geordian next," he said firmly, for the benefit of everyone at the table.

Mrs. Vantauge, still not tasting the masterpiece in front of her, gave a shaky nod, then turned her attention once again to the princess. "And will you travel as yourself or as a commoner?"

"I've found that it's easier to travel as one of the people of Tyralt, rather than as someone above them." Aurelia retrieved a slice of bread, tore it in two, and held out half of it to Robert.

He accepted the half.

His mother's fork clanged against her plate.

But it was Mr. Vantauge who spoke, his voice as harsh as it had been all morning. "And what will your expedition be worth if you refuse to bring with it the authority of the crown?"

"A leader is not defined by a crown," Aurelia replied, rephrasing one of Robert's statements to her—a quote Robert himself had retrieved from his father.

Mr. Vantauge stood abruptly. Plates slid and cider splashed. Robert's mother rescued the pitcher, though a beech-wood bowl of apples rolled onto Aurelia's lap, then tumbled to the floor. His father paid no heed. Instead, he stormed from the cabin.

Robert rose, furious. But two hands from opposite corners captured his wrists.

"I need your help," his mother said, pointedly handing him the pitcher.

Aurelia's eyes focused on the still open doorway, a dangerous look on her face.

He started in front of her, but she tugged him back.

"Stay here." And with that, she strode after his father.

Chapter Thirteen
LOVE OR DEATH

"LET HER GO, ROBERT." HIS MOTHER CROSSED IN front of him and shut the door.

"Mother, you don't know—," he started to say. Aurelia might feign strength, but she was more than capable of being damaged.

"No, Robert, *you're* the one who doesn't know." His mother's blue eyes met his. "And it's time you did." She ducked her head, though her thin shoulders remained straight. "Perhaps too late, but there's nothing any of us can do about that now."

"About what?"

Mrs. Vantauge plucked the pitcher from his hand. "You realize this charade of hers can never last. The rumors have been up and down the Gate for months. Even here, your father and I heard about you traveling north. With her." She tilted the pitcher over the nearby cider bucket.

His stomach sloshed along with the pulpy gold liquid, the fear that had stalked him from Fort Jenkins confirmed. If the rumors were that rampant, sooner or later they were bound to reach the palace. "Does Father think the assassins will follow her across the Gate?"

"Your father isn't worried about *her,* Robert." His mother set the emptied pitcher onto the table. "He and I are worried about *you.*"

"She's the one in danger, not me."

"You are in at least as much danger as she is." His mother eyed the fallen apple wedges and crouched down, rapidly beginning to pick up the fruit. "Robert, she is a princess."

"I know that, mother." He bent to help, retrieving the overturned bowl.

"But you don't seem to understand what it means." She thrust a bench to the side. "It's not something you can ignore. Or pretend doesn't exist. And you can't help her pretend either. Sooner or later, she's going to realize she can't run away from who she is. And she will go back." The blue eyes looked up at him. "Have you asked yourself where you will be then?"

He had, more times than his mother had any right to know. And he had come to one conclusion: it did not matter. Because he would not, and could not, do anything differently. He couldn't *not* be in love with Aurelia.

"I'm aware of who she is," he said softly. "She is a person who deserves to be treated like one."

His mother snatched the bowl from his hands and carried it to the opposite side of the table. "Your father used to believe that about the king."

Robert stood, his shoulders stiffening. She had no right to compare Aurelia to her father.

His mother lowered the bowl to the table, her head down, obscuring her face, then rested a hand on the back of her husband's chair. "Brian was raised for his position," she said. "As a son of the Vantauge family, there was never any question that he would serve the king. Your uncle, of course, inherited his father's place, but both boys were raised to believe it was a duty, and an honor, to support their ruler."

The stiffness drained from Robert's shoulders. He did very much want to understand his father's relationship with the king. "But Father changed his mind. Why?"

His mother's face paled. "Because of me."

The pull to know the truth drew Robert closer. "Tell me what happened, Mother. Why did we really leave the palace?"

She sank down into her husband's chair. "I wanted your father to tell you before you left, but he was so upset, and . . . I wasn't strong enough to talk about it."

Strong enough? Was Robert asking too much? But if he had learned one thing from his failure at the palace, it was that he needed to understand the forces controlling his life. "Please tell me," he said, taking her hand.

She stared across the room at the blank wall beneath the loft.

"I came to the palace when I was fifteen. My parents had passed away from a fever, and I moved to live with my grandfather, Colonel Lorance. You have no memories of him, do you?"

Robert shook his head. As long as he could recall, he and his father had been his mother's only family. "He was a soldier?"

"A lord by birth, but he served the former king in the cavalry and always preferred his military title. He taught your father how to ride."

Robert had known that his mother came from an aristocratic background and had married *down,* as Chris put it, but he had never known any real details.

"They became very close," she continued, "and that is how I met your father; Colonel Lorance introduced us. He thought Brian had potential and believed that, despite your father's upbringing, he could learn to make up his own mind."

Robert bristled at the idea that his father had ever needed to be taught to form his own opinions.

"Brian admired Colonel Lorance very much, but your father wanted, more than anything, to prove his own worth, and he was so, so proud of being named royal spy."

Of course he was. No one had managed to fill Mr. Vantauge's role at the palace since. Including his son. Robert slowly released his mother's hand and made his way over to the hearth.

"But the royal spy works for the king, Robert, not for himself."

Yes, well that was a lesson he had learned the hard way. Crouching down, he stirred the gray cinders with a metal prong.

"And the king . . ." She stopped.

"Isn't always worth supporting." He said the treasonous words for her.

"You've learned that lesson," she whispered. "I was afraid you might."

His gaze turned of its own volition to the sword now hanging on the wall beside his parents' bed. "How did my father learn it?"

"The king was worried about a group of people who were gathering to protest poor working conditions. He wanted to know who was behind the meetings. Your father was assigned to find the ringleaders."

Again Robert stirred the cinders, watching them swirl. He knew the story could not end well.

"Colonel Lorance tried to convince your father that the people were doing nothing wrong. He showed Brian the drudgery of the children hired by bricklayers to pour clay. Your father agreed that the situation was bad, but he believed if the people behind the meetings talked directly to the king, they could make their points heard; and Brian didn't support their secrecy. He found out the names and gave them to His Majesty."

Her voice stopped. Robert looked up to see her lips moving with no sound coming forth.

"And what did the king do with the names?" he prompted softly.

"He called in the men on the list," she said, her voice shaking. "They all told the same story . . . were stripped of their jobs, and allowed to leave."

But?

She continued, "They bought their freedom by telling the king the names of the aristocrats who had given money to their cause. Colonel Lorance was the greatest contributor."

The metal prong fell from Robert's fingers.

His mother's eyes turned gray with tears. "He was charged with attempting to incite public rebellion," she whispered. "And he was executed."

There were worse things than disapproval, Aurelia told herself, as she steeled her will and entered the gap at the edge of the sliding barn door. She had faced intimidation before, but unlike with the Lion and Lord Lester, she cared what Mr. Vantauge thought. This man, above all others, Robert admired most.

A high wall of tightly stacked hay bales blocked her path, rising clear to the loft and dropping down in steep double steps before her to the earthen floor. The potency of straw and dust clung to the air, and her sinuses stung as she eased her way along the narrow path to her right, then cornered the bales and found herself blinded by a slashing wall of sunlight. She winced, opened her eyes, and tried to regain her bearings, then plunged through the radiance.

Mr. Vantauge stood with his back to her, both hands planted against the far log wall, as if he were trying to push it away. The stance, the set to his shoulders, the dropped head—everything about him screamed that he wished to be left alone.

She was intruding. She knew that.

But sometimes intrusion was necessary. "You aren't happy to have me here," she said, entering the pungent corner inhabited by the barn's lone dairy cow.

He did not move, failing to react when taken by surprise.

A rare skill. No wonder her father had assigned him his post.

"I admit I can't even milk a cow." She let her gaze fall on the welcome barrier of the buttermilk-colored animal. "And I've never worked on a farm. I suppose most people on the frontier would be less than pleased with a guest in the midst of harvest."

"What do you know about frontiersmen?" Mr. Vantauge pushed his way off the wall.

"They're stronger than the people in central Tyralt," she said, stepping closer to the cow. "Maybe because of what they go through to get here. Or how desperate they have to be to come in the first place."

"Don't heroize them." He hefted a shovel at his side and turned to face her. "They're rougher too, harsher . . . and less tolerant."

"Yes, but they know what they want—what's important."

"And what is that?" The shovel's point hit the earth.

"Freedom."

His brown eyes drilled into hers. All his other features—his build, his hair, his hands, the muscles in his face—all these Robert had inherited. But not the eyes. There was nothing calm or comforting in those dark spheres. They were direct. Jaded. And hostile. "Does that frighten you?" he asked.

"No." She stroked the cow's warm buttermilk side. "Of course not. It's what we have in common. I needed the freedom to go on this journey, to explore my country and see who the people are."

"It frightens your father," he said.

She considered the statement. Her father had never cared for anything that challenged tradition. "Maybe."

"Definitely." He scooped a pile of fresh manure with the shovel, walked past the cow and her, and pitched the manure out the window, then flung the shovel to the ground. "How will you rule if what the people want is to be free of your control?"

"I don't want to control them. I want to help them." She thought about the kuro boy back in Transcontina. She had begun to understand, after the rigors of crossing the Gate, how children could be desperate enough to sell themselves for survival. But she could never accept any law that allowed people to become property. "And to ensure they protect and respect one another."

"Ah," said Mr. Vantauge, plucking a low stool from beneath the window. "By virtue of the crown."

Her temper rose at his sarcasm. "The people of Tyralt ultimately control their own destiny."

He froze. "You realize it's treason, what you just said."

It wasn't. It was common sense. "The role of a leader is to help guide that destiny, not shape it."

"And a leader . . ." He quoted her statement from breakfast haltingly. "Is not defined . . . by a crown."

"Exact—"

"My son told you that."

Had he?

Mr. Vantauge slammed the stool into the dirt. "And is that why you're here? To find out where he got his ideas?!"

Her eyes widened. *No, of course not.* She raised her hands to her hips. "Robert is more than able to make up his own mind."

"Then why is he obeying your orders?" He shoved the stool with his boot.

"I *asked* him to come on this expedition," she said. "I didn't order him."

"Why?" he demanded. "Why did you ask *my* son?"

She staggered back from the question. There was more to the answer than he had a right to know. But she would not lie to this man. "Because"—the reasons spilled out of her—"he's not afraid to argue with me or ask what I think; he'll tell me when I'm being stupid or foolish or blind; and he doesn't patronize me. He respects my ideas and isn't afraid of a challenge. We can fight . . . and still forgive each other. And he"—she blushed—"he looks at me with those eyes, and I know I can trust him."

The truth.

She knew now, as she had not a month ago, that Robert's thoughts of leaving her at the Fortress had not been betrayal. He could make hard decisions—ones she might not agree with—but he made them for the right reasons. And up on the high jagged Gate, she had learned to admire that quality.

Something shifted in Mr. Vantauge's stance. His voice and

head were low as he slid the squat stool over beside the dairy cow. "And you think it wise to continue your expedition, despite the obvious danger?"

"Wise?" She knew this question mattered to him, his son's safety. Still, all she could do was answer honestly. She shook her head. "But it isn't about me"—she paused—"or your son. It's about Tyralt. There is so much I need to learn."

His head came up, a new light glowing in those direct brown eyes. The line between his lips cracked, and the hardness in his chin relaxed. "Well, Aurelia." He said her name for the first time, then gestured at the stool. "I imagine I could teach you something."

Robert struggled with the revelation of his great-grandfather's death as he helped his mother clean up the rest of the breakfast, his mind swirling like the darkening dishwater in the bucket around her hands. How had he managed to grow up in the palace never hearing about Colonel Lorance's execution? Could such a thing be hushed? "Was it public?" he asked at last.

"Very," his mother replied softly "To send a message."

"Then why haven't I ever heard of it?" He tried to hand her the heavy cast-iron skillet.

But she rejected it. "You were so young at the time, and then"—she shook her head, motioning at a knife—"other events overshadowed it."

What could overshadow an execution? "Which events?"

"The death of the crown prince."

He dropped the iron pan.

"And the queen's disappearance," his mother added.

Yes, he supposed those would overshadow the death of a minor lord, though not, judging by the pain on his mother's face, for his parents.

"And yet you stayed at the palace until I was fourteen," Robert said, scraping the skillet with the knife. The crusted grime on the bottom of the pan refused to break free.

"It wasn't easy for your father to leave."

No, it wouldn't be. Not with Uncle Henry there, and the Vantauge family legacy.

"But something changed?" Robert asked.

"The king started to ask about your training."

He stopped scraping to look at her. "Mine?"

Her face muscles were tight. "The thought of you in that web of deceit made up your father's mind. And we left."

No wonder his father had been so angry when Robert had decided to return to the palace.

His mother wrenched the skillet from her son's hands and began scraping it herself. "Your father is afraid the princess will drag you back into that same web, Robert. She is her father's child. She was raised to expect things, and while she may be embarking on this expedition with the best of intentions, there's more than enough evidence of danger."

"And you think I should leave her to face it alone?"

"She's a *princess*, Robert."

How many times was he going to have this conversation? "Aurelia needs my help."

"She could find someone else, and I know it's not easy to accept, but eventually, she will." Mrs. Vantauge wiped the skillet with a rag, then dropped the pan on the table.

Robert stared at the black iron circle. Could Aurelia make other friends? He didn't doubt it. Could she find another guide? Perhaps. Could she one day develop a relationship with another man that was stronger than the one she had with him? *Yes.* But curse it if he was going to step back and let it happen!

"If you really believe in this cause, Robert, your father and I can understand. If you need to travel and go on this expedition for your country, then go. We won't stop you. But don't do it for this girl. Don't convince yourself she needs you more than any other person she could hire off the trail. Your father just wants what's best for you. He doesn't want to receive a letter someday saying that you've been executed in the street."

The image was vibrant. Red. Like the blood pooling beneath Chris's chest. But Robert saw another vision as well—that of the murderous flames devouring the princess's tent.

Her life meant more to him than his own.

The cabin door swung open, shattering the harsh vision, and in its place entered Aurelia. Laughing. And smelling like the barn. Her eyes were glowing, her hair loose. In her hand, she carried a metal pail. Hefting the container, she showed Robert the inches of foaming white milk. "I think I squirted as much on my smock as I did in the pail," she said.

Then Mr. Vantauge emerged behind her. Gone were the stiff, hard eyes and the rigid bearing. His warm chuckle rippled through the cabin, and he clapped his hand on Aurelia's shoulder. "Well, that's a start. You should have seen my shirt the first time I tried it." He grinned up at his wife and son. "I'm telling you both, she'll make a frontier girl before the week is out."

Chapter Fourteen
HARVEST

IT WAS THE MOST GLORIOUS WEEK OF AURELIA'S life. After that first morning, she was treated not as a title but as herself, a young woman who wished to learn all she could about the golden, ruthless landscape around her.

And she was taught to gather wheat. Six days she spent in the fields, beside Mary Vantauge, pitching and tossing the golden stalks severed by the scythes. Talking, laughing, asking questions. And feeling truly useful. Though no one appeared to trust her with a blade.

Ironically, the knife Robert had thrown her in the Asyan remained tucked in the waistband of her skirt, the hard sheath pressing into her stomach every time Aurelia bent to lower the pitchfork. But she refused to remove the weapon, finding comfort in its discomfort.

Like the bittersweet pain of her time with Robert's parents. With Mr. Vantauge, who never mocked her questions but taught her how to gather eggs and feed the chickens, to hitch the workhorses to the wagon and drive it through the fields, and to heave the wheat in a giant net up to the barn loft.

And with Mrs. Vantauge—Mary, she had asked Aurelia to call her after that first disastrous breakfast—who thought to explain the tiny everyday things without being asked, suggested rest before Aurelia ever had to beg for it, and dispensed kindness throughout the long hard hours of work. It was Mary, Aurelia learned, who was the source of her son's deepest strengths: his warmth, his patience, and his compassion.

How Robert could bear to leave this place, Aurelia could not fathom. His parents were all she had ever wished for in her own. And still more. They spoke to Robert as if his viewpoint mattered. His time, his effort, his work. And even though he had told her he preferred the horse-training aspects to the farming, it was clear he had played an integral part in the building and running of the entire homestead.

She should not have been surprised.

It had been evident to her, for some time, that Robert was no longer a boy, but a man.

A fact that did not preclude him from capturing her at the well the morning after the cutting was finished. His right arm circled her waist. "Close your eyes."

"Robert, what—"

"Trust me," he said, lowering his voice.

Did solemn vows include being captured before breakfast? But the feel of his touch, absent since her arrival here, was hard to refuse. She followed his wishes.

His hands urged her to the left, sliding around her as he circled in front, then took both her palms and guided her forward. "Don't worry," he said. "I won't let you fall."

Fall? What term would he use for the tumbling in her stomach? The long wild grasses snagged at her feet, and she tried to focus on her steps, but her mind caught on the calluses of his palms, the strength of his grip, and the knowledge that her skin had missed his. She tripped, losing her equilibrium. And felt his chest against her own, his hands on her shoulders.

"Are you all right?"

Mm-hmm.

Again he took her hands, pulling her forward.

"Robert—" She had no idea what she was going to say.

But a rustling in the grass told her they were no longer alone.

He circled behind her, his hands rising to her closed eyelids, and turned her slowly toward the sound. "Did you think I'd forget?" his breath whispered in her ear.

"Forget what?"

"Aurelia, you're eighteen." He laughed, his parents' voices joining in from nearby.

Her birthday. She was the one who had forgotten.

"I'd like to give you a gift," he said, "but you have to promise not to refuse."

"Why would I refuse?"

"Promise."

Her mind scrambled, trying to heed the warning pulsing through her veins. But she fell victim to her curiosity. "Yes." She opened her eyes.

His fingers slid from her face....

To reveal the cocked ears of the chestnut filly. The red and brown mane sprang up wildly behind those ears, and the matching tail arched above the glowing bronze back. The soft pale muzzle stretched eagerly in Aurelia's direction, the filly's reach held in check by Mr. Vantauge.

Falcon. Bridled, saddled, and determined.

Aurelia felt her heart break. Robert *couldn't* give her this beautiful, strong-willed horse. Her own mare had already paid the ultimate price.

The filly strained forward, no doubt anticipating one of the treats Aurelia always brought when she and Robert came out to visit the horses. She felt him slip something into her hand before subtly retreating.

Mr. Vantauge released the bridle.

And Falcon broke forward, her muzzle diving down and nibbling until Aurelia opened her fingers, exposing the oats just placed there. The filly stole the food. Then, instead of backing away, stepped close.

No, Aurelia thought. But the questing nose was so insistent, sniffing her chin, her cheeks, her hair. *Don't let yourself fall in love with her.* The black eyes were so wide. The red-brown neck so soft. She let her face fall against the filly's shoulder and lost her heart.

Then she whirled, flung her arms around Robert's neck, and kissed him.

Fast.

In fact, Aurelia had already mounted Falcon before she realized what she had done. And in front of his parents.

The tears in her eyes obscured the others' reactions. Her hand rose, but she forced it down. "Thank you."

Surely they would realize there was nothing intentioned in the kiss. Nothing . . .

Except for the way she felt about him.

She buried her face in the horse's mane, and within moments, she and Falcon were flying over the grasses of the frontier.

He wanted to go after her. But both his parents were standing there. Watching. He could feel their eyes drilling into him, and he knew they were thinking he would misinterpret the kiss, let himself believe it meant more than gratitude.

The contact had been so swift. So brief. How could he imagine it meant anything?

But she had never kissed him before.

Once, months ago, he had kissed her. Frightening her. And she had run away.

Now she had run again, but this time he had not caused her fear. Something else had. Like her own feelings.

If the kiss had meant nothing, would she have fled?

He was a fool.

His father's hand clapped down on his shoulder, a light in the older man's eyes.

Robert knew the breeze chasing Aurelia had caused that light. With a wind, the threshing could commence. And he would have to resign himself to a long day of beating grain with a flail. Beside her. Within inches of her. And without a moment alone with her.

Sure enough, as Robert had anticipated, she insisted on helping with the threshing. And after her delayed birthday breakfast, he, his father, and Aurelia all scaled the barn ladder to confront the massive pile of wheat under the eaves. Golden stalks, long spiky heads, and, somewhere in the midst of those pointed beards, the precious kernels of grain.

Mr. Vantauge began pitching the wheat.

And Aurelia, hefting a pitchfork, moved to help rake the long golden stalks into a smaller pile at the room's center.

Robert shoved open the large sliding door on one end of the loft, crossed the room, and tugged open the other door so that not only the light but the breeze could fly through the entire space. Then he turned to watch her, trying to take in how the same young woman who had appeared before him several months ago, draped in violet silk and a diamond tiara, could now be here, hundreds of miles north, in battered boots and borrowed clothes, her hair bound in his mother's blue scarf, and her hands wielding a pitchfork as though she had been born to it.

His father was saying something, but Robert blocked out the words. He knew the job.

Lifting the flail, he brought the tapered end swinging down onto the wheat, beating the grain from the husk, expelling his emotions. All he wanted was a minute alone with her. Though what he would say, he could not decide. His mind kept taunting him, about all the days—and nights—he had spent with her on his way here. Saying nothing. Or rather, saying everything except what he felt.

But something had changed. The moment he had relinquished his father's sword, the guilt that had clung to Robert's chest had retracted its fangs, and the pool of blood that had haunted his nightmares for months no longer held sway.

Instead, every night this week when he had closed his eyes, he saw *her.* A hundred images of her: stepping out from the trees in the Asyan to defend him; confronting her father, her stepfather, and the Lion; dancing in common clothes while somehow outshining everyone at the fort.

And now another image. The blue fabric around her head coming loose, slipping forward. She reached to push it back, but the entire scarf unraveled, falling in a blue ripple to the floor. Exposing her hair to the sunlight.

The flail in Robert's grip stilled, useless. All he could do was stare.

"Can you manage that, son?" His father was saying something.

"What?"

Mr. Vantauge sighed. "Show her how to clean the grain while I go help your mother."

His father was leaving! Giving Robert the chance he had craved all morning.

And then Mr. Vantauge was gone, not even waiting for his son's response.

Aurelia waited, the blue scarf forgotten, her dark eyes on Robert.

He opened his mouth.

And still had no idea what to say. All this time, and the words refused to come. He could have flailed himself.

Instead he dropped the tool, bent down, filled his arms with the separated wheat, and tossed the pieces into the air. The grain plummeted, and the chaff floated east, drifting in the breeze, the lightest pieces swirling between him and Aurelia in a dancing veil.

She bent down, filling her own arms, then flung them upward, shutting her eyes. Gold shimmered over her, attaching to her brown skin, tiny specks glittering from her cheeks, her throat, her eyelids.

And it occurred to Robert that the feeling storming in his veins had nothing to do with speech. He stepped through the wheat, toward her.

Her eyes flew open—her arms still over her head—and she stumbled back as if giving him space.

He didn't want space. Instead, his hands ended her flight, and he lowered his mouth to her lips. Not questioning. Telling. Telling her his feelings the only way he knew how.

He could sense her entire body shiver.

Her arms hovered over his, her hands trembling. And then her fingers threaded through his hair, pulling him closer, and her lips spoke back. Warm. Saying in no uncertain terms that they also had no desire for talk.

Chapter Fifteen
HUNTED

THAT NIGHT HE TASTED BLOOD, DRIPPING ON HIS face, one … drop … at a time, from the rafters of the barn. Robert didn't scream. The blood had drowned him before. Instead he rolled to a crouch, the floorboards creaking beneath him, the unthreshed wheat stabbing his back.

An eerie red light flooded the loft. Compelled, he looked up to confront the boy with the sword in his torso. His cousin, Chris. Absent his lackadaisical manner, the jesting irony. Blood oozed from the wound, spreading in a wide crimson stain upon the silk shirt.

Robert backed away. He had been here before. And won. But now he had no weapon.

The muscles in Chris's arms strained, and inch by reluctant inch, the blade slid from the cavity beneath his rib cage. Metal tore free, and blood poured, drenching shirt, breeches, and stockings.

Then, with a trembling, halting movement, the blade pointed.

At the closed loft door.

Chris's lips moved, forming one familiar, hideous word. Fire!

And then the door peeled open, revealing the screams.

Robert ran, but not fast enough, the ladder battering his shins, the door fighting his weight, the grass clutching at his ankles. Red flames swarmed the cabin, scaling every log and crevice, sweeping out the front window, and covering the door in an upward inferno.

He plunged into the blaze. The smoke had no smell, but it assaulted his eyes, flaming cinders stinging his pupils. And he followed the screams.

To his mother, afire by the table. He reached for her arms, and her skin came off in his hands. His father, a bonfire of flames before Robert could even reach him. His parents' screams died.

And Aurelia? Robert yelled for her. The flames attacked his voice, leaping over his limbs and face and down his throat.

He swallowed them. And they went out.

Blackness tumbled, leaving a hollow, barren pit. Cold. *A wind blew through the gutted interior of the cabin. From the west window.*

And close outside the window, a gray figure. Her. *Motionless.*

He said her name, then reached to touch her shoulder.

And it crumbled into charred ash.

Robert woke to his own screams. He had told himself the

nightmares were gone, relinquished with the sword. A fallacy that had burned away and left a scar.

He choked, rolled from his pallet, and fled out of the loft into the predawn gray.

His father stood just outside the barn, breathing hard, a fallen milk pail twenty feet behind him. Abandoned. No question he had heard his son's delusional screams.

Not able to face those brown eyes, Robert swerved away toward the empty paddock, a vacant ring of horizontal rails. He propped his elbows against the wood and buried his head in his hands, struggling to corral his cowardice.

"I know what it is to kill a man." His father's voice tore through Robert's chest.

Chris's body shuddering on the end of my sword.

The silence was long. And hideous. But his father refused to walk away.

Finally the words came from Robert's own throat. "He didn't deserve to die."

"He tried to kill you."

Yes, and there was no solace in that fact, only fodder for more nightmares.

"Chris was guilty, Robert."

Guilty? He himself was guilty. Aurelia was guilty. The king. The queen. Melony. "It was not my place to dispense justice."

He felt his father move up beside the rails.

"Justice is an illusion," said Mr. Vantauge.

Illusion? Was that what the nightmare had been? Paranoia?

But Robert knew the gutted cabin and crumbling ash had signified more than ancient memories. "I should never have come home." His voice rasped as he dug his fingers into the thick waves of his hair. "I told myself I had to come to return the sword."

"I gave you the sword, Robert."

"I can't . . ." The fingers pulled his hair tight. "I can't use it."

"Are you sure?"

He thought about Aurelia's assailant at Fort Jenkins. "I don't want to use it, ever again."

"Ah, that's different." There was no judgment.

But there should have been. Robert let the rough wood slice into his forehead. He had placed his mother, his father, and the young woman he loved in danger. "The assassins will know to search here. If they find her under your roof . . ." He let the words trail off, certain his father was already well aware of the threat.

"Who are they working for, Robert?" The tone was all business. "Is Melony powerful enough to hire the palace guards?"

"I don't know." His hands fell.

"Is that because you can't figure it out, or you're afraid to ask the question?"

Both. Robert pushed off the rails and whirled, ramming his back against the wood. "I think a man whose daughter has gone missing should come looking for her, and if he does not, there is something wrong."

"Then you believe the king might have ordered the most recent attack?"

He linked his fingers behind his head and pulled his elbows tight. "Aurelia loves her father." He had seen the way her eyes fell whenever the king was mentioned.

"But does *he* love her?"

An image sprang into Robert's mind, one that had been buried under the harsh memory of his own exile: the king, as he had been that morning in the arena, gray and trembling at the possibility of his eldest daughter's death. "Maybe."

Again silence filled the air as the purple reflection of dawn climbed up the cabin in front of him. "But if the king doesn't know about the recent assassination attempt"—Robert dropped his hands and rapped his knuckles against the wood, voicing the fear that had nagged at the fringes of his mind for months—"then his own men are obeying someone else."

"Would they obey his youngest daughter?" Mr. Vantauge did not look at his son, instead continuing to stare through the empty paddock.

Could she have that kind of power? Enough not only to hire ten of her father's own men, but to keep the rest from searching for her sister? Robert pictured the blond fifteen-year-old princess waltzing in her father's arms. "It seems ludicrous." Then he visualized his cousin's death. "But Melony is very persuasive."

"Never ignore the obvious or the unknown."

Robert winced. He had committed both errors when he had returned to the palace. "I had no place pretending I was the royal spy," he said. "You were right."

His father finally turned toward him, one hand closing on his son's shoulder. "No," he said softly, "I wasn't."

The absolution was worse than any reprisal. Robert found himself shaking, his utter failure washing over him. "I almost killed her," he said. Then the words, every flaw, every error he had made on his journey, spilled from his gut. "And after all that," he finished, "look where she is now."

The grip on his shoulder tightened, and his father's other hand flattened against the side of his son's face, forcing Robert's eyes to meet his own. "I *am* looking, Robert. She is alive, and you have yourself to thank for that. You didn't fail."

"How can you say that?"

But the brown depths were in earnest. "Because you didn't go back to become the royal spy." Mr. Vantauge prompted, "Did you?"

"I went back for *her.*"

The grip on his face released. "And you don't regret that?"

Self-recrimination blew out in the path of defiance. "No!"

The muscles above his father's mouth crinkled, and the brown eyes began to dance. "I never regretted marrying your mother."

Confusion churned through Robert's body. Was his father mocking him? But the words had not condemned. They had, in fact, done the opposite.

"I suppose any woman," his father continued, "who has the guts to travel this far, is worth a trip back to the palace." Warm light flickered from those eyes as they rose up from Robert's face.

His father—his *father*—approved of his choice.

And then the light went out. A horse snorted.

Still struggling to take in what he had just been told, Robert turned.

And met the flared nostrils of a compact brown mustang. With a man on its back. *I should not be seen.* Warning ripped through Robert's chest. But the dark eyes in the sun-blackened face sparked with familiarity.

"Zhensen." Mr. Vantauge's voice betrayed no surprise.

"See ya've finished with the cuttin'." The neighbor propped a hand on a muscular thigh.

"I have. And you?"

The man slapped his hat on his knee. "Threshin's done. Grain's sacked and taken to town. Must admit it's a pleasure beatin' ya at somethin', Brian."

Robert began to inch backward.

The dark eyes turned on him. "See yer son didn't leave ya high and dry after all."

"He's done more than his share," said Mr. Vantauge. "I suspect you had a crew of five men to accomplish what we've done with two."

Zhensen didn't take the bait. "Truth to tell, Brian"—his eyes remained on Robert—"I've heard your son has been up to a bit more than workin' harvest. Rumor has it he's been travelin', and not alone."

"My son has been right here for the past two months." Mr. Vantauge lied without flicking an eyelash.

"Mm-hmm, and in Fort Jenkins, Fyonna Township, and Transcontina."

Robert struggled not to cringe. The rumors were specific then. Not general anymore.

"They say Her Royal Highness is on a mission." Zhensen picked a tooth with his thumbnail. "Course, ya' know, folks out here ain't too keen on anyone tellin' 'em what to do; but they're claimin' she ain't afraid of an argument. And just might make some decisions as aren't centered clear over there in Tyralt City. Whad'ya think of that, Brian?"

Mr. Vantauge remained still. "I think that would not be a bad thing, Zhensen."

"Na." The man grinned.

He was not here to judge then? Robert opened his mouth.

Suddenly the neighbor's hand rose, fingers splayed. "And if someone were to ask me about yer son"—the words came fast—"I'd have to say I haven't spoken with him since nigh last winter. Same as I told the stranger askin' round town."

Robert's heart beat cold within his chest.

"What did this stranger look like?" Mr. Vantauge's voice was ice.

"Not from 'round here, that's certain. Long black coat in the heat a' summer." *A bounty hunter*? "Had a buncha men with him, lingerin' on his tail," Zhensen continued. "Hired guns, maybe. Didn't dress like soldiers. Didn't stand like 'em either, but they were watchin'. Saw everythin'. I'm 'fraid I was in too big a hurry to give 'em good directions."

"Did the man say who he was?" Mr. Vantauge tightened his left hand around a paddock rail.

"Seemed anxious not to."

A hunter. *Hired by the palace guard to track us across the frontier.* The logic made sense. For someone determined to kill her.

The wood rattled. "How far behind do you think they are, Zhensen?"

The neighbor smoothed his fingers on his hat. "Three, maybe four days, dependin' on how fer they got afore they realized I mixed up east with west. I came pretty fast. Left a wagon behind with my brother. Course if they ran into somebody, they might've turned round quick. But I don't reckon too many folks were headin' down Crossin' Canyon in the middle a' harvest." Zhensen grinned. "You?"

"No." Mr. Vantauge's reply was cool.

The grin sobered, and the hat returned to Zhensen's head. "You be sure and tell your son to stay safe, Brian."

The kindness of the words pierced Robert's chest. And his parents? Were they also to stay safe? Tongues of nightmare still burned within his mind. His eyes shot to his father.

The formal royal spy appeared calm.

I have to trust him. He will keep mother protected. And as long as Aurelia and I are gone, he'll see to it that there is no evidence we were ever here.

As had Zhensen. Robert held out his palm in a gesture of thanks, and the neighbor who had risked his own life for him took it, then urged the sturdy mustang around and cut a path cross-country. That was it then. Mr. Vantauge's hand closed on his son's shoulder.

Robert knew the assassins had traversed the Gate. And he and Aurelia were being hunted once again.

Chapter Sixteen
SANDSTORM

AURELIA SAW THE SHADOW ON ROBERT'S FACE AS soon as he entered the cabin. *He is afraid.* She did not have to ask why. He told her the truth—about the assassins. As Robert spoke, she could picture the fall of his thoughts, from fear to guilt to self-recrimination, but she had no time to head off the slide. Because first came the departure, from the most wondrous week she had ever known and the two people who had made that week possible. But this—she knew—was not about her. She forced herself to heed her much-disdained royal training and to make her own farewells with limited fanfare. Then she climbed onto Falcon's back. To watch.

It was hard. To see the long, long handshake between Robert and his father, in which neither seemed able to let go. And the tears of Mary Vantauge spilling over in her last embrace with her son.

Aurelia had no right to those tears. Though she found herself trying to imprint every detail of Robert's parents into her memory. The stiffness in his father's stance, which she now saw as a method of defense. As well as his constant advice. And Mary Vantauge: her blond braids unraveling from the rush, her hands passing the basket of parting foodstuffs from palm to palm, her blue eyes peering into the distance. Not south toward the danger, but north, where her son would be. To his future.

The entire leave-taking felt so . . .

Final. *Because everything is final when you're being hunted.*

At last Robert, now in his saddle, accepted the basket from his mother, giving her one more kiss. Then he whirled Horizon, and the stallion took off at a fast canter. Falcon kicked her heels at being left behind.

Aurelia lifted her hand in a wave, calling out her gratitude, then let the filly go.

The horses crested the slope, severing the chance of another glimpse at the Vantauge homestead, and instead of pulling up, Robert bent low. The stallion launched into a gallop, and Falcon accepted the challenge, racing amidst the wild grasses just as she had upon Aurelia's arrival.

This was about flight, not practical but emotional. Aurelia knew Robert was living and breathing and fleeing the danger behind them. And she knew what it meant. No stops. No idle conversations. And no more kisses. But for the glory of this one amazing week, she had known there would be a price to pay.

They fled north. Fast. For four weeks. And somehow avoided death. Robert had no choice but to maintain their earlier bearing. To the south lay danger. To the east the desert lands were restricted by treaty. And to the west lay only frontier, terrain sure to be known by their hunters.

Robert and Aurelia rose early and camped late, detouring around any settlement that broke their path and around the handful of travelers crossing the same route. He knew the solitude was the antithesis of the expedition but had promised her it was temporary, that once they reached the desert sands there would be no means for anyone to track them. He could only hope someone from the tribes would cross their path. For there were no towns.

Or maps. This he learned at the small trading post on the northern boundary of the frontier, from a woman behind a bartering counter. "Are ya hopin' ta be cheated?" she asked, then, taking pity on him, offered directions to the nearest oasis. "Though there's no tellin' if it'll be there on the morrow," she said. "The desert has currents. Ya never know when they might change."

For three days he and Aurelia traveled through a wasteland, neither frontier nor desert. No trees or canyons, fields or buildings, but one slope after another of sandy ground invaded by scrub grass.

And then, at the crest of a hill slightly higher than the others, the grass gave up. He heard Aurelia gasp at his side. A crimson sea of burnt red sand flared before them. No calm, flat, endless stretch, but a roiling of sculpted arcs. The dunes rose, then dropped in sharp fierce lines, their climax in a long dynamic ridge of defiant waves.

Something in his chest clenched. He had pictured the Geordian like an expanse of golden threshed grain, not this fierce lethal red before him. Scrambling, he reached for his pack. The compass was not at the top. He rummaged deeper.

"Robert?" Aurelia sounded annoyed. She must have said something to him that he had not heard.

But he continued the search. They could not go on until he found the compass.

She yanked the pack from his hands and glared. "Would you just stop?!" He could not have responded if he wanted to. "You've been dour for weeks!" she railed. "And I've put up with it because I know you're worried, and I know the danger is real, and we had to hurry. But Robert, it's the Geordian!" She flung her hand at the sculpted ridge. "Just look!" Her voice broke.

"That could be gone by morning," he said, trying to explain why he had been searching for the compass. "It's not a landmark. It's just sand, Aurelia. It moves."

She hurled the pack at the ground. "Admit it's spectacular!"

He blinked. Of course it was. "It's a challenge."

Her eyes narrowed. "Is that what draws you to it?"

"No." It was the story of his horse that had pulled him toward the Geordian. The possibility that Horizon's sire had come from the legendary herds of the desert tribes. "But that's what draws *you.*"

"Admit it's beautiful!"

She was so adamant. Determined. He could not resist testing her patience a bit further. "It's dangerous."

She stuck her tongue out at him.

"Oh, I see we've matured a lot on this trip," he said.

"Admit you can't wait to set foot in it."

True. There was something about that unmarred surface, daring him to step where no one had before. People had been living in the Geordian for thousands of years, but never *here.* Never quite in this exact place, due to the sand's shifting nature.

In answer to her statement, he dismounted, ignoring the fallen pack at his feet, and set one careful step into the crimson sea.

She swung off Falcon's back, landing beside him, then ran out ahead, spinning. Her brown hair flew, her face glowed, her arms rose to her surroundings. Embracing a dream. The ultimate goal, the edge of her kingdom, a place most people had only heard about in legend and myth.

He ran out after her, then raced ahead, skidded on the sand, and fell. She laughed, dodging his reach, and passed him. He pulled himself up, raced after her again, and within moments had her in his grasp, dragging her down.

"Admit it's beautiful," she demanded.

His nose was in her hair. His arms around her waist.

A thousand voices scolded him. His mother's. Drew's. And Robert's own. He tried to remember the reasons he had used to convince himself not to pursue her earlier. But the old arguments no longer held up. He was not supposed to love her because it would place her in danger. But she *was* in danger. Nothing could save her from that. He couldn't love her because she was a princess. Well, maybe he could not marry her. Or plan on the rest of his life at her side. But he was with her now. The only one. The only person in her life to share this moment, her achievement of this dream.

His breath came ragged and his arms ached. "Beautiful."

And then, to his horror, she pulled away, running back to the filly.

You see, his conscience taunted. *It's better to keep your emotional distance.*

What emotional distance? Exactly what about the last five months had been emotionally distant? When he had held Aurelia in his arms the night she yelled at him for not kissing her? When she had yelled at him for thinking of leaving her? Or when Robert *had* kissed her? That one long reciprocated kiss that had not died until his father's footsteps had returned to the barn.

Ruefully, Robert sat up, shaking the sand from his hair and eyeing the blasting red desert. Even that crimson view could not be more hazardous than love.

It took him another three days to learn he was wrong.

The sand had begun to blow. And to bite Aurelia's skin. She tightened the kerchief around her face. The dim red cloud had been stalking them for the entire afternoon, but Robert had insisted they continue. The oasis was near, offering the hope of real shelter. Though the closer they drew, the fiercer the wind and the more limited the hope.

No beckoning emerald paradise awaited, only a small stand of rocky ground with crippled, tightly bunched juniper. But even that meant water. And something solid enough that it would not rise to attack like the stinging grains that had swarmed above the filly's legs and begun to file away at Aurelia's arms. With a *hiss* like grating sandpaper.

If she and Robert did not reach cover soon, the sand would scrape the skin from their bodies.

Finally the horses reached the trees. She swung off and had barely touched the ground before Robert, his own mouth covered in a handkerchief, thrust the canteens into her hands. She accepted the task, knowing she needed to get the water now, as there was no telling whether it would be there later.

Wrapping the canteen cords over her neck, she scrambled into the inner trees, her vision impaired by the grains of sand that hurtled through the thin foliage and crooked limbs. There! A liquid pool beneath the shifting blur of red.

She closed her eyes and dropped down to her knees, completing the task by feel. Plunging each canteen beneath the wet surface and twisting on the lids. Then she stood up and hurried to help Robert.

The tent had decided to resist. No doubt a reaction to the fact that she had shunned it, rejecting its off-white walls for their similarity to the other tent burning in her nightmares. But she and Robert needed this one now. He had strung the rope from one juniper to the next and draped the canvas over it, but the stakes refused to sink into the ground. Or rather the sand spit them back out. The intensity of the wind had grown brutal, and the debris began to block out the light. Panic started to well up within her.

But Robert pocketed the stakes and hefted a rock, dropping it on the inner edge of the canvas. The material stayed down.

Of course!

Aurelia hefted two more weights and hurried to the other end of the fabric. Soon the worst of the wind was blocked, the sand pelting upon the canvas wall, and she and Robert tackled the opposite side, pulling the walls together as narrowly as possible, then curving the edges and lashing them together with leather rawhide ties, leaving only a low opening for an entrance.

At last the tent stood secure. As secure as it could in this barrage.

Robert gestured for her to enter, while he headed toward the horses. But she went after him. The supplies would be retrieved faster if she helped.

He didn't argue. He had no means. Even if he had spoken through the handkerchief, she would never have heard him over the howling wind and pelting sand. They removed the packs and the bedding, then tugged the horses as close to the leeward wall of canvas as possible.

Aurelia gave Falcon one last desperate hug, then hefted her supplies and hurried into the tent. But Robert did not follow. Binding her courage to fury, she plunged once again into the storm.

He was still with the horses.

She understood. She did. And had no desire to be responsible for Falcon's death. But if the horses could not survive outside without him, they would not survive. Aurelia moved up behind him, closed her grip around his arms, and pressed her fingers into the muscle. She would draw blood if she had to.

He detached her hold as though it were nothing, then locked his arms around her chest and pulled her into the tent, where she wanted to go; but then he tried to leave. She flung herself upon him, wrapping her arms around his neck and yelling, though she knew he could not hear amidst the growing roar outside. And then what was left of light went out.

Finally Robert gave way, dropping his attempt to leave and sinking to the ground instead, taking her with him. She relinquished her death grip around his neck, but he gathered her close.

Together they waited. For what, she was not sure, except for life. Death hammered on all sides, and she did not want it—could not accept it without a fight. But there was no way to fight the wind. Any more than there had been a means to fight the jagged cliffs of the Gate. And if she died, there would be no way to fight anything else. Not her sister. Or the hunters. Or corruption.

So Aurelia waited. She would never know how long. It was impossible to tell without light.

But at last the roar eased to its former sandpaper hiss.

And Robert withdrew. Into the night. A genuine dark.

She followed, though she did not want to, her left hand on his back, the fingers of her right tracing the leeward side of the tent. She remembered all too well Bianca's corpse and had no desire to find another. The sand still blew, but Aurelia could not feel its bite because she was numb with fear.

Then Robert pulled away. And her feet hit solidity. She bent, her hands trembling as they touched the gritty surface of a long, broad, sand-caked back. Horizon. She waited for a moan or a cry from Robert, but instead felt a harsh, uneasy cough. From beneath her. The horse was alive.

Aurelia flung herself forward, seeking Falcon. Her fingers found the filly's mane, traveled along the still head, and then quickly but carefully swept the sand from the horse's eyelids and nostrils. Falcon snorted. *Thank Tyralt!*

The filly thrust herself to her feet. Falcon's coat, despite the grit, had never felt so good against Aurelia's forehead. *You are a stubborn, stubborn horse,* Aurelia thought with pride.

Not to be outdone, the stallion rose as well. Robert reached for one of the metal containers, long forgotten, around her neck, and she handed him the canteen, then opened another one, offering the liquid to her horse and finally allowing the cool oasis water to trickle down her own throat.

Perhaps the small pool and rocky stand of gnarled juniper were no paradise, but they had saved her life. And Falcon's, Horizon's, and Robert's. They stayed there together, long enough to be certain the stallion's cough had gone. And long enough for Aurelia to admit to herself that the young filly in front of her was just as precious to her heart as her beautiful gray mare had been.

If it had been necessary, Aurelia would willingly have stayed at Falcon's side all night, but eventually Robert's fingers threaded through her own, pulling her back into the tent, and untied the kerchief from her face.

He did not speak. She did not need him to.

They both needed sleep.

Unrolling the pallets side by side, for there was nowhere else to put them, she and he both collapsed, the storm's remnants still hissing upon the canvas.

However, sleep and the need for it were two different things. Her mind refused to let go, insisting on reliving the past five months. Usually she shunned these memories, the cycle of powerlessness, nightmare, and flight. This was different. This was not about fear.

It was about the young man at her side who had come back into her life five months ago. Would she undo everything if she could? Go back to the time when she had felt safe?

No. Because it had never been real.

And what if it had been? Would she go back to that life, if her father had been the man she had believed him to be? If her sister had been the supporter she had pretended to be? If it meant Aurelia would never see Robert again?

The answer came even more forcefully than the first. *No!*

She would not go back to that life either. Feeling trapped and useless, despite her best attempts, not able to convince her father that her dreams were more important than her marriage. Duty and respect: those were the things drilled into her for most of her lifetime. And they were not enough.

Robert had understood that, perhaps even better than she had. He had given her the push she needed, the voice saying, "Why don't you go then? It will all be under your leadership one day. Shouldn't you find out about it?" His attempt to leave the Fortress had forced her past her fear. His hand had propelled her forward over the Gate. And he had left his home a second time to help her pursue her dream.

True, they had argued far more often than they had touched. Even now, they did not. They had spent months of nights together, but never this close.

And she kept coming back to the same thoughts. Sensations. The look in his eyes on that day when she had asked him to guide her expedition. The understanding in his arms when she had railed against slavery. And his kiss. The first one so tender. And fragile. And then the one in the loft, shooting feeling into her body. Her skin tingled.

He was asleep, she told herself. Had been asleep for hours. Dreaming of tomorrow.

She could not . . .

But without conscious thought, without permission, the backs of her fingers reached across the space and skimmed his.

That was it.

One light, almost imperceptible touch.

And Robert moved. In a single motion his chest came over hers, his right hand cupped her left ear, and his entire body returned the touch.

Chapter Seventeen
AFTER

CURSE IT! AURELIA STARED INTO THE SPLINTERED juniper and sputtering white light of the predawn campfire. Last night had been . . . she would be lying if she did not admit it had been more than she could have fathomed. His kisses. His touch. His heart beating against hers.

No distance or space between them. Together, within one another's embrace.

She shot a glance at the tent where Robert was still sleeping, then hugged her stomach and tried, really tried, to imagine a life as a wife and mother on the frontier. It did not work—had not worked from the moment it had occurred to her that if they continued, if they took one more step, Aurelia could risk bearing a child.

She had stopped him.

He had not argued or questioned. Instead, he had folded her in his arms, kissed her, and slept.

But she had not. The thought of becoming pregnant had never occurred to her before. Obviously! If it had, she would have seen the repercussions: the fact that if she had a baby out of royal wedlock, she would never be allowed to claim her right to the throne. A right she had already forfeited.

But deep down she must not have accepted that loss, because the thought of a child had elicited one awesome driving fear.

That there would be no going back. Ever.

No chance to convince her father he had been wrong. Or expose her sister's evil actions. Or fix the myriad problems Aurelia had seen throughout this vast journey. And only now did she realize she was not yet ready to give that up.

Would it be so terrible to marry Robert and let her past go?

Yes, came the harsh response. She could not explain why. It had something to do with all those years of training in which she had been taught that she had a larger duty. A greater responsibility. And no matter how often she had railed against those terms and the way they impaired her own actions, the larger truth had soaked into her veins and become something she could not sever.

Not even for love.

There came a rustling from the tent. In the name of Tyralt, how could she tell him? That after last night, after all she had felt and all he had made her feel, that they could never be more to each other than friends. Because she would not give up the crown she had already lost.

His mother had been right. And his father.

Even Daria had warned Aurelia not to hurt Robert.

He stepped from the tent.

And she could not look into those fathomless blue eyes. Because she could not allow herself to be lost.

Her mind turned to a charred blur as Robert bent to stir the dying fire. What he was thinking, she could not interpret. What he was feeling, she did not know. She only knew she must find a way through this dilemma herself before she could speak.

He let the silence come, ate his morning ration, then went to check the horses. She knew he would find them both brushed and cleaned, their abrasions dipped in his mother's salve. Aurelia had been up for hours. Had gone over every patch of missing horsehair and found nothing worse than a surface wound along the stallion's thigh.

Dousing the camp flames, she began to prepare to leave, a habit instilled in her over the past month. Wake early, pack, ride. She removed the rocks from the base of the tent, folded the canvas, and rewound the rope. The other actions could be completed by rote.

Again her reality blurred, until the horses were saddled and the supplies were strapped into place. Then she looked up. To find Robert gone.

At first she tried to dismiss his absence. He had a right, she told herself. A right to his own silence—his own space, after what had happened last night. But as the moments stretched, a new concern crept through her charcoal haze.

What if he had no plan? The disturbing idea drifted forward as she gathered the reins of both horses and began to skirt the brush. He had had no directions beyond the oasis, and the storm had wiped out any tribal prints he might have tracked. The assassins may well have perished or lost the scent, but she knew better by now than to count on their demise.

And she knew Robert would feel the threat even more keenly.

She found him along the edge of the juniper, staring east. Sunrise glittered over a high crest of red rock, less than an hour away, running north to south, severing the desert's stretch. The crest rose and sloped, like the underside of a wave, its curved lines defying gravity, its upper ridge arching a hundred feet above the ripples now molding the crimson tide.

"That is where we will go," he whispered, his voice so soft at first she thought she might have imagined it. "From the top of that ridge, if we can scale it, we should be able to see . . . everything."

Meaning danger, she thought. Of what use would it be to spot her pursuers? But no—he was right. She had come to see the tribes of the Geordian, and that ridge might also provide their location.

Either way, it was a goal, a purpose. A reason to continue forward.

On the trip to the crest, little entered her mind beyond the turmoil within her own heart. The same thoughts cycled over and over: She could not be with Robert—could not marry him. Because she could not forego her hopes for her kingdom. All this time she had disdained the crown and proclaimed that the purpose for her expedition was to know her people, yet she had refused to see the implications for her own future—had refused to see herself.

As she and Robert drew closer, the spectacular vision of the ridge tried to break through her thoughts. From the oasis, the rock had looked red, the same color as the sand, but now the high crest swirled with layers of reds and whites, golds and oranges, cutting across the concave arc in dizzying, unbroken lines.

Then a shadow. Diagonal. Thin. Nothing compared to the spectacle before her. But if there was a shadow, it must reflect off something.

Robert too had seen it. And she let him go. Let him be the first to reach the cleft between the outer rock face and the hidden one. Let him test his stallion's hooves upon the natural path at the base of the crevice. And let his horse lead the way up the slanted route between the two walls, despite Falcon's protests.

Aurelia's vision blurred once more behind the coil of her inner terrain. Half the trail slipped past her mind's eye, and she almost commanded her horse into a cliff face before spotting the tunnel climbing to her left. The sound of Horizon's hooves clattered from the shadows, and Falcon took over, clearly feeling that she knew better than the daft human upon her back.

Again Aurelia's mind detached, and it did not return until full light struck her face. As Horizon crested the ridge above her, Robert turned his head, aiming those blue eyes dangerously in her direction. It never occurred to her that he had entered a new landscape. Or that anything could be on the other side of that crest.

Not until the strange sound snapped above her, followed by a quick *whirr*.

And the arrow pierced Robert's flesh.

Though she was the one who screamed.

Chapter Eighteen
DISCORD

AURELIA WOKE TO DARKNESS. NOT NIGHT. A THIN net draped over her body, vision, and mind. The cushion beneath her was soft—seductive—and the taste of overripe melon coiled in her throat. From beyond came the murmur of female voices. Low. In a language she did not understand. But the cadence—the rise and fall of the tones. She had heard that rhythm before.

Memory filtered through the net: an arrow, blood, Horizon's fury. The stunned look on Robert's face as he fell, the pain as he crashed, and the absence of pain as a dark boot slammed onto his shoulder, snapping the arrowhead and Robert's consciousness.

She had hurled herself off Falcon's back, despite the pointed arrows aimed in her direction. And the six riders in white desert robes had not fired at her, being more consumed with battling the red-brown stallion. But the man with the dark boot had sprayed her with something, a sickness still clinging to the passages of her nostrils.

Though her mind had begun to tear free.

Her fingers tugged aside the netting—to reveal the interior of a large tent filled with women. The figures, dressed in brilliant caftans and kneeling in a circle on a golden rug, clutched a plethora of prized goods: vibrant silk, radiant jewels, ribboned baskets—all being ogled and passed around.

At the ring's center stood a girl, no more than Aurelia's age, with toffee-colored skin and a spiral of jet-dark hair at the back of her neck. She turned with her hands flat toward the opulent gifts as if saying she did not deserve them. Vines curled and wove upon her palms—tattoos matched only by the immaculate black lace hugging her torso, hips, and thighs.

The paint on her hands was red. Like blood.

Again Aurelia saw her last vision of Robert, his body limp, life seeping through his shirt. She spoke before questioning whether the women would understand. The southern half of the desert had been part of Tyralt since her grandfather's reign. Surely someone here must speak Tyralian. "Where is he?" She struggled up, then sank back, her limbs too weak to comply. Her voice broke. "Is he alive?"

The young woman with the painted hands glanced up, then flicked a wrist. And the entire circle grew silent. Her elaborate gown clung to her body like a second skin as her bare feet stepped outside the human ring. Then the girl tugged a deep violet curtain across the tent, separating herself, and Aurelia, from the other women.

A pair of cool gray eyes lifted. "Your companion is captive. He has been bound in the prisoner's tent beyond the tribal sphere and shall remain there until the Oracle has pronounced him guilty."

Relief warred with fear. "Guilty of what?"

The gowned figure crouched beside a laden ivory-white platform that appeared to serve as a table. "I am Mirai. You are my guest. The Jaheem do not arrest women."

Am I supposed to be grateful? As though women cannot commit heinous crimes. Aurelia thought of her sister, then thrust away the image. This was about Robert. "Your men shot him without provocation."

"His wound has been cleaned." Mirai tossed off the comment as though it exempted the tribe of any blame, then lifted a carafe and poured a dark red liquid into a glass. "He shall not die . . . of that."

Again Aurelia struggled to get up, this time grasping the netting and managing to stand, but the fabric was not sturdy enough to support her, and once more, she sank down. "Robert has done nothing wrong!"

"Robert." The girl's tongue curled around the word as though testing it. "This is your man's name?"

"He is not mine."

"Of course he is. This is obvious." The girl lifted the drink and a platter of exotic fruit, then held out the glass toward Aurelia.

Who rejected it, having no desire to again lose consciousness. "What is he accused of? He has committed no crime."

Mirai's eyebrow arched. "You claim to be unaware, then, that he was riding a stolen horse?"

Horizon! Of course. The tribe thought the bay was desert-bred. Reason began to thread its way through emotion. "Robert is not a thief." Aurelia took a ragged breath, then told Horizon's story as she had first heard it. About the trapper who had been nursed back to health by Mrs. Vantauge. And about the bay's sire, whom the trapper had given to the family as a gift.

The gray eyes drilled into hers. "Then why are you here? And who are you?"

Aurelia chose not to answer the second question. "We came to meet the people of the Geordian. To learn about your culture and customs and, yes, your spectacular horses. Can you blame us for wanting to see them?"

Venom spit back at her. "They will not be spectacular for long if our best are no longer here."

What did that mean?

"You!" the girl snarled. "And the other raiders. You do not understand that it takes more than a great horse to create a great line. For this you must have many horses and the Oracle to make the wise decisions."

Aurelia grasped for comprehension. Robert's life might depend upon it. "What raiders?"

"Indeed. You would say the same if you were among them."

True. But Aurelia was not. And the problems of the tribe

were hers as well. In the heat of emotion and her fear for Robert, it might have been easy to forget. But she had learned from the citizens of Sterling, the Asyan, and Transcontina, as well as from the travelers across the Gate and the people of the frontier, that first impressions were nearly always flawed. *The Jaheem are my people as well.* "What is it these raiders take?"

"Our horses. What else? From all across the southern half of the Geordian." Fury built behind the gray eyes, and Mirai thrust out the plate of untouched fruit, no doubt in a challenge to her guest.

Aurelia accepted a dark green slice, the rich taste oozing through her teeth and rinsing the sickness from her throat. *Raiders across the entire width of the desert?* That did not sound like tribal warfare. "When did these raids begin?"

Lowering the plate, Mirai murmured. "It has been four months. During that time, ten tribes have lost horses, including two Cherished Ones."

"I thought the tribes cherished all their mounts."

"Yes, but the Cherished Ones are special. There is only one in every tribe, and it is in this horse that the history and spirit of our people are bonded. To lose a Cherished One before that spirit has been passed down to another horse is devastation. The tribe must forego its identity. Even the Oracle can do nothing to repair such a great loss."

"The Oracle?" Aurelia asked. It was the third time the girl had mentioned this title.

"Our spiritual guide. He who records the history of the

horses, their strengths and weaknesses, to be kept with the knowledge of their ancestors. So that matches can be made."

A breeder, Aurelia decided as she struggled to wade through the unique beliefs. "This Oracle is your leader then?"

Mirai nodded. "For all the people of the Geordian. He sees the truth of the future and past with clarity." Her tone left no doubt that she believed her own words. "It is he who will determine the guilt, or innocence, of your Robert."

Aurelia felt a chill run through her flesh. She had lived in denial for so long, there was no comfort in truth. Not that she believed anyone could read the future. If this man claimed the ability, she did not trust him. But if the Oracle held the power to decide Robert's fate, then it was he she must address. "I wish to speak with him then."

"That shall not be permitted."

Her response was quelling. "It will." She did not care if the statement sounded like a command. Letting Robert die while she did nothing? *That* was not going to happen. She stood and this time managed to cross the space to the edge of the violet curtain.

The girl's voice snatched her from behind. "No one from outside his own family may speak to the Oracle without an invitation. You are a guest. Will you betray our customs and mark yourself a foe?"

Aurelia gripped the nearby tent pole to hold herself steady. Was this the line she walked? The same line her father treaded as leader of all Tyralt. Where one act, one simple show of human strength, could be read as enmity. Anger pulsed through her, not at Mirai, but at herself, for her own physical weakness. She did not dare quit, not with Robert's fate on the line. Her voice fell, not a demand this time, but a plea. "I must see your leader."

The figure in the black lace gown held up a tattooed palm. "You shall. At my wedding tomorrow. And if you promise not to approach him yourself, I will speak with my father on your behalf." The voice hardened. "Though I can assure you he will disregard anyone who does not offer so much as a name."

Torture arrived midmorning on Robert's second day as captive. Dissonant tones invaded the narrow width of his canvas prison, not music, but the clatter of strings, flute, and percussion. Scraping his mind like the blond spikes of twisted rope chafing his bound wrist.

The wrist on the side of his injured shoulder. *The same cursed shoulder!* A new wound just below the scarred flesh along his collarbone.

He could not believe his own stupidity. Why had it never occurred to him that the tribes might take offense and assume his horse was stolen? Hadn't he watched Aurelia stumble into one mess after the next on her way to the frontier because she did not yet understand the culture? And now here he was, tethered to a tent pole, with his shoulder sliced through as he waited for the return of his interrogator.

Three times yesterday the man had come. Always the same tribesman with the dark boots. At first Robert had had no concept of the other's purpose. The world had dissolved, and he had struggled just to wrench himself out of the bruising blackness, then had been so confused he could not have answered the interrogator's questions if he had wanted to. On the second visit, he had managed to take in the fact that the tribe believed he had stolen his horse. And on the third, he had learned that the accusation ran far deeper than theft.

Murder. Raids. And sacrilege. Those were the crimes the interrogator had leveled as he lifted a boot, set it on the injured shoulder, and pressed down. The man had disdained the real story about the stallion. He did not want truth. He wanted vengeance. And the names and location of other raiders.

The tuneless notes from beyond the tent now rose in an anguished swell. Robert rolled his head, trying to block out the sound and his own fears. Where was Aurelia? The last he had heard from her was her scream. After the arrow.

His eyes fell to the wrapped injury, then the bound wrist. Superfluous. He had no chance of escape. There was no way to survive the desert without supplies, not even if he took the stallion whose shrill whistle Robert had heard twice.

Of course, the tribesmen thought he had conspirators. That he might have the means of sending them a signal. Though such a thing would be impossible to hear now.

Screeching strings, howling flutes, clanging metal, and banging drums all shattered in crescendo.

Then silence. Sudden and sharp.

And it was then he heard the call of the jay.

The bird's scalding cry ripped through Aurelia's mind, ending in a piercing whistle that mirrored her own emotions. She hated weddings. Had hated them ever since being excluded from her father's second one. And the dissonant noise from the desert instruments did nothing to alter her outlook. Nor did the veil obscuring her gaze. Or the shoulders pressed tight against hers as the entire tribe stood crammed around the circle within the ceremonial tent.

Incense sucked the air. She could not breathe. The tent's lone entrance had been bound, shutting out the breeze. First the dark outer layer of the canvas, then the pale inner fabric layer, with leather strips to bind the wedded couple for all time.

It was not the unique symbolism that made Aurelia feel ill, but the larger concept: that all a woman was—all she owned, possessed, and dreamed—must now be defined by her husband. A concept no different for the female offspring of a king than for the daughter of a desert tribesman.

In black, Mirai stood alone at the center of the tent, upon a pool of turquoise stone. Her feet bare.

Then the bridegroom emerged from the crowd. Young. Shaven. And familiar.

The man who had set Robert unconscious. Aurelia jolted, pushing back futilely against the crowd as she yearned for flight. Her eyes reached up with desperation toward the tent's ceiling and the embroidered phoenix spreading its wings over the entire tribe.

You do not know this man, the ripple of the desert harp seemed to say as its calm notes glided through the back doors of her mind. He was a scout. Someone who had ridden out to face danger. She had learned that much in the past day. And enough to know that the raiders who served as the threat had committed both rape and murder. Her anger on Robert's behalf refused to release, but she knew she had little right to judge.

Harmony formed between the harp and a long end-blown flute, reeling her focus back down to the young couple. Who kneeled. Before the Oracle.

He wore white, his skin and eyes the same as his daughter's, but his garments with nothing to set them apart from the simple cloth robes and turbans around him. No braid or jewels. And although his lips moved as he spoke, he could not be heard from where Aurelia stood. His words were for the young couple at the heart of the tent, not the audience, though every head, every eye, had hinged in his direction. He was the sole focus of the tribe.

The man bowed, and the dulcimer sang as he backed away to the pool's edge, close by, but now Aurelia could see only a fraction of his profile.

Notes from the harp, flute, and dulcimer wound about each other, and the couple stood. The drums beat softly in syncopation and began to build. A hum swelled from the crowd, and the drummers' hands shifted from leather to carved frames, ceramics to hollow wood. The jingling of metal rings joined in.

And then song, a tremendous outpouring as hands opened and the tribe began to shower the young couple with golden grains of sugar.

The bridegroom swept Mirai up into his arms, strode across the turquoise pool and waited at its fringe, still within the human circle, while someone cut the leather ties on the inner layer of canvas.

Then a scream ripped the joyous harmony to shreds as the inner layer separated to reveal a canvas wall of flame.

Chapter Nineteen
TERROR

THE CRY OF THE COASTAL JAY SEARED ROBERT'S MIND. *The palace guards' signal of attack. From the night in the forest.* He rolled up from his pallet, cringing at the pain in his shoulder as his bare torso leaned against the unforgiving tent pole.

The call's significance splintered in his brain. The guards must have tracked Aurelia—which meant she must be here. But she would never recognize the call. She had been asleep that night. And neither he, nor she, had ever discussed their own experiences after the event.

He had to get out. To warn her. And he was tied to this blasted pole! Robert struggled to his feet, lifted the fingers of his left hand, and released a shrill whistle.

Hoofbeats answered.

Too soon. Not Horizon's. He counted the shadows crossing the canvas of his narrow tent. *A dozen mounts.* All headed toward the camp and the rising swell of music.

Then one slowed, circling. The rider's silhouette was clear, the unmistakable length of a musket in one hand. And something else in the other.

Robert prepared to die.

It would do him no good to yell. No one from the tribe would come.

Swoosh! Not gunfire, but the long swift swipe of a torch across the southern canvas wall.

And then a whistle, close. His own stallion. Robert turned to see Horizon's silhouette rise up against that of the other horse. *Crunch!* The musket fell. And the rider. There was a second of confusion in the blur of shadows.

Then a figure rolled under the tent flap. Pale. Wiry. Eyes etched with fear.

The stallion pounded the ground outside.

Inside, flames pierced the thin wall and began to scale the ceiling. "Help me!" Robert yelled, prepared to feign an alliance. "And I'll call off the stallion." He tugged the rope to the bottom of the pole and tried to yank free. To no avail. He had no strength in his right arm.

A strange slur came as a response, then brutal mockery with a heavy accent. "You will burn first."

Sparks began to drip from the ceiling. "Bastard!" Robert

kicked his pallet away from the fire. "How many people will you kill just to get your hands on her?"

"Her?" The man shifted, his trousers dragging on the floor. A strange fold lay low on one pant leg. *A knife,* Robert thought, *beneath the fabric.* If he could somehow get close enough to steal that weapon . . .

I would have to kill him. The response came swift and harsh.

He could not kill—could not allow himself to become that person again.

But the flames were coming, eating their way up the thin canvas.

And the man was still talking. "Is your Cherish-ed One a mare then?"

He is a raider, Robert realized, *not a palace guard.* Though this made no sense.

It had been the same birdcall!

"Who sent you?" Robert yanked at the pole. The flames were almost above him.

"What does make you think we have been sent?" The voice lost its mockery.

"I've heard your call before." There was a connection. There had to be, between the guards who had attacked Aurelia and the men committing the raids. And that meant there had to be someone higher up.

Again Robert fought the pole, then cried out as sparks burned his bare flesh.

Horizon attacked the tent flap.

And the raider took another step into the smoke. "You have witnessed"—*cough!*—"the strength of the Anthone military before."

Anthone. That was the accent.

Robert crouched low, his eyes watering from the smoke's sting. "Edward ordered men onto Tyralian land?"

"Why not?" The raider took another step. "Your king will never know. Or care."

What was that supposed to mean? That even the soldiers of Anthone had heard of the Tyralian king's apathy toward the northern half of his country? "His daughter will."

"She is the one who gave her blessing."

And then Robert knew. In that instant, he understood. The connection. Everything.

Melony. She had bought Anthone's help. Had let the neighboring military into her father's guard and hired them to murder her sister. She, not the king, had chosen Aurelia's escort. And as payment to Anthone, the blond princess had bartered the desert horses of the southern Geordian.

Was she powerful enough to hire palace guards? Robert's father had wanted to know.

The answer was that she was even more powerful. Powerful enough to destroy a treaty, devious enough to let a foreign power infiltrate her father's defenses, and foolish enough to invite another country onto Tyralian land.

But Anthone was a fool as well. "Has she married him?" Robert demanded. Because what else could she have promised to convince the old monarch that her own vendetta was his?

"No."

"And she won't," Robert replied. "Your king is deceived. He's bartered away peace to support the wrong successor. And I assure you her sister will care!"

If she lived. *In the name of Tyralt, let Aurelia survive.* He thought about the raids the interrogator had described, the deaths and other crimes committed by the attackers. Drew had been right. And Thomas. And way down deep, Robert himself. Because he had always known, from the very beginning of the expedition, that Melony could not become queen.

The smoke had grown so thick he could see nothing beyond the base of the raider's trousers, the fold in the cloth, and the lure of the blade that would sever his own soul.

Somewhere beyond, music still played, rising and swelling louder than ever.

And then a deep, soul-wrenching cry ripped through the harmony as an entire people raised their voices in terror.

Darkness enveloped Aurelia. Not smoke. But another scalding, choking blackness that stopped her heart and clogged her lungs. Her own barrier. Clotting her skull and crushing her mind.

She could not let the flames enter.

But they were already there. Inside her. Smoldering in her

nightmares. Disguised in denial, and doubt, and even the great need to prove herself.

Now she would die as she had been meant to die that night in the forest.

We all will.

The thought jarred the blackness from her mind.

The screams continued, one long uninterrupted howl that bled from every corner of the tent. Bodies scrambled over her: hands, legs, elbows. Not people anymore but parts, plowing against one another, slamming, tangling, piling away from the entrance. Trampling each other.

Memory jolted her back in time. To Tyralt City. And the day the people in the marketplace, angry over a new tax, had unleashed their anger against the stone image of her father. They had formed a mob—a group as unhinged as this. And *she* had stopped them—had spoken and stepped into the crowd.

But here she was invisible, too invisible to even have lost her weapon. Her hand clutched the hard metal in her waistband. The knife was useless. She could not carve her way through panic. Nothing would stop these people. Nothing meant more to them than their own lives.

Except, perhaps, the life of one man.

She thrust her gaze into the chaos of tangled bodies. The Oracle was close, though out of reach. She squeezed under an arm and around a hip, then lost ground, a length of turban catching her throat, pulling her down. She wrenched it away, then had to fight the undertow. The bodies pushed, kicked, and jabbed, but she battled her way up. There before her was her only hope.

Aurelia pulled the blade from her waistband and thrust it to the Oracle's neck.

Stop! Her mind cried beneath the screams, not at the man, but at the people in panic. *Please stop!*

And they did. First those close enough to see the blade. And then others, the silence peeling out in a stunning swath, its power stronger in the midst of chaos than a thousand shouts. Heads turned; eyes hinged on the man in peril. He had not moved. Had not resisted the blade at his neck. Instead, he held perfectly still until the final screams were sucked into the silence.

Then his fingers closed ever so slightly upon her wrist. "And what will you do now?" he whispered in perfect Tyralian.

Aurelia's heart thudded as she took in the status of the fire. The flames had not yet spread past the entrance. Instead, they had risen, eating their way up the canvas exterior and catching on the edges of the inner divide, forming a gap—a narrow gap beneath a blazing arrow-shaped curtain of dripping cinders and burning fabric. Her fist tightened on the knife. She could cut her own exit, but the breeze would suck its way through, sweeping the flames ahead. Over everyone.

Instead she guided the Oracle forward, straight up to the blazing curtain. She flung the knife through the gap in a public gesture, then pointed the man toward the blade. If she led, no one would follow. "Go!" she pleaded.

But the Oracle declined, holding the flat of his hand to her chest and calling out in words she did not understand. Then a surge of men swept forward, released from the crowd at even the farthest reaches of the tent. Not boys. Not old men. Warriors. They formed a column, then stormed beneath the flaming exit.

Their voices erupted outside in a fierce battle cry. Answered by birdlike shrieks and cracks of gunfire. *The raiders,* Aurelia realized. Death waited outside.

But her eyes followed the flames. The fire had scaled the open inner canvas and reached the wingtip of the phoenix on the ceiling. Now it was only a matter of time before the tent began to fall.

She tugged the veil from her face and met the solemn gray eyes of the Oracle. He knew the danger, yet was telling her to wait. Together they watched the flames stretch and reach, spreading their way over the crowd, bringing with them the choking, stinging smoke that could be just as deadly as the heat.

Still the hand blocked her chest.

Then a warrior, blood spattered on his face and arms, burst back inside. Had she not been so close, she would never have recognized him as the bridegroom. He was motioning for people to come.

The Oracle stepped back. "You may go," he said.

But she could not, not with their people still here. "After the tribe." She took her own step back, aligning herself with the edge of the flames so that she and the spiritual leader formed the posts of a gate to the flaming exit.

His response was to turn to the Jaheem. He spoke and they poured through—the same people who had almost trampled one another before, now working together. Children carried babies. Elders guided youngsters. Mothers helped the elderly. A woman's skirt caught on fire, but an old man smothered the flames in the folds. A girl dropped her doll, and the boy behind her picked it up before she had time to cry.

The Oracle said something to each person, and Aurelia wished she could understand the words because as the black smoke coiled its way down, infecting the air and thrusting the remnants of the group forward, her own turn became imminent. And fear grappled her soul.

Could she do it? Could she face the flames? Because everything in her mind said that this was her fault. That somehow, by eluding the fire in her past, she had brought it here, upon these people. And she could not—must not leave until every last one of them had escaped.

And even then . . . did she have the right—if this was her fate?

The line for escape had dwindled down to two. A woman, frozen in fear, and a boy, screaming and clutching at his mother's waist.

Without thinking or wasting time, Aurelia wrenched the boy from his mother and hauled him kicking and screaming through the gap.

Out.

Beyond the flames.

Bodies littered the ground. She dared not look at them. She could do nothing for the dead.

Instead she looked up. The Oracle and the woman had escaped the burning curtain, and without Aurelia noticing, the screaming boy had detached himself from her grip and run back to his mother. There were people all over. Though no raiders that she could see. Not living. Only the Jaheem. Black with soot. Coughing. And staring at the chaos around them.

Horses were everywhere, eyes wild and rolling, hooves pounding without direction, heads tossing and flinching away from the flames. Heavy smoke rose in a thick solid cloud. The tents were burning. All the tents.

Robert! He was in one. *Bound.*

Aurelia sprinted then, not sure where she was going, but past the tribal sphere. She fought her way through a charred gap, not heeding the smoke beneath her boots.

There! Across the sand. Another bonfire. "No!" Her feet raced, her heart pounding with denial. For there was no way to enter the tent before her. No barren canvas. Barely a structure. A familiar red stallion reared nearby, screaming at the top of his lungs.

"No!" she yelled, and thrust herself toward the flames.

A hand grabbed her, holding her back, the fierce grip digging into the flesh beneath her elbow.

No! She screamed and fought the restraint. Only one grip, but it would not tear free. She jabbed with her heels, tripped and fell to her knees, tugging her captor down with her, then flailed backward with her right arm.

"Curse it, Aurelia! Stop!"

The use of her name brought her to a halt as the captor pulled her up against his hard chest.

"I'm all right." Robert's voice was in her hair, beside her ear.

Emotion poured out of her, relief ricocheting through her insides and violently shaking its way from her body. He was alive. *Alive.*

She whirled and flung her arms around his neck.

He flinched, and then she remembered his injury, camouflaged by the soot. He had been in the fire. As close to the flames as she had been. Dropping her hold, she traced his face, the sharp furrows of his forehead, the dark streaks across his cheekbones, and those blue, blue eyes she had rejected the last time she had seen him.

His left hand was on her neck, caressing her hairline, and then his lips were on hers. Fierce. Tight. And there was nothing she would have or could have done to stop them. For this one moment, there was no future or past or destiny. Only Robert.

Her hands wavered, palms skimming down his chest, afraid of hurting him, then they found the raw marks on his right wrist.

He stiffened and pulled away.

Her gaze fell to the rope burns. "How did you—"

"The raider who tried to burn down the tent." Robert's voice was harsh. "He had a knife."

Chapter Twenty
THE ORACLE

"YOU DID NOT KILL HIM." THE LOW VOICE DRILLED into Robert as he stepped across the blackened threshold the next morning.

The spiritual leader of the Geordian sat directly upon the sand at the heart of the barren tent. His long white robes disguised the limbs crossed underneath, and despite the hardship of the past day, his face was smooth. Expressionless. Two knives lay before him, one tinted black.

Obtained from the ashes.

Robert relived those final moments in the burning tent. The screams of an entire tribe echoing in his eardrums, smoke tearing through his lungs and shredding its way through his chest. And the desperate grab he had made for the knife.

He had been prepared to kill. Had been certain once the hilt was in his hands he would have no other option. But the blade had remained a tool, not a weapon. The rope had severed. And the raider who had started the fire had chosen to use Robert as a human shield rather than an enemy.

Not cowardice. A change in judgment. The type that came when death was imminent.

Robert forced himself to respond to the Oracle's statement. "I've killed before," he said. "I had no wish to do it again."

Gray eyes delved into his soul. "The men who brought you here three days ago could not tell me your name, or hers." The leader nodded toward the tent flap. "I think it always wise to know whom one is capturing; do you not, Robert Vantauge?" The name dropped like shoveled ash.

Without response.

Robert too knew the art of testing a theory.

The Oracle spun the blackened blade in a slow circle. "I had heard of a man from both the north and the south who traveled toward the desert on a magnificent stallion," he continued, "but at no time was I told that this stallion belonged to the Geordian."

"The stallion is mine," Robert replied. "His sire was given to my family by a trapper who claimed to have won the horse from a desert tribe in a gambling match."

"My people do not play cards." The Oracle traced a line in the sand with the blade.

"No, but that does not mean they do not gamble."

A thin curve crept up the corner of the Oracle's mouth, and

the sketch in the sand began to wind in a long connected spiral. "Six years ago, a trader came to the desert on a frontier mustang. My people laughed at him, not only because they had no need of his furs, but because they found his horse to be dull and ugly. He challenged them to a horse race, the prize for which would be a steed. My people, of course, did not want the mustang, but the bargain was made to defend their honor. And the race was won by the man and his ugly brown horse."

The blade came to a stop, then switched directions. "An important lesson was learned that day, I think," the spiritual leader continued. "Though the tribe members involved in the bargain were not gracious in their loss. The trapper *was* given a Geordian stallion, a wild red with a violent temper. This, I believe, may have been the sire of your horse."

"Then you admit Horizon is Robert's." Aurelia's voice swept in from the tent's entrance, followed by her disheveled figure. There was ash on her skirt and sand in her hair. Blood streaked her right cheekbone. She had been helping to dig the graves.

"Ah." The Oracle lifted the second knife. "On this point, we differ, Your Highness."

Robert's veins tightened.

But Aurelia's voice remained cool. *When had she developed such calm?* "You just stated that Horizon's sire was fairly won."

The Oracle acquiesced. "It was not illegal for the Geordian red to be given away or for your companion's family to accept the gift." He swept a swift X through the spiral. "However, it was illegal for them to keep the stallion's offspring."

"That is politics, not truth," she replied. "Your men saw how angry the stallion became when Robert was shot with the arrow. And yesterday Horizon helped capture the raider that set fire to the prisoner's tent. You believe in the bond between man and horse, do you not?"

There was more to this conversation than Robert could divine. What had happened between her and this leader of the desert while Robert had been tied to a tent pole?

The Oracle sheathed the blade and handed it to her. "Your Royal Highness."

"Aurelia," she said, tucking the knife in her skirt. "My name is Aurelia Lauzon. You may address me as such."

"And you may refer to me . . . ," he said, drawing out the pause as though the bestowal of his name was an even greater honor than that of her own, "as Barak ze Geordian." He lowered his hands to his lap. "You have helped save the people of the Jaheem. I owe you a great debt."

She pounced upon the statement. "Then you may repay it by releasing Robert and Horizon."

"A debt cannot be paid on behalf of another," came the response. But for the first time since Aurelia's entrance, the Oracle's gaze flicked back to Robert. "The man you did not kill," the Oracle said. "His life was worth more than his death. Without him, we would know nothing about who sent the raiders. You have earned your own freedom, Robert Vantauge, and that of your half-desert stallion."

Relief warred with anguish as Robert watched Aurelia react

to the words. He had not yet had the chance to tell her what he had learned about the attacks. He had been under guard since right after their reunion and had spent most of the night helping round up panicked horses, including her own.

The sudden joy on her face tumbled rapidly beneath intensity. "Who is it?" she probed. "Who is behind the raids?" Her attention hinged on the Oracle.

And Robert allowed the other man to answer, then let his own eyes trace the crossed-out spiral in the sand as she and the spiritual leader discussed the involvement of Anthone.

Finally she said, "Why would Edward do this?"

"The king of Anthone has always wanted what he cannot have," replied the Oracle.

True.

"He's testing my father," she said, her voice tight. "To see if he will respond to a few raids clear out on the border."

Her father would never risk his claim to a century of peace for the sake of a few horses and desert tribesmen. Anthone *was* a threat to Tyralt—a real one—but not the greatest.

I have to tell her. Robert stretched out his fingers toward hers, wishing he did not have to do this in front of an audience. "We should discuss this outside," he whispered.

"No." She pulled away.

Perhaps she was right. The Oracle had lost some of his own people in this conflict. Had nearly lost far more. This was no longer only about her but about all of Tyralt.

"Aurelia," Robert breathed, aware that his own life would

change as soon as he told her. "Your sister is bartering with Anthone."

My sister? Her mind whirled at the accusation. Memories hovered in the tainted air: Melony as a young child clinging to Aurelia's skirts and pleading for attention, later as a fellow student bemoaning the demands of royalty, and as a sibling sharing their father's love.

The memories ripped apart as Robert explained about the call of the jay, first in the forest and then the desert—a connection between the attacks. Then the raider's revelation about Melony giving her blessing.

Aurelia had already known that her sister was spiteful, selfish, power-hungry—the most likely culprit behind the fire in the forest.

But this was different. Because the nightmares now were no longer of a single tent burning in isolation, but of an entire tribe consumed with panic before the flames.

Turning, Aurelia drifted toward the tent flap, then lifted the singed edge and stared out across the charred destruction: crimson mounds of fresh graves amidst a wasteland of blackened silk and canvas, the homeless members of the Jaheem sifting through the ashes.

"My sister did this?" she whispered.

Robert had followed her to the tent's edge. "Yes."

"With Edward of Anthone?"

"Yes."

"And there are Anthonian soldiers in the royal guard?" she said.

"Yes."

"We have to warn my father."

"Will he listen?" Robert touched her arm gently.

She did not know. "This is not about him."

"No."

"It's about Tyralt." Lifting her head, Aurelia looked up at the young man who had guided her all this way, had given her not a dream but the reality that was her kingdom. The man who had been exiled from the capital. "I have to go back."

Chapter Twenty-One
THE KEY

THEY MET THE HUNTERS TWO DAYS AFTER TURNING around. At high noon. The desert had foregone its dalliance with the breeze, and a harsh orange sun beat down without forgiveness on Aurelia's travel-roughened skin. The burnished crimson sand reflected the heat and painted a bloody backdrop against the dark winglike formation of the approaching assassins.

Eleven riders pulled up in a sharp forward V: the leader front and center, his black coat folded across the skirt of his saddle, with five men behind him on each side.

He was young, Aurelia realized. Perhaps only a few years older than she. Dark hair fletched from his face, the sharp eyes piercing from his perfect skin. Not a drop of sweat marred its pale surface, despite the heat and the arrows aimed straight at his chest.

The Oracle had sent her a guard. Five men. More than he could spare, but she had known better than to insult his desert pride. And known she would have to face the assassins.

Their leader lifted his hand, palm flat toward the ground, and lowered it in subtle command. The men behind him, all wearing long beige coats, dismounted in trained unison.

"Your Royal Highness," he spoke.

Falcon's reins bit into her left palm as Robert pulled his horse close on her opposite side. Too close. *He will never allow me to die first.*

"You have my identity," she said to the man before her. "I would have yours."

Then to her stunned surprise, he swung free of his ebony mount and dropped to one knee in the sand. "Valerian Siudek, Heir of Valshone, at your command."

The words splintered within her skull. Why would her mother's people be trying to kill her? "Who sent you?" she demanded.

His head sank, and his arm covered his chest in an abject bow. "My father, the Lord of Valshone."

"My g-grandfather?" she stuttered.

"Your mother's father passed from this realm more than ten years ago. I am the son of his successor and no blood relation."

She tried to inhale, but her thoughts were torn in too many

places. "Why claim to be the Heir of Valshone? There is no such title any longer. My father has ended the contract."

Slowly, without permission, the stranger stood, his narrow shoulders pulling back, a slender scabbard and finely coiled black sword hilt rising with him at his hip. "His Majesty *tried* to end the contract. The Valshone do not recognize that attempt. I was sent to the palace to claim the Right."

Had the blasting heat gone to her head? Or was it possible this man had just proclaimed his intent to marry her?

Robert chose that moment to interrupt. "If you were truly sent to the palace, the king would have denounced you."

The men behind the stranger shifted to reveal an array of silver sword hilts from beneath their merciless coats. Their eyes had not once left the arrows still pointed at the young Valshone's chest. As if, she thought, he was not their leader, but their charge.

For nigh half a minute, the tableau froze. Until the young man before her seemed to grasp that she did not know whether to believe him. He reached for the buckle on his scabbard, unlaced it, and placed the embellished weapon symbolically upon the ground. "I am sorry, Your Highness, to inform you of this, but the king is too ill to denounce anyone."

A brown cloud rife with splinters formed within her chest. *Don't listen. I have no cause to believe what he says.*

The Heir's head lowered almost to the crimson ground. "I believe His Majesty is dying."

No.

She had no cause to believe her father was ill.

Except that he had not come for her. Had not sought her out after her disappearance. Or even, to her knowledge, ever publicly renounced her right to the throne.

"What manner of death?" Robert spoke.

Her eyes shot to his. Surely he could not believe this!

But the look in those blue orbs was far from mocking.

The Heir's gaze flicked his way, then traveled back to her. "Permission to relay the events of my visit to the palace as they happened, Your Highness?"

She managed to nod. This must be a ploy, but why would someone trying to kill her bother with such an elaborate ruse?

"I arrived at the palace to learn I had missed your departure," the Heir said, "by a matter of days. I wished to follow at once but knew I must first present myself to His Majesty. However"—he paused—"there was much turmoil at court. The king was absent, and, forgive me, Your Highness, but there were rumors that he had in fact chosen to name his younger daughter as his legal heir, though no one seemed to have witnessed the documents with this change. Then came the news that His Majesty had fallen ill. None but his physician, family members, and adviser were allowed in his presence. I admit to having grown impatient.

"When other rumors came that Your Highness had either run away or met with some tragic fate, I made ready to proceed without approval. Then Her Majesty the Queen called me in for a private audience and informed me that if I wished to claim the Right of Valshone, it would be her daughter, and not Your Highness, whose royal hand I must request. I asked to confirm this with her husband, and she refused my petition. At which point I admit to going outside normal channels."

Aurelia waited, but the Heir had stalled, his fingers catching knots in the long strands of his ebony mount's mane. "There were . . . those who believed the king's illness, in conjunction with your disappearance . . . was suspect."

She should argue, but what could she say? That her father was perfectly safe with her stepmother, who may have killed her first husband, and with Melony, who had already proven she would murder for the crown. *Don't think of that!*

"At last," the Heir continued, "I spoke with the king's adviser about a private audience."

Henry. Yes, Henry would be the correct person to ask. Though the fact that the Heir—he had said his name was Valerian—knew to trust Robert's uncle gave the story a validation she could no longer deny.

"Was it granted?" Robert prompted, the intensity in his voice making her shudder.

"Yes," said the other man. "I waited at His Majesty's bedside for several hours before he awoke, by which point we had been left in complete isolation. I am afraid, Your Highness, that your father *was* in very poor condition, his skin pale, his breathing unsteady."

Robert's fingers reached across her saddle horn and rested

on the hand that seemed to have pressed Falcon's reins through her own flesh and into her bloodstream.

Valerian went on, "It was then that His Majesty told me he wished me to find you."

My father asked for me. She grappled with the knowledge.

"He wished me to deliver you a gift," the Heir added.

Why would her father have sent her a gift through a stranger, instead of asking her to return? Unless . . . unless he feared he might not live until she returned.

Her chest was tight. She should not cry. Not after how her father had treated her. But she had left under the worst circumstances, with too much unsaid. And she was too far away now.

"I'll never make it to the palace in time," she whispered.

"You don't know that." Robert's hand strengthened around hers.

"Eight weeks," she argued, unwilling to pretend. "It will take us eight weeks to journey back! And that is if no one stops us." If the assassins were not here, though, they would be elsewhere. Perhaps not chasing her, but waiting. At the foot of the Gate.

The Heir gestured backward. "My men and I can escort—"

"We should sail." Robert cut him off.

"What?" Aurelia asked.

"From Darzai," he replied.

Darzai? The outpost at the mouth of the Fallchutes. An isolated settlement thrust upon the Geordian more than a hundred years ago by a king wishing to control the great northern waterway. *And,* she remembered slowly, *the deepest port on the southern coast.* Robert was right. If they could cross restricted tribal lands, she could sail.

"How long?" she whispered, unwrapping the reins from her hand.

"We could save two, maybe three weeks," Robert replied, "with safe passage across the southeastern portion of the desert." He turned to question the only member of the Jaheem escort who spoke Tyralian. "We respect the treaty," Robert stated, "and we know the desert lands east of the frontier are restricted from nonnative travel. But we would ask your help. If we can return to the capital soon enough, we can report the threat from Anthone. If we cannot"—his voice lowered—"all of Tyralt may suffer."

Aurelia could not absorb the meaning behind those final words. She knew only that she must go back. Swiftly.

The translator conferred with the other members of the Jaheem, then turned again to Robert and spoke. "The Oracle has said we may bring Her Highness, and you, across all tribal lands. To their edge. At which point we must turn back. This will leave you within a day's ride of Darzai." The translator's gaze traveled slowly over the armed men of the Valshone. "None but those with the Oracle's word may cross sacred lands."

Valerian's shoulders stiffened, and his face muscles tightened.

But Aurelia, tugging in her frayed emotions, placed her palm over her heart in thanks to the Jaheem, then turned to the Heir and held out her hand in diplomacy. "I shall never forget your grand gesture, sir, in bringing me this message. Though I can offer you only my sincerest gratitude and the knowledge that you have completed your mission."

"No, Your Highness." The stiffness vanished from his stance as he pressed her fingers to his lips, then stood and reached below his shirt collar to retrieve a silver chain. "My mission was to bring you this." He drew the chain over his head and held it out to her. A long train of linked silver circlets, and at the center, a key.

An object that throughout her entire life had been worn around the neck of solely one person. A symbol to be passed from monarch to royal heir only when the current leader reached the end of his or her reign. The key of Tyralt.

Chapter Twenty-Two
DARZAI

THE BLACK FLAG OF ROYAL MOURNING DRAPED OVER the blood-red sandstone wall of Darzai, heavy thick cloth weighed down by the oppression of late-summer heat. Everything else faded from Aurelia's view: the high dark cliffs of the Quartian Shelf looming above the southern edge of the desert, the final tract of crimson sand reaching almost to the Shelf, and the eastward flow of the Fallchutes River, the only barrier between the stark contrast in landscapes, its final blue stretch disappearing beneath that towering curved wall. With the flag.

The royal crown against the background of her father's death.

Aurelia felt the veins in her limbs constrict, trapping the blood in her heart. Somehow she had lost her grip on the leather reins. Her fingers reached down for the fallen strands but seemed unable to find purchase.

Robert's hand grazed hers.

No! She pulled away.

If he touched her, there would be no way to restrain the sobs battering her rib cage in search of escape.

She should not cry. Should not. Her father had hurt her. Had rejected her. Had tried to sell her into marriage for his own peace of mind. But that fact did not change the trembling of her hands or her torso.

Robert's arms came around her now, pulling her to his chest and rupturing her own into a million asymmetrical pieces. The tears broke free. "I don't . . ." She gasped for breath. "I don't know why . . ."

"Shh," he whispered. "You don't need a reason."

And that was the truth. The cold, hard reality. That whatever her father had done or not done, she did not need a reason to cry over his death. She did not have to obey his orders or trust his judgment or admire his choices. But she did love him.

And she could not suppress the pain of that loss.

It rocked and jarred and crashed through her until she was as stripped of ornamentation as the desert sands. And then, because there was nowhere else to go and because she could not turn around, she urged Falcon on. Toward the blood-red sandstone wall and the ominous black fabric of her father's death.

Robert felt his throat catch as he approached the royal emblem. He did not know why. He had had no time to consider the meaning of this death for himself. The death of a king—a man who had paid the inevitable consequences for his own weakness, yet still, the only monarch to have served Tyralt throughout Robert's entire life. His throat reacted to that loss.

Though it could not compare to hers.

The unthinkable. A father.

Robert's gaze stretched toward Aurelia, but she had pulled out of reach. He longed to stop her, to warn her of possible danger before she entered Darzai. But she was beyond listening. And he knew he had no right to hold her back. He had known, when she had made the choice to return to the capital, that to support her meant accepting that risk.

Her spine and head were stiff as she urged Falcon nearer the fortifications. The barrier was thick, almost as deep as the legendary Tyralian wall, and rose over three times higher. Red sandstone plastered the black backdrop of the Quartian Shelf, then slung out over the river, past the sole gate, and curved around on Robert's left beyond his vision.

City guards littered the edifice. Frozen like gargoyles upon the upper echelons of the stone surface. Perched in the shadows of deep indented cubicles built straight into the wall. And the same guards, in what appeared to be white tribal robes, clogged the gateway.

"*Zat!*" The cry came from a voice at the Gate.

And Horizon halted. Falcon took several more steps, but the

guards rode toward them and stretched out into a circle, closing in around both horses and riders. Three guards came inward, bearing down upon the filly, with drawn arrows. A fourth man stepped before the stallion with an upraised hand, then began to speak in the language of the desert.

Robert watched Aurelia. He should have urged her to wait and gather herself before—

But then a hand reached for his reins, and he had no time to think as his horse launched onto hind legs. Robert looped the leather around his palm and curled against the stallion's neck.

Every weapon in the circle now twisted his way.

"Barak ze Geordian!" Aurelia's voice ripped through the air.

Thrice the Jaheem escort had used those words as their party crossed the paths of other tribesmen. And each time, the words had caused the same reaction. As they did now amid the Darzai. The weapons tilted downward, diffusing the tension, and the circle backed away.

Though it did not open.

Horizon put forth one last display of powerful kicking, then dropped his forelegs to the ground. But the man in front did not lower his hand. Dark eyes met Robert's and held there for a prolonged minute, then the guard spoke again, this time in Tyralian. "There are those who seek the stallion with the heart of the desert."

I'll not go through this again, Robert thought as his grip tightened.

The man continued, "And the mare of the bronze sun."

Why would the tribes of the Geordian hold an interest in Falcon? Unless…

"Who?" Robert asked, though he had received no permission to speak. "Who seeks us?"

"Those from the capital," the man replied.

Palace guards. Robert felt the old shot of failure fire through him. He had brought her to Darzai to take her home, to give her one last moment with her father. Instead her father was dead. And the assassins were here.

"Let us bring the horses into the city for you," said the man. "You may retrieve them at the wharf. At the Inn of the Rising Shadow."

The speaker shot a quick glance toward Aurelia. "We make this offer to protect Her Royal Highness, Aurelia Lauzon…"

Why? Robert's grip lost its hold on the stallion's reins.

"Whom the queen has charged with treason."

Treason! The word snagged on the crags of Aurelia's mind. Did treason mean defiance? Or murder? Or the threat to her sister's claim to the throne? The thought scalded her interior as she dismounted before the city guards. She didn't know whether to trust them. They were not friends or neighbors or tribe members with whom she had shared a life-threatening experience.

But these robed figures *had* recognized the name of the Oracle. And they had the power and strength of numbers. If these men had wished to kill or arrest her, they could have done so right there. Immediately.

She had been betrayed more than once by those she knew.

But during this journey, she had also been saved as many times by those she did not.

Aurelia handed over the reins, then waited as Robert worked his own way to the same unavoidable choice and gave up his horse's reins as well.

On foot, she and he crossed beneath the thickly guarded barrier.

And entered Darzai.

The brilliance of their new surroundings clashed against Aurelia's inner turmoil. For this place was no struggling outpost, as she had imagined. But a city. Red-stoned streets wound in every direction. Buildings, all composed of the same sandstone, curled their way in long connected strips, arching over roads and canals with no thought of separation. And walkways spread out in wide-open paths abloom with life. Island lilies and speckled tigereyes clustered about rows of Minthonian lemon trees and tropical mandarins. Geordian women hawked jewelry beneath rainbow-colored canvases, and men taller than Drew balanced paint jars along scaffolding, while clusters of children ran below, their heads blond, brown, black, red—some even covered in the inked scarves of the Distant Isles.

She tried to inhale the beauty, but darkness warded her inner gates. Had her expedition held any worth? Or had it only given Melony more power—the chance to plot in safety against their father and now to wait out the mourning period, without challenge, under Elise's temporary rule?

Aurelia knew hate was wrong—that it could suck all the beauty from her heart—but as she and Robert traveled down the city's natural slope, the streets themselves began to fall victim to the shadows. Here the walls were stripped of canvas, and the stone was pitted with old scars. The archways, cracked and unpainted, grew lower and closer together, forming a tunnel that conspired with the saltwater breeze to bombard her with the scent of home.

They spit her out onto a wharf teeming with soldiers. Not a dozen men, or fifty, but an entire company of Tyralian military crawling over the docks. And only then did she truly comprehend that the hunt had changed. Not her main adversary. Her sister remained the ultimate danger. But there would be no more secret assassins. No more covert palace guards.

Her sister was the law.

Robert grabbed Aurelia's wrist, pulling her back into the tunnel and up against the concave wall, then clasped her palm in what she knew was meant to be a gesture of comfort. "Wait here, I'll locate the inn and then find us passage . . . somewhere."

Us.

Guilt crashed over her as he slipped away into danger. She should never have let him travel back with her this far. For the past month, she had known she must tell him good-bye. Under her father's rule, Robert would have faced prison if he had returned to the palace. And now . . . what could she offer him but a spot beside her at her own execution?

Perhaps, as he said, he would find passage, but passage where? Even if she boarded a ship for escape, what nation would allow her to disembark? Who could afford the ire of the Tyralian government? She edged from the shadows, her eyes immediately picking him out amid the swarm of military uniforms and duck-clothed sailors. The departure would be easier if she left now, but she could not do it. She owed him the truth.

Rough pressure brushed against her. "Ye seen this girl?" The wool gray of a man's uniform scratched her arm, and a paper was thrust into her hand.

She looked down.

At a sketch of her own face.

The paper tumbled.

"Hey!" The soldier snatched it back up, then jerked her arm. "I asked ye a question."

"I haven't seen her," Aurelia replied.

His fingers dug into her skin. "Ye'll address me with respect."

She had missed the insignia on the upper corner of his jacket. "Yes, Corporal."

"And ye'll look at me!"

She faced up, desperately hoping he would not see past her desert-burned skin.

A leer edged across his face. "Reckon I can come up with a proper apology." His tongue curled toward her throat. Then he turned behind him to a group of other figures in uniform. "Here boys, lookin' for some flesh to ease your duties?"

She jammed her boot into his shin and tore free, then ran.

The shouts rose behind her.

Dodging a moving wagon, she plunged into the port at full tilt. Three ships—no, four—crowded the docks, their tall masts cluttering the sky, their cargo sprawled across the wharf. She leaped over a rope, sprinted across a ream of fishing nets, and wove in between the crates.

But footsteps followed her. She must not be caught. If the soldiers found her now, they would see. Or ask questions she would not be able to answer. Vaulting over a chicken crate, she ducked behind a tower of grain sacks and plunged into the refuse from the second vessel.

Whistles shrilled from behind. Which meant more eyes. Aurelia craned her head toward the streets, but the blur of soldiers loomed in every exit.

She had to hide. But where? If she stopped in the open, it was only a matter of time.

And then, up ahead, she saw the sign, over an old cracked doorway. *The Inn of the Rising Shadow.* Dashing behind a row of barrels, she swerved toward the inn, burst across the remaining space, and tugged on the door.

It stuck.

Then she swung inward, yanked it closed behind her, and spun around.

To see cold stone, shuttered windows, and a tall figure, in long robes, blocking the opposite exit.

The figure stepped forward, releasing the daylight from behind him. And revealing the unusual blue and green stripes on his robes and the familiar gleam in his eyes. *Drew?* "Well, Your Highness," the mocking tone confirmed, "I see you finally managed to deprive yourself of that hangnail of an escort."

How dare he criticize Robert's loyalty!

The door opened again, and Robert burst through, slamming it shut. His gaze sought hers, and she knew he must have chased down the disturbance on the wharf.

"Then again"—Drew grinned—"some things never change."

Except that my father is dead, and I have been charged with treason. "Why are you here, Drew?" She banged her hip on a dusty table.

The horseman rubbed his chin, then reached around the back side of the wall as if to retrieve something. "Arrived three weeks ago. Planned to head to Tyralt City, see if I couldn't persuade His Majesty to put an end to these desert raids, but before I could float a passage, a boatload of soldiers disembarked. Brought their own weapons, a flag of royal mourning, and a warrant for a friend of mine." He tossed Falcon's bridle onto the table. "I wasn't too keen on sailing then. Thought I'd stick around and help out. Heard you'd crossed the Gate. Figured you wouldn't risk it on the way back. Unfortunately, someone in the capital figured the same thing."

"The horses are here?" Robert edged toward Drew.

"In the stable out back."

"You recruited the local guard?" Aurelia asked, incredulous.

"Darzai is a city unto itself," Drew replied. "The locals are none too keen on having Tyralian military in their wharf."

He was right. Obviously. So why did she still feel angry?

The conversation stalled as she struggled to grapple with the chaos that was her life.

Robert finally broke the silence. "You have a plan," he said to the horseman. It was not a question.

"There's a ship in the harbor," Drew replied. "Claims she's a trader from the Distant Isles, but fact is she's a smuggler. Captain's a friend of mine. He'll take Your Highness off Tyralian shores."

"No," she replied.

Drew acted as if she had not spoken. "Hate to say it, Vantauge, but you'd have to leave that stallion of yours behind. There's no way to get those horses shipboard without attracting every musket in the harbor. You and the lass, though—I can make that happen."

You cannot.

"Where would the ship take us?" Robert asked.

Nowhere.

"The Outer Realms." As soon as Drew said it, the answer was obvious. No one in the Outer Realms would care about the good graces of the Tyralian government. Because legally, there was no relationship between the two countries. Which meant it was the one place she could go. *Except she couldn't.*

She could not abandon her countrymen: the orphans on the frontier, the travelers at the mercy of the Lion, the tribes under attack. And she could not disappoint all the people who had helped her on her journey: the Oracle, the Vantauges, Valerian, the Jaheem. "I have to return to the palace." Her fingers fumbled for the chain around her neck. "I can fight Melony's claim to the throne." Aurelia pulled out the glimmering silver symbol.

The horseman's eyes widened at the sight of the key, then closed, and he took a step back, again cutting off the light. "You don't understand, Your Highness."

No, *he* did not understand. She knew there was an entire company of men out in that harbor, wanting to arrest her. And there would be far more guarding the port at the capital. But she had to return now. Before it was too late.

"Your sister is already queen," he said.

Not plausible.

"She's completed the coronation."

"She can't—"

"She has," the horseman concluded. "And your stepmother has confirmed her daughter's right to the throne. They thwarted the period of mourning by claiming your father was poisoned and that justice must be done. The trial has already been held, Aurelia, and you were found guilty."

None of this made sense. Not in any world except the tainted, foul corruption that was her sister's reality. Where falsehoods were murder weapons and avarice was greater than love. Where lives—Aurelia's own, her father's, and those of her people—meant nothing!

All the anger that had been building since the news that her sister had charged *her* with a crime ripped loose. Aurelia whirled and slammed the shuttered window with her hand. "I can't—," she yelled. "I can't let Melony win!"

Silence exuded behind her, then the sound of retreating footsteps. And she crumpled against the boards, jabbing them with her knuckles. This was not about Drew, or the ship, or the plan.

Gently Robert's hand smoothed over the back of her head. He should understand. He had seen the flames, and the cinders, and heard the screams of the Jaheem. "I can't flee," she whispered, easing off the boards. "I can't betray my people."

His hand moved to her face, brushing away tears she had not known were there. "You won't betray them, Aurelia, as long as you are alive."

"I can't . . ." She trembled.

"Melony won't win." The blue eyes were sincere. He reached up and tugged back the shutters, forcing her to face the view of the hundreds of soldiers swarming the wharf. "The only way she wins is if you gift her with your death."

As he ducked beneath a massive cobweb to enter the small stables an hour later, Robert could not regret the harshness of his words. He had not wanted to frighten Aurelia, or to inflict any more hurt than she had already suffered. She had a right to her anger, but he could not allow her to ignore the truth. And he could not protect her from the pain of saying good-bye.

Falcon nickered over the warped boards beside the door. Robert ran his hand gently along her bronze snout, then crossed the ill-lit space and entered the final stall.

Horizon thrust his way forward, trying to break free of the cramped interior, to no avail, as Robert shut the latch.

Turning, he buried his face in the stallion's warm coat, trying to imprint the feel in his memory.

Images flashed in his mind: of a little bay colt, kicking and tossing his heels in the fresh green fields of spring, the blur of those same fields as the stallion took his rider on their first genuine run, and the silhouette of avenging hooves outside a burning tent. "You saved my life," Robert murmured.

And Aurelia's. That mist-filled morning in the palace arena.

He babbled then. Explaining. Though he knew the stallion would not care about the reason for the departure. The bay would only know his rider was gone and would wait for him to come back. Robert had to struggle not to make promises he had no power to keep. "Remember, you are in charge. If Drew takes one misstep, you break the boards."

Horizon snorted, and Robert laughed, then buried a sudden rush of tears in the stallion's neck. "I'll miss you," he murmured. "I'll miss you."

"No, Robert." Her voice came from behind him.

He tried to wipe his eyes on the red-brown coat, but his vision remained blurry.

"I can't ask you to come with me," she said. He struggled to comprehend the statement. "I can't ask you to leave Horizon and your family, and Tyralt—" Her breath caught. "I know you love this country as much as I do. I would never have understood half of what I have seen on this expedition if you had not been the one to show me. And I'm grateful. I'm so . . ."

He turned, this time obliterating the tears from his face without any attempt at disguise. "You don't need to ask me, Aurelia. I am coming anyway."

She was biting her lip and staring at the sandy floor, her fingers threading aimlessly through Falcon's coat. "Robert, I know you think you love me."

He *thought*?

"But I . . . I *can't* . . ."

The dagger shredded his insides like a blackened knife. He had not expected her to profess her love. She had lost her father and her country all in one day. But—

"I can't marry you," she finished.

Marry?! He vaulted out of the stall. Who had said anything about marriage?

"Your parents were right," she told the stable floor.

His parents? What had they said to her? When?

"And Daria—even Daria tried to tell me, but I didn't listen."

Tell her what? These other people had no right to wreak havoc on his life!

"But I'm not ready, Robert." Her hand fell from the filly's

neck. "I can't give it up. It's not the crown. Or the palace. Or the power—that is, I don't even have any, but the thought of giving up forever the chance to help, to change things. I don't know *why* I can't be like Daria or your mother or—"

That was quite enough.

"Stop." He crossed the gap and put his hands on her shoulders. This was his fault for not telling her how he felt about her.

While apparently other people had been telling her nonsense.

"If I wanted a girl like that," he said, "I'd have stayed on the frontier and married one." Then he looked, really looked at her. In her travel-stained clothing and her tangled hair. With her natural brown skin burned darker by the desert and her boots worn through. She was so much *more* than any other girl he had ever met.

And he had not even known when he returned to the palace—had not fathomed half the emotions that ran beneath her confident exterior. "What I *love* about you, Aurelia," he said, very clearly, "is that you aren't satisfied with life as it is." He thought about the kuro and the Lion and the desert raids. "I love that you refuse to accept problems just because they exist and that you want to learn more about everything. I love that you don't have your future all planned out and that you're messy and contradictory and you feel too much." He understood that. He had felt too much his entire life. Looking into her dark eyes, he found the person below the surface, the person who was so scared of letting people down that she had even tried to save him from her own heart. "And Aurelia, I would never—I could never fault you for caring too much for your people."

She had stiffened in his arms, and now he felt her shudder. "How can you say that when I'm abandoning them to my sister's rule?"

"You aren't abandoning them."

She was the least selfish person he knew. He had learned, from the Oracle himself, about what she had done to save the Jaheem. And it rang true, with every wild, insane, gut-wrenching action she had taken on this journey.

Everything she did, every risk she took, was for her people.

"If I don't speak for them," she said, "who will?"

"They can speak for themselves."

"Then of what use am—"

"Hope," he cut her off. "As long as you're alive, they'll have hope. Aurelia, you aren't the voice of Tyralt. You're its heart."

Something reverberated through her frame.

"And mine too," he added. "I *am* going with you." He had already made that commitment. Had known what he was choosing on that dark night in the stables when he had found her asleep on Horizon's back. And had known when this moment came—or something far worse—he would be with her.

His hand touched her cheek. The sacrifice he could not make—the one thing he could not live without—was her. "I love *you*, Aurelia."

The thought flowed through her blood, her brain, her body. It wasn't something she could deny. Or relinquish. Or put off until a later time when she was somehow better equipped to sort out her contradictory life. He loved *her.* Not some mental fiction, some facade she performed, or even some childhood fantasy.

The past six months had blown through all those ill-fitting versions of her in a hail of blood, flames, and tears. She returned to the unanswered question: Had the expedition held worth?

Yes. It had taught her how much she did not know. About the Valshone and the role they played in Tyralt's defense. About the outlaws of the Asyan who had built a community after being proscribed as useless. About the travelers to the north who risked everything to begin new lives, the frontiersmen who had the grit to survive that dream, and the tribes who maintained their beliefs despite a barrage of indignations.

She could not regret knowing her kingdom.

You're its heart.

Was that what her sister really feared?

Aurelia had lost Tyralt, and everything and everyone.

Except the young man before her.

The expedition had taught her about him as well—the companion who somehow knew her kingdom better than she did. Who knew *her.* Whose arms around her were gentle and strong all at once. And who was waiting, patiently, with those deep blue eyes, for a response after spilling his heart into her hands.

She leaned forward, closing the final space between them, and cradled his head in those hands, then found his lips with her own and spilled back all of her messy, contradictory, passionate heart.

Epilogue

AURELIA SCRAMBLED UP THE LADDER FROM THE hold and the secret compartment that, according to the captain, had provided sanctuary to hundreds of refugees. She had promised to stay out of sight as long as the ship's deck remained within view of the dock. But the heaving scrape of the anchor against the wooden exterior, the shouts of the sailors, and the sudden jerk that had nearly knocked her from her feet had all indicated that the vessel had pulled away. And the more gentle rocking motion suggested the ship had settled in for its journey.

She could not wait a moment longer. Her hand reached for the upper hatch and thrust up the square panel. Salt air assailed her nostrils, and bright sunlight invaded her eyes. She stumbled the final steps to the deck, then propped herself against the rigging.

Slowly the ocean revealed itself. A magnificent stretch of turquoise waters, pulsing and glimmering under a beckoning sun. Who knew what lay before her, across its vibrant waves? As a child, she had dreamed about distant shores beyond the ocean.

But that was not what she had climbed to see. Regaining her footing, she hurried to the ship's side. *There!*

She gripped the smooth surface of the railing and hung on, savoring every last detail of the view. The melded buildings of the red-stone city rose in unison like a mythical castle upon the sand. On their right stretched the everlasting beach of crimson, and above towered the glossy cliffs of the Quartian. She could understand now why people chose to defy them. There was something in the challenge, something that could not be taken away once achieved.

She would look toward other challenges soon.

But now was the time to secure forever in her heart and mind this final vision of the Tyralian Shore. A sorrow, unlike any she had ever known, lodged in her throat, and she could not swallow or wash away the grief. Because she could not afford to cry and lose her last chance to witness this incredible view. It was more than a place. It was a set of dreams and hopes and a future that had defined her for as long as she could remember. How could she watch it drift from her life? But she must—she must because it was happening and there was nothing she could do but bear witness to the moment.

Despite herself, the emotion broke free from her throat and began to seep through the corners of her eyes.

Then a strong warm arm encircled her stomach, and she sank back against Robert's chest. His chin rested on her head. When had he grown so tall? She supposed she should have noticed, as she should have heard him come up behind her. But neither lapse mattered. She could feel him. The warm, companionable comfort that came from sharing her deepest sorrow. They didn't speak. Did not need to. All they needed was to be there for one another. As together they watched their home drift away into oblivion.